Ray Wilcox began work as a messenger boy at the *Daily Mirror* in London. Later followed a successful 30 year career, working in 25 UK prisons.

Lock-Down Blues evolved as a result of his knowledge and experiences as both uniformed officer and governor.

He now lives in Spain with his wife and is busy writing a sequel.

LOCK-DOWN BLUES

Dedications

Margaret, my Wife

Who makes everything possible

All you need is love

....

Marcus & Giorgio

Our beautiful boys

....

Elena & Ray

My Mum & Dad

Ray Wilcox

LOCK-DOWN BLUES

AUSTIN MACAULEY
PUBLISHERS LTD.

Copyright © Ray Wilcox

The right of Ray Wilcox to be identified as author of this work has been asserted by him in accordance with section 77 and 78 of the Copyright, Designs and Patents Act 1988.

All rights reserved. No part of this publication may be reproduced, stored in a retrieval system, or transmitted in any form or by any means, electronic, mechanical, photocopying, recording, or otherwise, without the prior permission of the publishers.

Any person who commits any unauthorized act in relation to this publication may be liable to criminal prosecution and civil claims for damages.

A CIP catalogue record for this title is available from the British Library.

All characters appearing in this work are fictitious. Any resemblance to real persons, living or dead, is purely coincidental.

ISBN 978 184963 582 0

www.austinmacauley.com

First Published (2014)
Austin Macauley Publishers Ltd.
25 Canada Square
Canary Wharf
London
E14 5LB

Printed and bound in Great Britain

Acknowledgments

Lock-Down Blues has been a long time coming and I've been lucky to have been blessed with such supportive friends. In particular, Wilf & Sheila, John & Mo and Billy. John & Kate in the UK have never been far from my thoughts as John travelled the same Prison Service road as I did.
Katie & Ian at SR Print Design (Pedreguer) for their patience and Roddy Braithwaite for convincing me to join the Prison Service all those years ago. Finally, the regulars at Taverna 'El Laurel'. Thanks.

Foreword

Prison is a place where ones darkest fears and emotions are dragged to the surface and cannot be ignored. They are visible to be pored over, laughed at and misunderstood. Casual cruelty can sometimes feed on the laughter and the perpetrator will rarely spare the victim.

Violence is commonplace and has a life of its own. Fear is a reality and should not have shame attached to it. The individuals who manage and control fear are the true warriors, be they staff or prisoner.

Although this is a work of fiction the events which I describe happen more often than is common knowledge. Fortunately, violent death is still a rare event and long may it remain so. I offer the opinion that both staff and prisoners would not want it any other way.

The bell is ringing
It won't stop now
There's nothing for you to choose
If you fight the man
He will lay you down
And play you the Lock-Down Blues.

Ray Wilcox
2013

Prologue

Hello, welcome to my high-security room with a view. I bet you thought I'd be a Dave or a Ronnie. Pleasantly surprised, I hope? I'm more the Marlon-type. Not the one in Emmerdale, silly girl, the film star. Talks through his nose and starred in a film about God. No? Well, never mind.

I know that you've been told something of my background so there's no need for you to speculate about my tendencies. I tolerate most people but I hate nonces and kiddie fiddlers. But you're not here to listen to me ramble on, you're here to see where I live. Let me show you around.

I call it a room because the word 'cell' is so final, so institutionalized. I won't become institutionalized and I'll kill any bastard who says I will. Sorry, I'm going off on one again. It will, however, be my home for the rest of my natural life. There are a small number of 'natural lifers' and I feel quite privileged to be amongst the elite. They might move me to different prisons but the room will still be the same.

This particular room is ten feet by six. They do vary in size particularly if they have to house two prisoners. The screws, officers, would never put me in a two-man cell because, very quickly, it would become a one-man cell if you get my drift.

The door is made of re-enforced steel. My particular door can open outwards if the screws want it to. Something to do with preventing a barricade. I've seen a barricade and it's a piece of nonsense not even worth thinking about. If I need to make a serious point, I shed blood.

All cell doors have a spy hole in the middle, near the top. The screws look in to make sure I've not escaped and to watch me knocking one out. There's one particular female screw or screwess as I call them, Geordie girl, who seems to linger longer at the hole. If I know it's her I put on a bit of a show, make the sheet go up and down, dribble and shout out things like, 'go on my son, nearly there'. I think she gets embarrassed but it doesn't stop her looking. When I'm out on the landing I wink at her and lick my lips. She goes as red as a beetroot.

I've got my own toilet with a modesty screen. If a screw is looking in I make out like I'm giving birth. My bed has a base which is moulded concrete. I have prison issue mattress, sheets and pillow cases. The duvet is my own, I was allowed to send away for it. Thirty quid from Argos. It's blue and has a nice picture of a bear with a hat on. My mate Dennis is a whiz with a needle so I gave him a little job to do. When the screws search my room they still haven't noticed the balloon next to the bears mouth with the legend 'all screws are cunts', picked out in black cotton. Nice one Dennis.

On the back wall I've got a small window. I used to be able to open the middle pane until two screws came in and welded it shut. Apparently, some clever cunt on B wing had managed to secure a torn sheet to the window opening, made a noose and hanged himself. I can still see out, the screws' houses and overgrown gardens never change. I asked the wing principal screw if I could be let out to tidy the gardens and make the place look nice. He laughed so hard I thought he was going to piss himself. Sarcasm is the lowest form of wit. My room is on the threes. The threes means the third landing up from the ground floor. A most sought after location. Top of the shop, so to speak.

I've got two small cupboards which, pushed together, form a work surface. I do a lot of writing so it comes in handy. I used to write to the relatives of my business activities but the screws stopped the letters. I thought it was good of me to let them know how their loved ones had behaved up to the last moment. Give them closure. The governor told me it was bad form, whatever that means.

I attended education classes, after I was sentenced; it was a better option than sitting in my cell. The teacher, nice old bird, said that I had a way with words and that I should write a story. So I did. It's about a young boy I met in prison. I knew his mum on the outside, used to give her one when I was at a loose end. I suppose you would call it a sympathy shag. Anyway, his story touched me because he topped himself.

Waste of a young life. He used to scratch his arse the way I do when I'm bored. Funny the things you notice. I'll read it to you. It's called 'Josh'.

Josh

The prison stank, was freezing cold and loved its lifers. Over the 134 years of its existence, the walls and buildings had witnessed every kind of torment and deprivation, including death.

Josh didn't give a shit about the place or its history. Cutting the nonce a new smile had earned him months in segregation but also a cell to himself when he got back on A wing. Doing a life sentence meant nothing to him.

Although fit, he cared little about his appearance. At 27 he looked a few years older. He'd hated the children's homes they'd put him in after Daddy had left. The other kids seemed to enjoy the school work but Josh didn't. He could speak enough to make himself understood but silence was bliss.

The other cons knew he liked hurting people but never ventured opinions after the 'new smile' incident. In fact, only a couple of selected cons and the screws spoke to him.

For Josh, 17 July had a special meaning. It was the day, when he was four and a half, that Mummy rose into the clouds.

He'd seen the rope which had been used to pull her up through the clouds and into heaven and he'd cried because Mummy had always made tea and she had left him hungry. Josh had always been hungry since Mummy went to heaven. He remembered being punched by Daddy because he had wet himself. He still did it but nobody knew.

He'd felt good, powerful, when he beat up the old poofs as they laughed at him with their painted mouths and black eyes. Shame he'd got caught. Selfish cunt didn't need to die. Slags. Josh sat on the end of the bunk bed and stroked his acoustic guitar. It was his only possession other than the picture of Mummy.

Midnight turned into 17 July and, softly, he started to play and sing,

'My clothes were old and second hand
I know it wasn't fair
I forced the door and stepped outside
But you weren't there

I tried to stop the things I did
I know, you know I care
My heart was breaking every night
But you weren't there

I want to answer all your questions
I know, I know you care
The light was burning late for me
But you weren't there

I'm stuck in here, I've lost my way
I couldn't raise a prayer
I do my best, I dream of you
But you're not there.

He played it twice and cried, the tears of a man with no hope. With his guitar placed carefully against the wall, he lay back with his head on the pillow. He closed his eyes and his right hand searched the edge of the mattress for the tiny tear. Carefully, he withdrew the pencil thin joint he'd bought earlier in the day for two phone cards. After sparking the joint into life he drew the fragrant smoke deep into his lungs. He didn't give a shit if the screws sussed him, not tonight.

The powerful weed took hold and he drifted off. The dream always started with him entering Mummy's room and seeing her being pulled up, with the water dripping down her legs on to the carpet. He called to her but she wouldn't answer. Perhaps she would tonight.

He gave the joint some real attention and his head started to heat up. His cock felt hot. He could hear Mummy in his head, he could fucking well hear her.

He'd rehearsed the words he would say to Mummy, rehearsed them so many times over the years. He liked to speak the words because it felt like he was speaking to her, in the cell with him.

'Mummy, I know you can hear me. There's never been a day when I haven't thought about you, wanted you with me. Once, I tried to speak to the Chaplain but I gave up when one of the cons heard me and started to laugh. I kicked and punched him until the screws pulled me off him. He won't cross me again. I want to tell you about today because I feel like I've crashed. The bastards told me that my parole application has been turned down and I won't be able to have another go for five years. Mummy, I can't wait that long.'

As he thought his head was going to explode, her voice cut into his brain.

'Josh, I love you, I've always loved you. You don't have to wait. Come to me now.' Her voice faded and was gone.

The joint wasn't working any more. Nothing was working any more. He couldn't do another day in prison. He needed to be with Mummy.

It was easy. He cut his bed sheet into long strips and knotted them together. He stood on his chair and looped the sheet around the one window bar that wasn't protected by mesh.

He tied one end to the bar and made a noose at the other end. The knot was hard.

He put the noose around his neck as he remembered Mummy had done it. It didn't hurt.

As he kicked the chair away, he smiled and began his journey.

Did you like it? Thanks, nice of you to say so. No, his mum wrote and asked me if I wanted to attend the funeral. I told her to fuck off, it wasn't like he was a relative was it? Anyway, I digress.

At the moment my only regular contact on the outside is a bird called Sandra. She's one of those birds who enjoys getting involved with long term prisoners. Turns her on. It's funny how they're always called Sandra, Babs or Kat. I notice things like that.

I bought her name and address from a con on C wing. Cost me an ounce of Drum tobacco and two phone cards. Well worth the investment. I wrote to introduce myself and she replied with a twelve page letter and a photo. Very, very nice. She had a red and black basque-type thing on with crotchless knickers. I don't think the screws noticed the knickers, or lack of, otherwise they would have confiscated the photo. She's a big bird, bit of a beer gut but nice legs. Her face isn't much to write home about but, you can't have it all. She's holding a bottle to her mouth and drinking what looks like milk. Dirty cow.

Sandra asked for a photo of me but it's not allowed so I couldn't oblige. When I say 'couldn't oblige' I really mean that I didn't want to. If I had wanted to I could have made it happen.

I replied with a detailed description of myself including the fact that I have a humongous cock. One of my redeeming features I'm told. She found out for herself when she first visited me a couple of months ago. The whole exercise cost me five ounces of Drum, three phone cards and a favour to be collected at a later date.

Five minutes after I'm seated across a table from Sandra in Visits, my mate Dennis cracks his old lady one in the gob, two tables away, and they really start going at it. As the screws start piling in to stop the ruck, Sandra slides her hand under the table, into me strides and gives me a very satisfactory one off the wrist. Now she knows what a big boy I am. Dennis spent a couple of days in Segregation and we had a good laugh when he got back on the wing. His old lady is a real trooper, salt of the earth.

Sandra and I have been 'going out' for just over three months and we're getting to the time when she'll want to marry me. They always fucking do. If I did allow myself to fall into that particular trap it would be a prison chapel wedding followed by Sandra being serialized in a Sunday rag telling about her life with Mr Long Term Prisoner. No, no, not for me.

There's a lifer on D wing who's interested in Sandra, so I'm seriously considering selling her on. She won't mind, it's all a big game. Play by the rules and nobody gets hurt.

Once again, I digress. I have a small wardrobe, made out of cheap wood, where I hang my spare strides and perfectly pressed tee shirts. I use a nonce, who lives on the twos, to clean my room twice a week and do my washing and ironing when the need arises. I don't need to, but I do give him a couple of smokes when I remember. He makes sure that I'm satisfied because he knows that shoddy workmanship would lead to me cutting his cock off and tickling his tonsils with it. Standards must be maintained.

My walls are painted a fetching shade of grey. I've got a three foot by two pin board on the wall next to the crapper. It's normally bare but if I get wind that I'm about to get a cell search I pin up a choice selection of crumpet with plenty of beaver shots. If the Geordie screwess is one of the searchers, all the better.

A lifer on B wing, Johnny something-or-other, does a bit of hairdressing so I visit him twice a month. I like to keep my barnet short, always have. An old-fashioned barber used to come in from the outside until he nipped the top off of a mole that old Lenny's got on his neck. The geezer spent two weeks in hospital and, rumour has it, he's about to go back in for a second lot of surgery on his face.

I supplement my various 'interests' by making tea and clearing up after the gym screws. They know my reputation so they show respect and don't take the piss. I respond by ensuring that only the right sort of con gets to use the gym. No nonces on my watch.

So, that's about it with the guided tour. I expect to be in this particular shit hole for about another six months. Either I'll get bored or they'll decide that they've had enough of me. People can take me the wrong way and I don't know why. Live and let live is my motto. Oops, did I really say that?

You're going to meet a lot of prisoners but none will be as nice and generous as me.

Nice meeting you, but be careful, prison can be a dangerous place.

Part One

Chapter One

Prison Service Headquarters (HQ) is situated on a side street which runs parallel with Horseferry Road, a few minutes' walk from the Palaces of Westminster. The building is ugly but functional. A mixture of main-grade civil servants and operational staff provide the Orders and Instructions by which the prison establishments, in England and Wales, are governed. Area managers, directly accountable to the director general, are responsible for the performance of the prisons under their control.

The meeting was scheduled to begin at 20.00 hours. Prison Service director general (DG) Ron Miles was a stickler for punctuality and the other three men who were sat around the large, rectangular table had all arrived early. Miles had purposely called for an evening meeting because the building would be virtually empty. Just to be certain, Pete Richardson, his staff officer, had checked the other offices on the fourth floor and found them all to be empty.

Seated either side of Richardson was deputy director general Dennis Pearson and director of security Joe Malpas.

Pearson was popular across the service because he was considered to be honest, a man of his word. Although nearing retirement, he had the energy and enthusiasm of a much younger man. He had governed a number of the most difficult prisons in the system and never forgot how demanding the work could be for the officers dealing with prisoners every day. He made a point of visiting one prison each week and would spend equal amounts of time speaking with both staff and prisoners.

Malpas was a native of Birmingham and fiercely proud of it. After a short career in the police he had joined the Prison Service at Winson Green prison in Birmingham. In the 25 years leading up to his present position, he had moved around the prisons and staff colleges in the Midlands, never feeling the need to move his family from their home near Burntwood. He enjoyed being director of security and it was due, in a large part, to his forward-thinking approach to problem solving that the Service had recovered and moved on from the disasters at Whitemoor and Parkhurst a few years before.

'Right, let's begin. Pete will take a detailed note of the meeting. No other notes will be taken and no record of this meeting will find its way into any computer. Pete's notes will go straight into my personal safe at the end of the meeting. Any questions so far?' Miles asked as he sparked up the first of many Marlboro Lights that evening. Although smoking was banned in HQ, the restriction never found its way into the DG's office.

No one needed to say anything so Miles continued. 'First, I will put this meeting into context. On Monday I was summoned to the Home Office. I met with the Home Secretary and the Prisons Minister. The agenda items included the increasing levels of violence and drug taking in our prisons. The figures they produced, to support their concerns, appeared to be at odds with our own statistical information but still made worrying reading. I did remind them that the dramatic rise in the overall prison population, in the past five years, combined with the efficiency savings we have had to endure year-on-year, had not helped the situation. They were further concerned that, during Prime Minister's Questions (PMQs) next week, our illustrious leader was going to be placed firmly on the spot by the Opposition. I, of course, informed them that we are constantly looking at ways to address these problems. I am to report back to them, next Monday, with new initiatives and a way forward. Comments?'

There was a general discussion about the problems and the relative shortcomings of prominent politicians, which Richardson didn't bother to record. Bottles of mineral water were opened and chocolate biscuits consumed.

'Obviously, I've been giving the problems a great deal of my time, since the meeting, and I've come up with a suggestion which is radical in nature and has not been tested for its legality. Let me explain. Our system of rewarding certain prisoners for providing us with low-level security information is well established and need not be altered in any way. If it ain't broken don't fix it, is my motto.' This remark brought smiles and nods. Richardson was comfortably scribbling away, sucking on a Silk Cut.

'What I am proposing will take information-gathering to a whole new level. I have completely dismissed the idea of placing volunteer staff undercover because I believe that they would be exposed and their lives placed at risk. The Prime Minister will have to ride out the coming storm at PMQs because this can never enter the public domain. So, consider this,' Miles said as he rose from his leather chair and began pacing the room. He spoke, without interruption, for fifty minutes.

The meeting finally broke-up a few minutes before midnight and Joe Malpas knew that he was about to embark on the most important and sensitive piece of work he had ever been entrusted with.

After his scheduled meeting, the following Monday, Miles called Malpas to his office and said that the PM had agreed, reluctantly, to give the initiative the green light. Miles had, thoughtfully, provided the PM with a number of light-weight suggestions for use in the House during the coming week.

Over the next two weeks, Malpas visited each of the ten area managers who were responsible for the prisons in England and Wales. They set the performance targets for each establishment, and were ruthless in their expectations. The targets, known as key performance indicators, measured activities as diverse as the time prisoners spent unlocked and how the governing governor of each prison used his budget allocation.

Some of the area managers were opposed to the idea but accepted that it would happen. The area managers then visited each of the governing governors at their prisons and issued the order. Only the governor and head of security, in each prison, would know of the existence of the order and it would be their duty to ensure that it was complied with.

Chapter Two

In 1992 Johnny Scapes, aged 45, was making a good and steady career in hairdressing. His salon 'Scapes', situated just off Hampstead High Street, attracted a discreet and well-heeled clientèle. Scapes had personally designed the salon. The ground floor of the four storey terraced property had been converted for commercial use many years before so planning permissions and local council interference was kept to a minimum.

There was no conventional waiting area, just a room decorated with rich, dark carpet, a small counter in one corner and an assortment of well-nourished pot plants. The counter boasted a very expensive Italian coffee machine which was popular with clients and staff alike. When a client arrived they were shown directly into one of four 'style and cutting rooms'. The client would be offered coffee and pastry with the opportunity to browse copies of that day's Times and Daily Telegraph.

Two year old copies of Horse & Hounds, offers of 'something for the weekend' and enquiries about 'holiday arrangements' were definitely off the agenda at Scapes. He insisted that his staff demonstrate old fashioned manners and his clientèle obviously appreciated it. His staff consisted of Mo, salon manager plus Abbey and Sebby who were rapidly gaining reputations as skilled, inventive stylists. Both had followed Scape's example and graduated from the Vidal Sassoon Hairdressing Academy. Scapes and Mo had been romantically linked, some years before, but their relationship could best be described as on and off. They were, however, most certainly on with the other business conducted in the salon. Drugs dealing.

During the mid-60s, Scapes was a dyed-in-the-wool mod. A checked shirt, tonic mohair suit and Ravel shoes were his uniform and he was a known 'face' on the London club scene.

At that time he was already well into his apprenticeship in the hairdressing salons in Central London. The rapidly expanding Afro-Caribbean community in South London brought with it a ready supply of marijuana and he wasn't slow to recognise that there was good money to be made. By 1968 he had a well-established but discreet organisation. He was pulling in a steady income but, most importantly he wasn't greedy.

He lived in the well-appointed two bedroom flat over the salon. When he'd first met Mo, many years before, he'd recognised a kindred spirit and they had both benefited from their joint business prowess.

The fourth 'style and cutting room', although decorated in the same manner as the others, was Mo's office from which she managed both aspects of the business. Appointments for hairstyling were between ten and eight and made in person or on the salon number. Appointments to buy drugs were made by telephoning an answering machine. If Mo recognised the number or voice then the caller would be advised of a time between eight thirty and midnight. The drugs of choice, in London at that time, were cocaine, speed and marijuana. The drug clientèle were always well-heeled and attracted no attention from the local residents. Both sides of the business were operating very well indeed.

Physically fit and a gym rat before the term became fashionable, Scapes was fastidious about his appearance. He'd made the right decision when his rich, curly brown hair started to recede. He shaved the lot off and now sported a dome of well-tanned and deeply moisturised skin. A number of his clients had intimated in the 15 months of the salon's existence that a tip need not necessarily be of the monetary kind. Never one to mix business and pleasure, Scapes always declined. A fuck was never on the cards, no matter what financial inducements were on offer.

On 5th of May 1992, Scapes was enjoying a Gitanes in his office at the back of the salon. Although sparsely decorated, the office radiated a style which reflected the owners approach to life. Discreet, well-made furniture and framed prints of racy lithographs surprised and delighted those clients fortunate enough to be invited into his sanctuary.

It was just after seven and Scapes was reading the Evening Standard. With no further hairdressing appointments and the first of the evening's customers not due until 8.30, he'd given Mo time off to visit relatives in Leicester. As he was stubbing out his cigarette in a cut-glass ashtray, two men entered the salon. Both were white, well-muscled and expensively dressed. They sported long but well-cut hair which immediately put Scapes on alert. Growing up in North London had honed his sense of survival and he recognised a bad situation when it was standing in front of him. 'Hello, My name's Simon and this is Michael,' the slightly taller of the two addressed Scapes in a North London accent.

'Why would that be of interest to me, do you have an appointment?' Scapes replied, as the one named Michael turned and slipped the deadlock on the front door.

'No, but we have a business proposition for you.' Simon answered, a slight smile beginning to form on his wide mouth.

'Really?' Scapes answered.

'Yes, really,' Michael answered, 'let's get on with it.'

'Right, this is our proposition. We provide business insurance, which in these uncertain times is a must for any forward-thinking businessman. For a small monthly premium we will ensure that your business doesn't become a target for thugs and hooligans. We offer 24 hour cover and have many satisfied customers,' the smile now stretching from ear to ear.

Scapes stared at them. He'd thought that a situation like this might happen one day and he'd debated long and hard how he would deal with it. He was glad that he was on his own.

'Do you want me to repeat our proposition?' Simon asked.

'No, that won't be necessary,' Scapes answered as he walked slowly behind the counter. Michael started to move forward but stopped when Simon placed a hand on his shoulder.

'Why would a successful hairdresser in a respectable area of North London require business insurance?' Scapes asked, keeping his voice level.

'The hairdressing part of your business is of no interest to us, we are more interested in your evening activities,' Simon replied, the smile having now vanished like a wisp of smoke.

'And what might they be?' Scapes asked, elbows now resting on the counter.

'Let's stop playing fucking games. You know exactly what we mean so stop acting like a prick,' Michael shouted, spittle leaking out of the corners of his mouth.

'Your dog looks thirsty, would you like me to give him something to calm him down?' Scapes asked, his right hand reaching under the counter.

'That's it, I've had enough of this poncy cunt,' Michael spat and ran forward. Scapes found what he was looking for and as Michael reached the counter, he flipped the lid off of the canister of Elnett hairspray, raised it and sprayed the liquid into Michael's face. Michael stumbled, screamed and started clawing at his eyes. Scapes grabbed a handful of Michael's hair with his left hand and smashed the canister across the bridge of his nose. Michael fell backwards and crashed into Simon who was moving towards the counter. Simon fell and banged into the front door with the back of his head.

Scapes knew he had a chance if he could maximise the advantage the clowns had given him. He moved round the counter and, after kicking Michael in the side of the face as he was trying to stand, he jumped on Simon who was trying to pull something from his jacket pocket. He managed to sit astride Simon and hit him four times across the nose and mouth with the canister. Simon started to shout and blood sprayed across the front of Scapes's shirt. He leaned forward and, taking Simon's head in his hands, he smashed it down, repeatedly into the deep pile carpet. After a minute, or so, he stopped. Simon was still and his breathing was laboured. Scapes place both hands over Simon's mouth and pressed down hard. After what seemed like an eternity Simon stopped moving. Scapes checked for signs of life and knew that Simon was dead.

As he climbed off of Simon's lifeless body he remembered Michael. He looked over his shoulder to see Michael trying to sit up but failing miserably. It then started to dawn on Scapes that the visit from these two wannabe gangsters hadn't happened by accident. He had to find out how they knew about his evening activities otherwise he really was in deep trouble. The fact that he had just killed a man wasn't sinking in but his instinct for survival was.

He moved over to Michael and checked his pockets. Apart from an old fashioned flick knife and some change, he had nothing on him. He dragged Michael into number two style and cutting room and sat him in the chair. The man wasn't in good enough shape to fight but, ever the cautious one, Scapes ran back to his office and found the roll of brown parcel tape he kept in his desk drawer. He returned to Michael and, after taping his wrists securely to the arms of the leather and chrome chair, he cut a small strip and pressed it over Michael's mouth.

Scapes slapped Michael repeatedly round the face until he got a mumbled response. He then emptied a full bottle of ice cold Evian water over Michael's head. He knew that the small refrigerators he'd installed in each of the room would come in handy one day.

"Michael, I know you can hear me. Nod to say you can." Scapes waited for a reply.

Nothing, just rage blazing in Michael's eyes and snot dribbled from his nose. He remained still until Scapes slapped him hard across his damaged, taped mouth. He nodded.

'Good, now we can have a sensible conversation. But, sorry, of course we can't with you all trussed up like a turkey. So,' and with that Scapes ripped the tape from Michael's mouth taking a badly damaged front tooth with it.

'How does that feel, better?' Scapes asked, feigning interest.

Michael responded with something resembling 'fuck off'. Scapes smiled.

'I've one question for you. Answer me with the truth or I'll kill you here, right now. Do you understand?'

Michael nodded and his chin dropped and rested on his chest.

'Who sent you here today?'

Michael stared at the ceiling and remained silent.

'Wait one,' Scapes said and left the room. When he returned he was holding a gleaming pair of Jowell hairdressing scissors. They were his favourites and had just been returned from the manufacturers after having been sharpened. Scapes had once lost concentration and cut the top off a client's ear with his trusty Jowell's. When the client complained, Scapes offered to cut the top off the other ear free of charge. Michael flinched as Scapes stroked the blades against his groin.

'Last chance,' Scapes whispered

Michael spat blood at Scapes and made a sound like 'more'.

'What, say again?'

Michael breathed in and said, 'Mo.'

'What?' Scapes shouted, placing the blades against the skin on Michael's neck.

'Mo, Mo,' Michael spluttered.

Scapes remained silent for a long minute and then came to a decision, 'Thanks,' he whispered as he plunged the scissors deep into Michael's neck.

Maureen Day, known to all as Mo, was born in the Midlands in 1947. After she'd left school with eight GCE 'O' levels and a brace of 'A' levels she'd drifted through temp agencies before finding her vocation in the world of public relations. At a petite five feet or so, her good looks, great dress sense and sharp intellect made her perfect for PR. It was at one of the many drink and nibbles functions hosted by Ryder Communications that she'd first crossed paths with Johnny Scapes.

Mo was instantly attracted to Scapes but drew the line when he'd offered to cut her hair. A drink, dinner and early to bed was acceptable but a haircut on a first date, no way.

As predicted by her close friends, their relationship was explosive, passionate and short lived. Scapes had decided that, variety being the spice of life, he'd try to pull Mo's best friend Essy. His massive lapse in judgement nearly cost him his crown jewels when Mo found out. She'd attacked him with a

Stanley knife but failed miserably when there were no blades in it.

Six months before the opening of Scapes they met again through a mutual friend. Over dinner at one of the many overpriced eateries in Soho, Mo told Scapes what a bastard he'd been and the pain he'd put her through. He murmured his apologies and seemed to be sincere. They parted having agreed to meet again for pie and mash the following Saturday. When Essy asked Mo if she'd forgiven him, her reply was a frosty 'you're having a laugh'.

Over lunch, Scapes explained his plans for the salon in Hampstead. Well into the second bottle of red, Mo described a business she been made aware of in Leicester. In essence, the concept was simple. In one of the few smart areas in Leicester, a shop sold expensive underwear during the day and operated a lucrative drug dealing business during the evening hours. Many of the clients shopped for both products on offer. No business was conducted after midnight so as to minimise the chances of a visit from the police. Mo said that the business worked because the owners weren't greedy, so they were no threat to the real heavy dealers and they were certainly operating under the police radar.

Scapes listened, fascinated, and decided that the concept would be ideal in the rich, corrupt areas of North and West London. The front of a highly respectable hairdressing salon was too good an opportunity to turn down.

They both agreed that theirs would be a shag-free relationship, concentrating solely on the business in hand, so to speak. They also agreed that Mo would become salon manager dealing with appointments for both areas of the business. They parted just after three and went their separate ways. Scapes was pleased, and not a little relieved that Mo had forgiven him and agreed to work in the salon. He also gave himself a pat on the back for displaying the famous Scapes gift of the gab. Mo was over the moon that, finally, she would get the opportunity to really hurt the bastard. It had been quite obvious, over lunch, that he had been paying lip service to the series of grovelling apologies which he'd uttered between mouthfuls of excellent pie and mash. Mo decided that she wouldn't need a Stanley knife this time.

The wood and glass door came off its hinges when it was struck with the battering ram for the second time. A police officer stepped in through the opening and pointed his Heckler & Koch assault rifle at Scapes who was trying to stand in the pool of rapidly spreading blood.

'Armed police. Remain in a kneeling position and place both hands behind your head. Do it now!' the officer shouted.

'But...' Scapes started to reply.

'Remain in a kneeling position and place your hands behind your head. Don't make me repeat myself again.' This time the officer's voice was quieter but devoid of emotion.

As the officer was speaking three more entered the room, two pointing their weapons at Scapes. After a few seconds he managed to balance himself on his knees. As he was placing his hands behind his head the unarmed officer walked forward, slightly to one side and forced Scapes face down in the pool of blood. In what seemed to take moments Scapes found himself with his hands secured behind his back by thin strips of plastic.

As he was trying to keep his face out of the pool of blood a fifth officer entered the room. He had sergeant's chevrons on his shoulder boards.

'Search the style and cutting rooms but start with number four,' he said with obvious disdain, all the while staring down at Scapes. Three of the officers secured their weapons across their chests and began the search. The remaining officer, who had first entered the room, stood with his weapon pointed at Scapes' now blood-splattered head.

Scapes knew that the past five or so minutes had not happened by chance. The fact that they were searching number four first set alarm bells ringing in his head. That they had found him holding scissors in a man's throat with a second one lying dead nearby hadn't really registered in his over worked brain. All he could focus on was the rifle pointing at his head and the noise coming from room number four.

After what seemed like hours, but was in fact 15 minutes, the search was complete. Moving from number four they had given the other three rooms no more than a cursory glance. But what they carried out of number four shocked the already stunned Scapes. There were two sacks which two of the officers were dragging out. They were followed by one carrying two Waitrose shopping bags and the last officer emerged carrying a further two Sainsbury's shopping bags. The bags appeared to be fit to burst.

If the bags contained drugs, which Scapes suspected they did, then something had gone seriously wrong. Mo was meticulous in her drug dealings, never having more product than was necessary for the evening's business. Scapes did not accept casual business so what could have happened?

As Scapes was trying to concentrate on his predicament he was dragged to his feet by two of the armed officers.

'John Patrick Scapes I…'

'It's Johnny not John.'

'Johnny Patrick Scapes, I'm arresting you on suspicion of the murder of two IC1 males, yet to be identified, and for the possession of a large quantity of Class A drugs with intent to supply. These alleged offences took place in your business premises known as Scalps Hair.'

'It's Scapes,' he shouted.

'What?' The sergeant replied.

'It's Scapes not Scalps.'

"I said Scapes," the sergeant stated, exasperation in his voice.

'You said Scalps. It's a stupid name and makes me sound like a red Indian!' Scapes screamed.

The officer holding Scapes' right forearm started to smile but he maintained his composure with a laughter-suppressing cough.

'Whatever. You do not have to say anything but it may harm your defence if you do not mention, when questioned, something which you later rely on in court. Anything you do say may be given in evidence. Do you understand what I have just said?'

'Yes I do. How do you know my middle name? Only one other person knows my middle name.'

'Interesting questions. No comment.'

"Was it Mo Day who shopped me?" Scapes whispered, tears running down his cheeks.

'Another interesting question. No comment.'

Scapes spent a long time on remand. He hired the best solicitor his not-inconsiderable funds could afford. The solicitor Michael Croft, known across the London underworld as a man who would do anything for the right amount of non-tax-deductible money, had the brief to slow down the proceedings as much as possible to give Scapes the chance to come up with some sort of plausible defence. They both knew that it was a fruitless exercise but carried on regardless.

Croft did, however, add to Scapes' bank balance by arranging to have the Hampstead salon burnt to the ground. Croft had used his underworld contacts to employ a firm who specialised in arson. The fee for the work included a twenty per cent bonus for Croft. Despite the cost, Scapes was content because he had the perfect alibi. The insurance company had no choice but to pay up because the police finally gave up on any chance of finding a culprit.

Mo Day was livid when she heard about the fire. She had promised Scapes that she would withdraw any statements she had made against him in the hope of having his eventual sentence reduced. She had also promised him that she would tell the police that she had pointed the two dead men in Scapes' direction because they were blackmailing her and that Scapes was only acting in self-defence. When the fire happened she was certain that Scapes was somehow responsible and that as far as she was concerned he could go to hell.

Scapes eventually appeared at Snaresbrook Crown Court to stand trial for the murders of Michael Waters and Simon Cresswell and for possession of Class A drugs with intent to supply. The trial lasted five days and the jury returned with unanimous guilty verdicts on all counts. A number of Scapes' famous clients did turn up for the trial but all refused, point-blank, to enter the dock and be a character witness.

The following day, the judge sentenced him to two life sentences plus an additional 10 years on the drugs charge. The 10 years would run concurrently with the life sentences. Scapes had been expecting the sentences but was devastated when the judge informed him that he would serve a minimum of 30 years before he became eligible to be considered for release on license.

As he was being led back to the cells to wait for transport back to prison he saw Mo and Essy in the public gallery waving at him and laughing. On his return to Belmarsh prison he soon settled back in to the mind-numbing routine. One evening he was playing pool when a fight started. It ended with a prisoner, who was the prison hairdresser, being taken to the healthcare centre with extensive upper-body injuries. He never returned to the wing.

Scapes decided that he wanted more time out of his cell so he volunteered to be the new hairdresser. His offer was accepted and after a few days he had a waiting list of clients, as he liked to call them.

He was allowed on to the other wings, which was virtually unheard of in Belmarsh, and he made a lot of contacts and learned a lot about what was really going on in the prison.

On the first of March he was informed that he would be transferred to Gartree prison in Leicestershire. Gartree, now a lifer assessment centre, had been a dumping ground in the 70s and 80s, for the psychopaths who were almost running amok across the Service.

Scapes was, at first, worried that a move to such a place would be a disaster. He made an application to see the wing governor to discuss the transfer. The young governor, who had worked for a short period at Gartree as a part of his accelerated promotion scheme training, assured Scapes that the move would be a positive aspect in the progress of his life sentence. Scapes came away from the meeting feeling upbeat, for the first time in months.

The following Tuesday he was collected by a national escort bus and driven to Gartree. He arrived during a thunderstorm, a regular feature at the prison which was sited on a disused airfield. He was informed that the assessment process would take as long as was necessary before he was transferred, again, to serve the next phase of his sentence. After a couple of weeks' induction he settled into the endless interviews with the prison psychologists. He also secured for himself the coveted job of prison hairdresser as his reputation had preceded him.

He got to know the real 'players' on the four wings and always paid particular attention to their hairdressing requirements. One gang leader on A wing gave him an invaluable piece of advice, which was to offer to cut the officers' hair free of charge. Scapes laughed but decided to give it a try. His reputation across the prison had grown so one young officer decided to give him a try. It was a success and he soon had a list of clients from both sides of the fence.

Just before Easter he summoned his solicitor to the prison. When he gave his instructions, Croft flatly refused, saying that he was out of his mind. He did, however, accept the work when informed that his fee would be £30.000. Scapes had kept a secret bank account where most of his wealth was held which included the payout from the salon fire. After warning Croft of the dire consequences if anything went wrong, he verbally detailed his requirements. As well as the £30,000, Croft was to withdraw an additional £40.000 to be split equally between the two individuals who would do the work.

Early in May, Scapes wrote to Mo asking her to visit him so that he could apologise and recompense her for all the trouble he had caused. After thinking long and hard Mo decided to agree to the visit. She asked Essy to go with her because, at the very least, it would be a good laugh.

They caught the train to Market Harborough and the shuttle bus to the prison. Essy had to wait outside because the visiting order only allowed Mo into the prison. She sat in the visits room waiting for Scapes. After twenty minutes a young, female officer walked over to Mo and told her that Scapes had refused to see her. Irritated, she asked the officer if he had given a reason. The officer replied that all Scapes had said was to tell Mo to 'take care'.

Mo stamped out of the room and eventually met Essy who was waiting in the car park. After explaining what had happened they began to make their way, arm in arm, over to the bus stop. Deep in conversation, they didn't notice the old Ford Cosworth start to move from where it was parked behind a line of cars. After suddenly accelerating, the car hit Mo and Essy pushing them on to the pavement by the bus stop. The car reversed, accelerated and mounted the pavement, stopping on them. The car seemed to rock, backwards and forwards, on them and then roared off. It was later found abandoned near the village of Great Glen. Mo was declared dead at the scene, her body a tangled mess. Essy lost her battle for life, two days later, in Leicester Royal Infirmary. Surgeons said that she would have been a tetraplegic, with extensive brain damage, if she had survived.

Croft visited Scapes, a few days later, to recount the events in the car park. Scapes made him repeat his commentary, smiling the whole way through. Croft had one last job to do. He met Sebby and Abbey in a pub in Soho, handing each of them an envelope containing £20,000. After checking the contents they both smiled and left. He never saw or heard of them again.

The daily routine at Gartree was predictable and he almost enjoyed it. Apart from his hairdressing work and the security limitations of living in a maximum security prison, his time was his own. The number of assessment interviews had now dwindled to a trickle and he'd gotten used to the questions and how to answer them.

He submitted his list of hairdressing 'clients' to his wing principal officer, at the beginning of each week, and he went about his work with virtually no interference. He carried messages for selected 'clients' but refused to carry packages to the various parts of the prison his work took him to. Early on, he had offered his hairdressing services to the staff and had been rewarded with a list of both male and female clients. Some of the younger members of staff would brag about the incidents which they had been involved in and he would nod but offer no comment.

Late one Thursday afternoon he was stopped, at the gates to his wing, by the young governor who was head of security. Scapes had seen him before and was mildly alarmed but tried to remain calm.

'Hello, Scapes, how's the hairdressing business?'

'Fine, thank you, am I in trouble?' he blurted, the words tumbling out before he could stop himself.

'Why would you think that, or is there something I should know about?' the man asked, smiling broadly.

'Nothing, it's just that you've never spoken to me before.' he replied, sensing that he probably wasn't in trouble.

'Okay, calm down. I've heard good reports about you and your work. Staff seem more than satisfied. So, I'll be coming to your wing, this evening, and you can cut my hair. We'll use the principal officers' office. About 7.30, alright with you?'

'Of course, I'll be happy to cut your hair. But if you don't mind me saying so, it looks as if you've just had it done.' Scapes answered, keeping his voice low.

'Exactly, see you this evening,' the man replied and let himself out of the wing before Scapes could react.

Scapes spent the tea time lock-up period worrying about the coming meeting with the head of security. He knew that he couldn't be in trouble because he would be sat in the segregation unit by now. But why on earth would the man want a haircut if he'd just had one. Strange.

Just before 7.30 he was unlocked and made his way down to the ground floor where the head of security was already waiting for him. He had, sensibly, brought his hairdressing bag with him although he sensed that it wouldn't be required. The man showed him into the room and, following him in, closed the door. Following instructions, Scapes prepared to cut the man's hair by placing a maroon sheet around his shoulders. Scapes started to ask....

'Okay, the charade stops here. Hold your comb and scissors as though you are cutting my hair in case we are interrupted.' Scapes did as he was told. 'Listen carefully to what I have to say and don't speak until I tell you. Understood?' Scapes nodded.

Scapes listened as instructed and with scissors and comb poised, and was flabbergasted at what the man was saying. Resisting the urge to ask questions, he listened. After almost 20 minutes the offer was made.

'So, Scapes, what I've just told you is not a work of fiction or a practical joke. It has come from headquarters and it is exactly, word for word, as told to me. Do you understand?

'I think so,' Scapes mumbled.

'Good. The concept is simple but does, as I've already explained, have its dangers. If it works then we both gain. If it doesn't, then you lose. I can't make it clearer than that. Shall I continue?'

'Yes.'

'If you now agree to work for us, inside the guidelines I have explained, we will ensure that your 30 year tariff is reduced, incrementally, so that you will have a realistic chance of being released before you are too old to appreciate it. The information you provide will be reliable and current. Rumour will just not do. You will be moved to other prisons as we see fit. Sometimes it will appear that you are being moved against your will. You will enter into the ploy to minimise the danger. You will be employed as the hairdresser, some time after each transfer to a new prison, because of your obvious skills in that department. You will never mention a word of this to any prisoner, member of staff or visitor. If you do, I am instructed to inform you that you will never be released from prison. You will die behind bars. Do you understand what I have said? A simple yes or no will suffice.'

'Yes.'

'Excellent. This is a genuine offer. If you agree, as a sign of good faith I will instruct the necessary authority to formally reduce your 30 year tariff to 29 years. You will be shown the reduction, in writing, but you will not be given a copy. There will have to be trust on both sides. I have given you a lot to digest but do you have any questions, now, which I may be able to answer?'

Scapes considered what was on offer and nothing was said for well over five minutes. He asked a couple of questions which were answered to his satisfaction.

'Okay. I will give you the weekend to consider the offer. I will come to your place of work, next Monday morning. If we have an agreement, you will offer to cut my hair, again, making sure that the other prisoners who are waiting hear you. I will politely refuse and walk away. By doing this we will both know that we have a deal which is binding. Clear?'

'Yes.'

'Excellent. Also, your first transfer could be tomorrow or next year. That is something which we cannot predict. Clear?'

'Yes,' and with that Scapes followed the man out of the office and was returned to his cell. He spent the majority of the weekend in his cell, explaining to staff and prisoners that he felt unwell. He refused offers of treatment, both legal and illegal, and emerged on Monday morning professing to feel much better.

Just before lunchtime his offer to cut the head of security's hair was politely refused, much to the amusement of three prisoners and a member of staff.

Chapter Three

HM Prison Rosmere came into being in 1904 near a village called Whittingham in the north west of England. Often shrouded in mist, it was foreboding with its high walls and fences. Its role in the penal system had changed down the years but in 1975 it became a specialist prison holding men who were serving life sentences. It could comfortably accommodate 224 and was close to that number on any given day.

Lifers from prisons all over the country could routinely apply for a transfer to Rosmere because it was reckoned to be a cushy number. If one could keep one's nose clean in Rosmere rumour had it that light might appear at the end of the life sentence tunnel.

Trouble did, however, raise its head during the summer of 1994.

The bus arrived just before two in the afternoon. It was cold, with a blustery wind which seemed to eat into the very fabric of the place. Two lifers had endured a six hour journey from prisons in London and the Midlands. The bus had entered through the outer gates and was waiting in the sterile area. Once the outer gates were closed and locked, the inner gates would open and allow the bus entry to the prison grounds. Well, that's what usually happened.

The mechanism which opened the inner gates finally gave up the ghost after years of make-do-and-mend maintenance. The Prison Officers Association had complained to successive governors about the state of the place but had always been fobbed off about the lack of resources to do the work.

After two frustrating hours the gates were finally opened, manually, and the van made its way to Reception. The two prisoners, Jerry Syston and Johnny Scapes, were processed through reception and taken to B wing which would be their home for the foreseeable future.

Syston had received his life sentence for the brutal murder of a drug dealer in Leicester. When the judge had ordered that Syston serve a minimum of 16 years before he would be eligible to be considered for release, Syston had smiled and wished everyone a very merry Christmas. Scapes was just another lifer on the move around the system.

The wing was much the same as the rest of the wings in Rosmere, tense but ticking over. An incident had happened on B wing in 1983 when a prisoner had set fire to cell B2.31, and had died in the ensuing blaze. For some years after the blaze cell B2.31 had been used as a storeroom after a civilian worker had reported seeing the ghost of the unfortunate prisoner walking through the locked cell door.

In May 1994 a new governing governor was drafted in. Charles Knight was known to be a dour, uncompromising man and he revelled in the reputation. He was a hard-liner and believed that lifers had it too cushy and should do their time the hard way. He changed the regime and rotated the staff into posts many had never worked before. Not surprisingly, for the first time in years there was a very real tension between the prisoners and staff.

The new governor had promised HQ that he would run Rosmere profitably so the legend of cell B2.31 was forgotten. Eventually, the cell was redecorated, a toilet installed and was ready for occupation. Jerry Syston was the first prisoner to occupy the newly refurbished cell.

Syston met some of the other prisoners on landing B2 and received some strange looks when he mentioned that he was in cell 31. He thought nothing of it because long term incarceration did strange things to men and resulted in strange behaviour. He spent the remainder of that first evening unpacking his belongings. His door was locked at exactly 9 o'clock. Syston lay on his bunk, rolled a smoke and read the *Daily Mirror* which another prisoner had lent him.

Just after midnight, Syston was drifting off to sleep when he heard what sounded like a whisper. He sat up and looked around the cell. A full moon was providing enough light to see by. There was nothing out of the ordinary so he lay back down, turned to face the wall and drifted off to sleep.

At 7.40 the following morning, 13 August, Officer Robert Jackson made his way along B2 landing to begin the unlock. Jackson was still getting used to the routines on B wing and decided to start at cell 31. He inserted his cell key, released the lock and pushed the door open. He turned to the right to walk the short distance to the next cell door. He never made it. Two hands reached out from the interior of cell 31 and dragged him in by his throat.

The exact sequence of the events which followed were never fully ascertained but, some fifteen minutes later when Officer Christine Saren stepped into the cell looking for Jackson the scene before her caused her to collapse in a dead faint. What she saw would haunt her for the rest of her life.

Jackson's head looked down at Saren from the top of the small television which was secured on a bracket to the wall in the top right-hand corner of the cell. Where there should have been eyes there were bloody holes. Blood had dripped down from the holes making Jackson look like he had cried blood. He probably had. The nose was intact and a roll-up cigarette was jammed between the blood encrusted lips. The cut which had separated the head from the rest of the body was fairly neat. The attacker had obviously taken his work seriously. Jackson's arms and legs had also been severed from the torso and were discarded behind the modesty screen which hid the toilet. The torso had been jammed, neck down, into the toilet pan. A knife, fork and spoon were sticking out of Jackson's anus.

When Saren had repeatedly failed to respond to enquiries on her personal radio, other staff were despatched to look for her. They found her where she had fainted. She appeared stunned and confused. Her face was covered in a white, sticky liquid which a nurse later identified as semen. Both Saren's and Jackson's keys were missing from their security chains.

Syston was nowhere to be found but now had access to cells and nearly every other part of the prison.

The duty governor, Rob Young, was already in the prison and ordered that no further prisoners be unlocked until Syston had been located and contained. Prisoners who had been working in the kitchen were returned to their cells with no explanations given. Johnny Scapes asked to see the governor and was advised to shut up and mind his own business. He did.

By 9.30, a full scale search for Syston was under way. Governor Knight arrived and immediately contacted area manager Mitchell Hagen, as he was required to do. Hagen, who had just taken command of the North West Area, offered to send staff from other prisons but Knight refused saying that he didn't need help sorting out his own problems. Hagen started to lose his temper, shouting that the murder of a prison officer was a Service problem, only to find that he was talking to himself. Knight had hung up the phone.

Police arrived shortly afterwards but were kept in the gate lodge whilst the prison was being searched. Although offered tea and excuses, the police knew that they were powerless to insist on admittance because the Prison Service was practically a law unto itself.

Just before midday the coroner's people arrived and took the remains of Robert Jackson to the central hospital in Carlisle. Christine Saren was under heavy sedation in the healthcare centre.

By 15.00 hours the search had been completed. There was still no sign of Jerry Syston. The police superintendent was finally allowed to meet with Governor Knight. The young superintendent patiently explained that by moving the body of Officer Jackson the crime scene had been compromised. Knight replied that a 'fucking crime scene' wasn't necessary as the culprit for the murder of Jackson was a prisoner called Jerry Syston and that no copper barely out of short trousers was coming into his prison to tell him how to do his job.

Superintendent Rice, normally a quiet and measured man, felt his temples starting to throb. He knew that losing his temper was not really an option but he also realised that Knight was testing him to the limit. Rice tried to calm himself by asking how the search for Syston had gone. Knight snapped that with a prison as old as Rosmere it was like looking for a needle in a haystack. When Rice insisted that it was the time for the police to become involved, Knight laughed and told him to leave. Rice left and, reaching his car, contacted police HQ in Carlisle. He was advised to back off but insist on a police presence in the prison incident room. This request was agreed to.

At 16.15 hours, Mitchell Hagen arrived. He was shown into the governor's office and noticed Knight trying to place a bottle in the top left-hand drawer of his desk. Senior colleagues in headquarters had warned Hagen that Knight liked a drop but he was shocked to see the advice proven to be true.

'Bit early for a drink, Charles?' Hagen left his remark hanging in the air.

'I don't need your fucking advice about my drinking habits. If your type had controlled this fucking place years earlier it wouldn't be down to me to clear up the mess,' Knight growled, foam bursting from the corners of his mouth as he walked unsteadily around the side of his desk.

'Charles, I've come here to help, not to be insulted and I really don't need to remind you that you should not be drinking on duty.'

'Mr High 'n' Fucking Mighty Area Manager comes into my prison and starts telling me how to behave. I was running places like this before you'd shit your first nappy, you arrogant bastard,' Knight shouted and sprawled onto the floor, having sat down into an empty space.

Hagen turned, walked to the office door and opened it. He called Knight's secretary and asked her to contact the security principal officer and request his presence immediately. It was clear by the look on her face that she had overheard the exchange which had taken place.

When the principal officer arrived, Hagen went back into Knight's office. Without preamble he informed Knight that he was suspended from duty with immediate effect and ordered the principal officer to escort him to the gate. Hagen telephoned the duty Governor and asked him to make arrangements for Knight to be driven home. It would not be the last occasion during his tenure as North West area manager that Mitchell Hagen would suspend one of his governing governors.

Hagen immediately took personal charge and noted that the incident management arrangements were running properly, one of the few things operating correctly as far as Hagen could ascertain.

By 18.00 hours the prisoners were still locked in their cells and the mood was decidedly ugly. Doors were being kicked and the odd window was being broken. Hagen had already requested that Operation Tornado be activated and the gold commander in headquarters had agreed. Tornado was a well rehearsed HQ plan to respond to major incidents and staff were being prepared to travel to Rosmere from the Midlands and North East of England.

As Hagen was discussing emergency plans to feed the prisoners he received an urgent message informing him that cells in A and B wings had, somehow been unlocked. Prisoners had started to attack the wing staff who had been forced to retreat to areas outside the wings. Senior staff informed Hagen that they had chained the wing gates shut but couldn't be sure if any prisoners had left the wings before the trouble had kicked off.

Evidence later came to light, from anonymous sources, that Syston had been seen on both wings unlocking cell doors. One of Hagen's biggest concerns was that Jackson's and Saren's bunches of keys were still missing.

Fires were being set in the effected wings and Hagen decided that the situation was too dangerous to allow the fire brigade admittance to the prison. Prisoners were wreaking wholesale destruction so staff had to wait for the anger to subside before attempting to enter and retake the wings. The arrival of staff responding to Operation Tornado would eventually enable this to happen.

The fires and rioting raged for two days and nights. Tornado staff attempted to start retaking the wings on day three but were beaten back by the flames. Headquarters staff voiced opinions, privately, that the prisoner who started the troubles should burn in hell. Publicly, they made assurances that every effort was being made to bring the incident to a swift conclusion. The press office was patiently dealing with a mountain of enquiries from the media and prisoners' families.

Staff eventually began to retake control, a wing at a time, and allowed the fire-fighters to enter and do their jobs. Prison transport arrived from across the country and started to transfer the inmates. Ringleaders were being identified but it would be a further 24 hours before Syston was found. From the air and on the ground, HM Prison Rosmere was a smoking mess.

The other fatality was a convicted paedophile who was found on C wing. He had been tortured, and beaten to a pulp. His penis and testicles were never found. The killers were later identified when staff found a note on the landing near Johnny Scapes's cell.

Syston was eventually cornered on C wing roof, again after a tip off. He appeared calm and seemed to be enjoying himself. He took obvious delight in telling the watching officers how he had dismembered Jackson. He seemed to particularly enjoy recounting how he had masturbated over officer Saren but became serious when he said that he wouldn't have fucked her because she was about as attractive as an anorexic stick insect. One of the watching staff couldn't stop herself and vomited.

Syston laughed, thanked her and stepped off the roof into oblivion.

Once the police were satisfied that they couldn't uncover any more evidence into the murders and assault on officer Saren, the Prison Service investigation swung into action. Many conclusions were arrived at, the main one being that nothing could have been done to predict the orgy of violence and destruction which would follow Syston's one-night stay in cell B2.31.

Stackley and always listened intently when he called them on their private lines.

Stackley also ran area office. It was a lean and efficient operation. It had the smallest number of staff of any area office and was a favourite of the director general who was a regular visitor and always smiled when Stackley called him boss.

Stackley was totally loyal to Hagen and didn't abuse their friendship. Hagen had offered him senior posts in the North West prisons but Stackley had always declined. He said that he would move on when Hagen retired and not until then. They were both happy with that arrangement.

'So, do we have a date when we can accept the first prisoner into my new establishment?' Hagen asked.

'Early 2003,' Williams replied with a smug look on his acne-scarred face.

'How confident are you of that, because I want David to prepare a press release?'

'Absolutely, one hundred per cent. The original infrastructure is mostly intact. The fire did damage the mains pipework above ground but I'm reliably informed that any work will be minor,' Williams replied.

'Great! Walter, are there any finance issues which I need to be aware of?'

'No. We have the necessary funding earmarked to rebuild, equip and staff a category B male establishment. Although overcrowding issues seem to fill our waking hours at the moment, long range predictors indicate that your new prison will open as a category B.'

'Excellent. David, any thoughts?'

'A number, as you would expect,' Stackley replied. He straightened up and continued, 'Long term, we need to be thinking about who might be the first governing governor of our new prison.'

'I've already given that some thought and have a couple of up-and-comers in mind,' Hagen offered, declining to elaborate.

Stackley smiled, already having discussed the list of candidates with Hagen. At the end of each day they would close Hagen's office door and discuss strategy over decaffeinated coffee and Marlboro Lights. They acted out what amounted to be a pantomime in front of the other two so that when the rumours leaked, early, Hagen would be portrayed as a benevolent manager, which he clearly wasn't.

'Anything else? I want David to work on the press release. The director general wants sight of it before we go public.'

'Just one,' Stackley offered, a smile stretching across his bearded face.

'Shoot,' Hagen replied, knowing what was coming.

'We need a name for our new prison.'

'Any thoughts?' Hagen said, looking from Stackley to Williams and from Williams to Sutton.

Sutton and Williams remained silent because they knew that a decision had already been reached.

'I think that we should call it Raymar,' Stackley offered, smiling at Hagen.

'And why would I want to have it called Raymar?' Hagen answered, fighting to keep a straight face.

'Because it combines Ray, my middle name, and part of my wife's name,' Stackley answered, clearly enjoying himself. It took seconds for Sutton and Williams to understand and then they laughed as was expected of them.

'I've never heard of a new prison being named after the area manager's staff officer and his wife? Absolute lunacy.'

'We could call it HMP Beelzebub but some people have short memories and we don't want to get off to a bad start do we?' Stackley smiled, 'and when they number the cells on B wing there won't be a 2.31.

The room fell silent. Hagen winked at Stackley.

'HMP Raymar it is, then,' Hagen said and the legend was born.

Chapter Four

If you don't come out we're coming in,' the young prison officer shouted at the door in front of him.

This was his first week at the South London prison after he had completed his training at the school in Wakefield. He had never, in his wildest dreams ever considered that he would be standing in front of a door in a prison trying to persuade a seriously angry prisoner called Masters that he was going to be transferred hundreds of miles away from London.

'Is that the new baby screw who is trying to make me piss my pants?' a smiling Anthony 'Tony' John Masters shouted back through the door. Masters is white and aged 32. Tall and well built, he knows that he is a bit of a handful and a good looking bastard. The distinctive mark above his right eye was the result of falling out of a tree and not a battle scar from his time in prison. He is serving seven years for assault and a number of robberies. He has been in and out of juvenile, young offender and adult establishments. He was born in Peckham, South London. Masters is quiet, racist and supports Spurs. He is convinced that, one day, he will kill someone.

Masters was fed up with his present incarceration in a London jail which he hated and where the staff hated him. He had done his remand time there and never considered that they would send him back when he had picked up his bird. His co-accused had been sentenced on the same day and were now settled nicely in cushy jails in the Midlands. He had imagined that he would be going with them. Wrong!

'I'm trying to be reasonable with you, Masters,' the young officer, called Arnold, shouted once again at the door. He knew that he was going to be given his first opportunity to participate in a forced cell entry and the idea did not fill him with happiness. During his months of training he had avoided as much as possible the sessions where violence was involved.

He was a passive man but the lure of regular money had been too much to ignore. The information which he had received prior to applying for the job had painted a picture where the prisoners were so occupied with education, work and in-cell television that violence was the last thing on their minds. The Service website had concentrated on the sparkling view of the job. New words such as key performance indicators and diversity sounded great but did not hint at the position he presently found himself in.

Arnold heard what sounded like wind chimes coming from the bottom of the door. When he looked down he saw a rapidly spreading pool of urine making its way towards his shiny new boots. He cursed this old London prison and its old, warped doors.

'I thought that you might be thirsty Mr Arnold so I did this just for you. Enjoy.'

'I'm asking you for the last time to come out. Nothing will happen to you if that's what you are worried about.'

Masters stepped backwards and kicked the door. He was now getting seriously pissed off with this young tosser. He was sure that he had heard the con in the next cell laugh. He knew that he would end up getting a few slaps but intended to ruin the day for at least one screw.

'Masters, I'm now giving you a direct order to stand away from the door.'

'Fuck off and tie yourself in a knot, you wanker!' Masters shouted.

'Masters, Mr Arnold has been very reasonable with you but, you being you, are unable to accept that we are coming in for you and you are going to be transferred. We've had enough of you here.'

This was a different voice but one that Tony Masters recognised immediately. Senior officer Ross, known by the cons as The Rat, was the type of screw who came and gave you a good kicking but always with three other screws as backup.

'Nice to hear your voice, Mr Rat, I wondered how long it would be until you showed up. Waxed our whiskers and shined our tail, have we? Who else is with you?'

'Just me, bonny lad, and I'm looking forward to our nice van ride up to Raymar. My friends up there know all about you and can't wait to meet you.'

'No way am I going up there, I'll get no fucking visits.'

'I'll tell that skinny slag who visits you where you've gone when I make her a happy bunny tonight.'

'Ross, you're a miserable bastard. Make sure you're first through the door, I've got a present for you.'

As Ross was about to reply the duty governor, Miss Trisha K Ford, arrived on the landing. Ross hated her because she was one of those fast-track wannabes who looked down on landing staff. She had spent about five minutes in uniform and thought she knew the lot. God, he hated her. Good body, smart clothes. Slut.

'Mr Masters, I am ordering you to allow us to enter the cell, you will not be hurt if you do exactly as I say,' Miss Ford said, trying to fill her voice with authority.

'Hello darling, got that nice tight skirt on today? A lot of the cons would love to try you on.'

Ford blushed and tried to turn away to avoid the stares and smirks of the officers waiting on the landing. Ross almost choked on his laughter but Arnold hoped the ground would open up. He knew that this situation was going to turn really nasty.

'Mr Arnold, go with Mr Locking, Mr Trembath and Miss Lakes and get suited up,' Ford snapped, 'This has gone on long enough.'

Masters knew what was coming. His years going in and out of jails had hardened him to the pain that was surely on its way.

Peckham, South London. Over the years, Peckham had been home to more than its fair share of thugs and villains. Great train robbers and gangsters who enjoyed pulling teeth out with pliers could be found in the dingy back streets. In the Sixties and Seventies it had been a vibrant community which did not encourage outsiders. There had always been a rivalry with the inhabitants of East London, just across the River Thames. Disputes were settled, in the traditional manner, using fists and boots. Unfortunately, the Nineteen Eighties proved to be a time of great change. The government of the day ripped the heart out of the community by demolishing the network of back streets and cul-de-sac's and, effectively, turned the heart of Peckham into a massive housing estate. The estate spawned its own gangs and the culture was one of indiscriminate violence and isolation. The older residents rarely ventured out after night fall and the police patrolled in pairs. So much for traditional values. His mind drifted back to the first beating in the children's home in Peckham.

Masters had wet himself and asked the nurse for some clean pants. The nurse, a big fat lad called Arthur, had taken him back to his room and had punched him so hard in the stomach that he had been sick over his shirt. Arthur then punched him again and again until he'd wet himself again. Masters never, again, asked Arthur for anything.

When Masters was 17 he saw Arthur coming out of a pub at the back of Rye Lane railway station. He followed Arthur to a dingy house on Lyndhurst Way and heard an old lady shouting at Arthur for coming home drunk. He laughed when Arthur started to cry as he was saying sorry.

Two days later and Masters was ready. Arthur came out of the same pub and started to walk towards Lyndhurst Way. As Arthur walked past a white van Masters stepped out behind him and hit him across the back of the neck with a lump hammer. Arthur staggered forward, fell down on his knees and then on to his face. As he was about to cut Arthur with his new Stanley knife he heard someone screaming at him from the upstairs window of a terraced house a few yards away. He legged it. A story in the South London Press described the attack and recorded that, although Arthur had survived the attack he would spend the rest of his life in a wheelchair.

Masters wedged the bunk bed against the cell door and stood behind it. There was a loud click and, as the door opened, he jumped away from the bed. As he started to raise his blade the shield hit him in the face and the officers pinned him to the floor using wrist locks. They got him up on his knees, dragged him out across the landing and down to the ground floor. They stopped and put handcuffs on him.

He was placed in a holding cell and, later that day a van took him to HM Prison Wakefield. His time in the maximum security conditions at Wakefield was uneventful and his next move was in April 2004.

Chapter Five

Roman 'Diamond' Perry is black and aged 34. He has long dreads and cleans them every day. He's a gym rat and his superb physique is a testament to hours on the weights. He has a sharp mouth and his scars were well earned. He is serving a life sentence for a gang-related murder and may be eligible to be considered for release on license, after having served 20 years. So far, he has served two years.

Perry was born in Stockwell, South London but always claimed that he was born in Brixton. He collected the nickname 'Diamond' at a young age because friends and enemies could see that he was hard and rough. He distinguished himself by being expelled from every school in the Stockwell, Brixton and Clapham areas. He couldn't go further afield because his mother couldn't afford the bus fares. His father had left the family penniless and had run off with a female traffic warden. It was fortunate that Perry had not found him because, if he had, then daddy would have suffered a painful death.

He liked living in London but he had always seen himself as the powerful leader of a gang based in Kingston, Jamaica. He had the regulation dreads but would not have been put out if they became unfashionable. He didn't give a fuck about Rastafarianism but nobody, not even his closest friends, had a clue about his true feelings.

Perry's mission in life was money. Not women, not clothes, not flash cars but cash, dosh, whatever it was known by. Since he was a kid he had dreamed of having a room full of money. Not coins but notes, beautiful notes. Millions and millions of pounds. It had the same effect that porn had on other men. It didn't make him abnormal. Did it?

His mum had opened a bank account for him on his eleventh birthday. She'd put a fiver in. The fiver was still there plus interest. There was no way that he was going to put money in a bank when some smart bastard might decide to rob it. Think of that, a brother taking his cash. No, not possible, not in his sight or thinking.

Until his early twenties he drifted in and out of gangs. He made a modest living selling blow and anything else he could lay his hands on. Despite the urgings of his mother and family he never applied for benefits. Not a penny. He reasoned that by claiming, the suits might try and make him get a job. Be respectable. Be boring. No fucking way, Jose. He had the usual succession of casual relationships but none had the lure or attraction of the great god quid. When he had just turned 24 his life took a memorable turn. Years later he never could decide if the turn was a good or bad one.

He was on his way into Brixton to sell some blow and chill when a white boy stopped him. Now, seriously, how would a white boy have the nerve to step in front of a brother on his way to the citadel. But he did.

'My name's Cutler Grove.'

'So what, fuck off out of my way.'

'No offence mate, just trying to score a little blow to chill out on a warm day.'

'Why would I want to deal with you, you could be nice Mr Plod.'

Grove looked around, satisfied that nobody was looking, and showed Perry a well decorated six inch blade and a fat roll of twenty pound notes.

As Perry reached inside his own pocket, Grove intervened, 'Listen man, chill. I only showed you my blade and roll to convince you that I'm not old bill.'

Perry thought hard, never once taking his eyes off Grove's hands. A lesson he had learned was that, when threatened with a weapon, keep your eyes on the weapon and the person's hands. Silly people look at the man's eyes. Big mistake. Keep your eyes on the hand that holds the weapon. The weapon can hurt or kill you, eyes can't. Good advice.

Perry relaxed, there were no brothers around to witness this show of disrespect so no harm done.

'So Mr Grove, what can I do for you?'

'Call me Cutler.'

'Whatever.'

'It's not what you can do for me, it's more what I can do for you.'

'Really, how might that be?'

'I might need some help scoring some drugs.'

'Why me? Does my black face say drug dealer, crack head or all together a piece of black shit? Listen, white boy, you have strayed into a dangerous area. Check.'

Grove was now considering the fact that he was in Brixton talking to a serious black boy. He was also debating with himself whether or not he was in the middle of a life-changing mistake. 'I was given your name by a good friend of mine called Tony.'

'Tony who?'

'Just Tony. He said that you were sound and could put something good together. Tony advised me to show respect so I thought I would just walk up to you and front it out. Looks like I got the wrong man. No offence, I'm off.'

Perry thought quick and hard. He knew the man known only as Tony. He had a good rep. For a white man he was cool, tough and treated all men the same. No racist shit. If you could cut it you were fine. If you couldn't, or didn't cut him in, he would cut you out.

'Listen man, maybe I was a bit hasty. Fancy a pint of Guinness?'

'Sure, where?

'Not here, let's go over to the Elephant. It's quiet over there.'

'Sound good to me.'

They walked back to where Grove had parked his car to find two black lads about to break into it. Grove was about to go for them when Perry stopped him. Perry shouted at the boys who froze. He walked over to them and spoke quietly, for a couple of minutes. They were nodding so hard Grove expected to see their heads fall off. The conversation ended and the kids walked off without a backward glance. Perry walked back over to Grove.

'Them boys won't apologise which is no big deal. What they will do is ensure that your wheels will always be safe in the future as long as you park them where you have today.'

Thanks man, respect,' Grove muttered.

'Don't overdo the honky shit, let's go.'

They drove in relative silence and parked opposite East Lane market.

'Got a boozer in mind?' Grove said, a familiar feeling of unease coming over him.

'The Temple Bar, just up on the right hand side of Walworth Road.'

'Excellent.' Shit I fucking hate being so near to Carter Street Police station, Grove thought.

'Is there a problem?' Perry asked, staring intently at Grove.

'No, fine, let's go.'

Ten minutes later they were sat nursing pints of Guinness in the back bar by the stage. Grove was still deeply unhappy at being so close to Carter Street nick, but decided to play it cool.

'So Mr Cutler Grove, how do you know Tony?'

'I do a bit of work for him, you know, this and that.'

'So, have you come to see me for yourself or on behalf of Tony the Man.'

'For me, for now, Tony knows nothing about it.

'Does he need to know anything about it?'

'Not yet, no.'

'What do you mean not yet?'

'Let's see how it pans out.'

'Listen man, you're talking in riddles and I don't like riddles. Are you after a little party smoke or something else? We could have done the business in Brixton and be gone.'
'Then why are we sat here then?' Grove whispered.

'Listen man, you answer my question,' Perry whispered, the menace in his voice was clear.

'Alright, I might have a bit of business which could benefit both of us.'

'What kind of business, selling Avon, double glazing, what?' Once again, Perry was having trouble controlling his temper.

'I happen to know where there is thirty kilos of blow and pills waiting to be had. They're stored in a protected lock-up near Spurs ground. The crew in possession are heavy and I need a little assistance to procure said items.'

'Why come to me?'

'I've heard that you might do it for the right wages.'

'Who put you on to me?'

'Davy Padget.'

'How do you know Padget?'

'We grew up together in Bromley.'

'Where's Padget now then?'

'Coming to the end of a ten in Coldingley. I visited him a couple of weeks ago and he spoke highly of you. He also asked for a little taste if the deal goes down.'

'For a white boy Padget is OK. But one thing you will understand is I don't take fucking wages for any fucking work I do. Understand. A percentage or nothing.'

Grove stared into the dregs of his pint and thought hard about his options. He was running short of cash and jobs were hard to come by. Well, certainly any kind of job he would consider. If this one came off there was big money to be made for a modicum of well planned and executed effort.

'Alright, thirty per cent,' Grove said.

Perry laughed, stood up and went to move away from the table. Grove put his hand on Perry's left wrist. The small, razor sharp knife in Perry's other hand was now resting comfortably just below Grove's left ear. The men stared into each other's eyes. Nobody in the crowded pub appeared to notice.

'Forty five per cent and you're on.'

'Done, fancy a refill?'

'Guinness and a vodka chaser?'

'Nice one.'

Perry saw a lot of Grove over the following days. They got on well and seemed to have the same opinions about the important things in life such as drugs, sport and a love of money. They carefully put together a team of players, which, interestingly, was an equal balance of black and white lads. They could all be relied upon if a ruck started combined with fully functioning brains in their heads.

Two of the lads were tucked safely in a white transit van which was parked a hundred yards away from the target lock-up. The back windows appeared to be completely blacked out when looked at from the outside. The lads did, in fact have a perfect view of the lock-up and the road leading up to it. They both had Pentax cameras and were shooting rolls of film detailing the comings and goings at the lock-up. There was definitely a routine established and this varied little over the five days that they were there.

Very little appeared to happen until about 5 o'clock in the afternoon. A black Mercedes would pull up. A big black man would climb out of the back of the vehicle. One of the watchers, Tag, recognised the man as a Yardie. Shit, this put a whole new complexion on the situation. The Yardies were serious players and had to be treated with respect. Tag left the van and made his way up the road away from the lock-up to where his motorbike was chained to some railings. He made his way back over the river and phoned Perry. After listening to Tag, Perry phoned Grove and they arranged to meet in a pub just off of Borough High Street. They no longer used the Temple Bar after Grove explained that it gave him the creeps being so close to a police station. Perry thought it was hilarious but went along with his new friend.

'Tag couldn't have been mistaken could he?' Grove ventured, trying to put the ramifications into some kind of order in his head.

'No, Tag is sound. He was born in Jamaica and still has a lot of good contacts. I've asked him to get on the blower, tonight, and check on the current status of this man.'

'Does this man have a name?'

'Linton Garner, which is the name he is using at the moment. I've asked Tag to meet us here at half past nine.

At 9.30, on the dot. Tag arrived. He dressed conservatively with his hair cut close to his skull. If anything, he looked like a university student on his way to meet his mates for a pint of cider.

'Hello boy, what can I get you?'

'I'll have a Guinness with a rum chaser please.'

Perry made small talk until Grove returned with the drinks.

'Well, what's the news from Trench Town?'

'Not good, Garner has been here for just over six months. Came in by private jet so he didn't have any contact with immigration. He's staying in a nice pad in Hampstead which is owned by some face in the music business. The business in the lock-up is being financed by a Yardie crew back home. Apparently, they intend to expand their operations into South London.'

'What kind of muscle is this Garner?' Grove asked.

'A grade one heavy. He's wanted by the filth back home. Apparently, a brother ignored him when he was visiting a club. Garner walked over to him and laid a blade in the guy's neck. He stood there and watched the mug bleed out. He then punched the mug's woman twice in the face, breaking her jaw and nose. He never said a word all the time it was happening. Cool, eh?'

'How did the filth find out it was him?'

'The injured woman didn't take kindly to having her face rearranged and, despite being warned by concerned brothers, she put Garner in the frame.'

'Did Garner get a pull?'

'No. The day after she had given the filth the good news she was found in a storm drain with her throat cut. Apparently, Garner was on the point of coming over here so he had no reason to delay his travel plans.'

The three men sat in silence as they sipped their drinks.

'Good work Tag. Keep our conversation just between the three of us.' Perry reached over and placed two fifty pound notes in Tag's jacket pocket. Tag smiled, finished his drink and left.

'Where do we go from here?' Grove asked.

Perry sat, deep in thought, before he replied.

'We've got to do a number on Garner otherwise we're wasting our time. I'm also concerned about their plans to expand south of the river. South London is nicely tied up at the moment. There are no greedy bastards because everyone is getting a nice taste. We'll actually be doing a public service by wasting the bastard.'

Grove thought hard about what Roman had just said. There was a fucking lot at stake and the last thing he wanted to do was to get on the wrong side of some crazy Rastas.

'Listen, let's sleep on it. I've got a bit of business to do on the Old Kent Road so I'll give you a bell in the morning.' With that, Grove finished his pint, squeezed Perry's shoulder and was gone.

Perry sat there staring at his glass. He'd thought that he'd judged Grove correctly and that he was a man he could rely on. He hadn't considered that Grove might be a bottle-less bastard but he had to now. He knew that if he hadn't heard from Grove by tomorrow lunchtime then he was on his own.

Grove finally phoned him two days later. He came up with some old bull about having hurt his back. He said that he was going to his cousins for a few days to convalesce.

'When are you coming back then?' Roman asked, not trying to disguise his anger.

'I don't know.'

'What do you mean, you don't fucking know.'

'I don't know.'

'It seems to me that we might be shitting our pants over some fucking Yardie,' Perry growled. Grove didn't answer.

'I can't hear you,'

'I'd better be going, I've got stuff to do,' Grove answered.

'One thing before you go. I'm going to move on this with or without you. If I get the slightest inkling that there is going to be interference, I'll come for you and if I do you'll have bigger problems than a fucking bad back.'

As Grove started to answer he realised that he was talking to the dialling tone. He knew that he could handle Perry, if push came to shove, but that it was best to let sleeping dogs lay. He was well off out of it. He would go to Margate for a few days. There was good money to be made in Margate.

Perry sat and pondered the future. So much for trusting a fucking white boy. Should have listened to his mates. Too much time and cash had been invested to stop now. He would be looking after both sides of the river by moving forward. It was the only way to go. He made his phone calls and arranged for the black crew members to meet him in a pub in Crystal Palace the following afternoon. He told the white crew members that he was cancelling the work but to meet him by the Oval tube station at seven that evening to collect their wages. He was on his own and intended to stay that way.

He paid off the white lads with generous wages. He met his black crew and added two new faces that he'd known since childhood. He made Tag his number two. Tag would also be his eyes and ears amongst the other crew members. When Tag asked about Grove, Perry said that he was taking a holiday and would not be back on the crew. That was the last time Grove was mentioned.

Perry was a meticulous planner and had taken this one to the line. He outlined the plan to Tag and the crew. They were going to launch a full-on attack on the lock-up the following Thursday afternoon at 6 o'clock on the dot. He had discussed his plan with his friend Tony, who had agreed to provide the tools and transport for 35 per cent of the profit. Agreed. All the crew members were well acquainted with firearms so there were no training issues. The transport would be a black Mercedes 4x4 and a Mercedes Sprinter. Perry, and a crew member called Split, would deal with Garner. The crew, led by Tag, would deal with the contents of the lock-up and the people guarding it.

The big day arrived and the crew assembled in a garage at the back of a block of flats in Stockwell at 4.15pm. It would take them at least an hour to reach the target so they left in plenty of time. When they reached the target they parked just around the corner. They were all dressed in black with the compulsory ski masks. Split was lying on his stomach looking over a low wall opposite the lock-up. When Garner arrived he phoned Perry on his mobile. It was a go.

The Sprinter was moved to within 100 yards of the lock-up. The crew waited. Split ran back to the 4x4 and jumped in. With Perry sat in the passenger seat, he started the vehicle and put it into drive. He turned the corner and headed towards the target. The lock-up was protected by two stout wooden doors. They were no match for the Mercedes 4x4 as Split smashed the vehicle in to the double doors. The old wood splintered and they were inside. The crew were out of the Transit and on their way in.

As Perry jumped from the vehicle he saw a figure rushing through a door just to the left of the Merc. It was Garner and he was not happy. Because of his size he almost filled the doorway. Perry took his chance and fired. He caught Garner just under the left eye. A fluke shot. Garner went down. The crew, led by Tag, ran past Garner and quickly secured the place. Garner's crew were obviously not ready for a ruck and when they heard that Garner was gone it was all over. Perry walked over to Garner and looked at the mess that was now the man's face. His mouth was moving and Roman could hear strange, gurgling sounds coming from it. He shot Garner, again, just above his nose. The sounds stopped.

Perry felt great. He wished that Grove had been there to see him deal with this Yardie bastard. If Grove had of been there he might have received a couple of rounds himself.

Perry looked around but couldn't see Split anywhere. Must be sorting out the goods. But no, Split was nowhere to be seen and Perry was seriously worried. Garner's crew caused no problems as no one had seen the shooting, no one could give evidence. But where the fuck was Split?

It took just over an hour to load the drugs into the transit. The crew sat in the back with the drugs and Perry drove them back over the river and dropped them off at the agreed places. The drugs were stored in the garage in Stockwell with Tag and a crew member on guard duty. Perry would make sure that Tag and the boys got good wages for a good day's work. But where the fuck was Split?

At 5.30 the following morning, Perry heard the sound of his front door breaking, in his dream. He realised that it was a nightmare when three armed police officers were pointing their weapons at him. As they dragged him from his bed and secured him with plastic handcuffs he was formally arrested for the murder of Linton Garner the previous evening in a lock-up in North London.

It had to be Split, the bastard. If he could get his hands on him he would rip his throat out and shove it up his arse. Bastard.

Six months later, Perry stood in the dock of court four of the Central Criminal Court Old Bailey. He received a life sentence for the murder of Linton Garner. The Judge said that he should serve a minimum of 20 years before he would be eligible to be considered for release on license.

He had expected the life sentence but the 20 year tariff came as a massive shock. His first instinct, as he stood shaking in the dock, was to call the judge a useless cunt but common sense prevailed and he said nothing. Respect was not earned by allowing weakness to show.

On his way back to Belmarsh prison from the Old Bailey one of the escorting officers informed him that he would be moving to Gartree, which was a lifer assessment centre in Leicestershire. Once again, he said nothing but he was sad because it would mean that he would have to move even further away from his beloved Brixton.

On his arrival he was further put out when he was taken to the healthcare centre. When he protested, saying that he wasn't sick or a nonce, the nurse laughed. When he started to lose his temper she patiently told him that it was a rule that when a person was sentenced to life imprisonment he or she would have to spend the first night under observation in the healthcare centre. Something to do with suicide prevention, she said. He decided that it wasn't worth pursuing so, after refusing pie and chips he climbed into the hospital bed and slept solidly until just before unlock at 7.30 the following morning.

For the next six days it was business as usual. Although now a sentenced prisoner, he was allowed to remain in the same cell he'd been in since his arrival at Belmarsh. On day seven he was informed that he would be travelling to Gartree the following Tuesday morning. Once again, he suppressed the urge to kick off, smash anything he could lay his hands on which might include the nearest screw. Tuesday arrived and he was on his way.

After leaving the M1 motorway the van passed through Market Harborough and Gartree came into view. It seemed to rise up, in the distance, and seemed desolate and unwelcoming. On arrival he was processed through reception and located on A wing in a single cell. He was happy to find that he knew a number of the other prisoners and quickly settled into the routine.

Part of the assessment process involved interviews with one of a number of psychologists who seemed to be everywhere. The guy in the next cell, Max, was a font of knowledge and quickly brought Perry up to speed. The most important thing, Max emphasised, was to play the game. Don't be too friendly but don't draw attention. Perry learned, quickly, that the coming months would probably go a long way in deciding where he would spend the first few years of his sentence.

For the first time in his life he wasn't sleeping well. Every night he seemed to slip into the same nightmare. He would find himself standing in the dock at the Old Bailey, as before, but he's naked and the people in the public gallery are laughing at him. His friends are laughing at him. All of a sudden, an eerie silence descends over the court as the judge starts to speak. Perry is straining to hear and he's cold, so cold. He tries to shout at the judge to speak up but he's lost his voice. As he's trying to concentrate on what the judge is saying, his whole body starts to shake and he collapses into the well of the dock. Two of the guards drag him to his feet and he hears the words 'and yours will be a whole life sentence which means that you will never be considered for release. Take him down.' His terror always jolts him wide awake at that point and, as usual, he's soaked in freezing cold sweat.

His poor sleep pattern and the constant pressure of just being in prison, was really starting to get to him. The psychologist who was in charge of his assessment was called Mac Hugh. He insisted on everyone, staff and prisoners alike, calling him Mac. So far, Perry had 'played' the game, by speaking a lot but saying very little.

'You're looking tired Roman, really tired. Can I help?'

'If you don't mind me saying so, it's none of your business so butt out.'

'Everything that is happening to you is my business, so I won't butt out. I'll ignore your rudeness. How can I help?' Mac replied, staring at Perry.

Perry was about to launch a fusillade of abuse at Mac but something deep inside stopped him. That feeling was new and it bothered him. But he knew he needed help and, in his present situation, Mac was his only option.

'I'm not sleeping very well. When I do get off I seem to have the same fucking nightmare every night.

'Tell me about it.'

'Do I really have to, can't you just give me some sleeping pills or something? Every other cunt in this place seems to get pills without having to spill their guts.'

'It doesn't work like that. If I'm going to try to help you to get back into a normal pattern of sleep it's essential that we look at what's causing the problem in the first place.' Mac sat back.

'Yea, well, alright but I'm not happy. All I want is a good night's sleep-'

Mac seemed to jump to his feet and stepped towards Perry. 'Okay, Mr Perry. It would seem that our relationship has now come to a grinding halt. This isn't the first time that you've displayed a complete disregard for how I work and, as far as I'm concerned, enough is enough. You've crossed the line. You've played the game, as you call it, but the game has now come to an end.' With that Mac stood, carefully placed his chair back under the table, turned and left the room.

Perry was stunned. As he was trying to make sense of what had happened, an officer entered the room and told him that he was taking him back to his cell. Perry stood and walked back to his cell in a trance. The officer asked him, twice, if there was a problem. Perry just shook his head and said nothing. He spent the next hour sat on his bed thinking about what had happened. He'd never been spoken to like that before and it had come as a shock.

That evening, on association, he bought a joint from one of his regular dealers and took it back to his cell. After smoking it he turned over and tried, once again, to make sense of what had happened with Mac.

Sleep came, as did the same nightmare. The only difference from previous nights was that Mac was the judge.

The following Monday morning, at unlock, Perry made an application to see Mac. He was surprised when at unlock after breakfast he was taken to an office in the psychology department. Mac was waiting, standing by a window in a Barbour coat that was dripping rain water.

'Mr Perry, I've not got much-'

Perry raised his hand, smiled and went straight into the speech which he'd been preparing for the past two days. 'I won't keep you long. I want to say that I regret behaving like a tool. This psychology stuff is still new to me and I don't always understand what is being said. I've had a lot of time to think about what happened last week and I've realised that I made a right pig's ear of things. I'm not good at saying sorry and this is about the best I can do.' Perry finished, took a deep breath and waited for Mac to respond.

Mac started at him for what seemed like an eternity. He knew that it had taken a lot for a tough, black lifer to admit that, just once, he might have been in the wrong. 'Okay

Roman, it would seem that, at last, we have started to make progress. No more game playing, eh? Let's start by you telling me about you. I think you'll find that the nightmares will take care of themselves.'

Perry nodded with a feeling of immense relief, 'Thanks.'

Perry's passage through Gartree was not without its problems. Although his time with Mac seemed to go well he wasn't totally convinced that it would affect his future. His nightmares did stop, and for that he was thankful. He constantly seemed to clash with authority and realised that if he didn't get a move he would find himself in serious trouble. At the end of March he was taken to see the wing governor and informed that he would be transferred to a prison near Carlisle the following month.

Chapter Six

Brian Lincoln sat in the prison van deep in thought. He'd got used to sitting around, waiting. A lot of the time he'd spent in his cell in Belmarsh prison had involved waiting for something. Waiting for a visit, waiting for the gym, waiting, waiting, waiting. He'd developed the knack of turning in on himself, almost like meditating, as an old lag had laughingly told him.

During evening association on his wing he was enjoying a quiet moment, leaning against the wall by the pool table, when he first noticed officer Esme Philips. He'd got used to the routines in Belmarsh and realised that it was time for a new bunch of screws to come on the wing. Philips was one of the new bunch and she was gorgeous. She was tall and slim with dark hair. He could only imagine that she had great legs because she was wearing trousers. She obviously had some foreign blood in her, not you-know-what, but European, probably Spanish or Italian. Nice, very nice.

On her first full day on the wing she'd unlocked him and said hello. He'd ignored her because it didn't do to be seen exchanging pleasantries with screws but she didn't seem to take offence. As she moved on to unlock the other cells on his landing he'd chanced a closer look. Very nice indeed.

That evening she'd unlocked him for association and, once again, said hello. He'd grunted and asked her if she fancied a shag. He'd expected a hard response and to end up on a governor's report but, to his astonishment, she'd laughed and carried on to unlock the other cells.

Over the next few days he'd found himself thinking about officer Philips more and more. It was as if she was renting space in his head. He knew that his head was in a mess, what with waiting for a date to appear at crown court and worrying about what the future would bring. Things started to change the following Monday morning at unlock.

'Hello Mr Lincoln, my name's Esme Philips and I'm your new personal officer.' Her voice was husky and very sexy.

'Say again,' he answered.

'My name's Esme Philips and I'm your new personal officer,' she replied, flashing him a beautiful smile.

'Yea, right,' Lincoln blurted, trying to recover, 'I didn't know I had an old personal officer.'

'You would have had one but the old guard in this place aren't interested in casework stuff, all they want to do is unlock doors and moan about the good old days. I didn't join the prison service just to be a turnkey, I want more out of the job than that. Sorry, I do go on.'

Lincoln had never heard a screw speak like that before and it took him a few seconds before he replied.

'Is that what I am, casework stuff?' he answered, 'and what's with the Mr stuff, are you taking the piss?'

'I'm sorry, I don't seem to have handled this very well. 'Casework stuff' was a poor choice of words. What I meant to say was that I take my personal officer duties seriously, because I take my job seriously,' and with that she smiled, turned and walked away.

Lincoln felt confused and was lost for words. Later that day he was getting ready to be unlocked for association when a folded sheet of paper appeared under his door. He picked it up, opened it and read,

'Mr Lincoln. Once again, I apologise for my tardy behaviour earlier today. I'm still in my probation year as a prison officer and the assessment process can be difficult. I came into the service on what is known as the accelerated promotion scheme. If I do well I could become a junior governor in five years. My years at university taught me to research any project and to never ignore anything I didn't understand. I have researched personal officer duties and I know that, if we work together, I can help you get something positive from your time in Belmarsh. If you think that we can

work together, let me know when I unlock you for breakfast tomorrow morning. Esme Philips.

Lincoln read it through again, folded it and placed it under his pillow. He played pool and watched the last ten minutes of Coronation Street before returning to his cell for the night. He had considered showing the letter to a couple of cons he was friendly with, and have a good laugh, but something had stopped him. He read the letter, again, but couldn't work out what the word 'tardy' meant. He satisfied himself that she wasn't taking the piss and decided to give the 'personal officer' stuff a go. He'd certainly never met a screw like her before.

'Good morning Mr Lincoln, I hope you slept well. Did you have the opportunity to read the note I left for you?' she asked, looking as fresh as a daisy.

'Yea, I have, I suppose I'll give it a go,' Lincoln replied, trying to sound bored.

'Good. I'll arrange for us to use a wing office early this afternoon. I'll need to know something of your background, family and interests. As I said before, if we work together we can get something positive from your time here.'

'Yea, whatever,' Lincoln answered and went down to collect his breakfast.

For the rest of the morning Lincoln sat in his cell deep in thought. He declined the one hour exercise period, which surprised the officer who unlocked him. Lincoln said that he had a headache and just wanted to sleep it off. The officer accepted the reason and moved on to the next cell. By the time Philips came to his cell to take him down to a wing office for their first interview, Lincoln had decided to tell her everything. Normally, he wouldn't have shared the time of day with anybody in uniform but in this instance he reckoned that it could do him no harm. He knew that the crown prosecution service had a cast iron case against him because his barrister was trying to cut a deal. So, when he got to court his barrister could stand up and tell the judge and jury that he had cooperated fully, in prison, whilst waiting for his trial. He had accepted help and advice concerning his offending behaviour and that a long prison sentence really wasn't necessary. Just after lunch he had managed a quick call to his barrister from a payphone on the ground floor of the wing. His barrister listened patiently as Lincoln outlined his plan and agreed that it could certainly improve his chances of a reduced term of imprisonment.

'So, are we ready to begin?' Philips asked, twirling a gold Mont Blanc fountain pen between her fingers.

'Yes, I suppose so,' Lincoln answered, his attention drawn to the expensive pen she was playing with.

Brian Lincoln is white and aged 27. Just under six feet tall he wears bespoke suits and nice brogues. He buys his shirts from Austin Reed and insists on getting his Y-fronts from C&A. He says that boxer shorts can't hold his meat and two veg in place. He is serving eighteen years for armed robbery. He is suspected of being involved in the death of another prisoner.

To Lincoln, London and particularly Deptford, was the centre of the universe. His early days growing up around Deptford, New Cross and Peckham were littered with incident and controversy. Very much a 'Jack the Lad' he quickly attracted the attention of one of South London's major players. Although only 13, Lincoln was welcomed in most of the pubs in the area. His sense of humour and quick fists marked him down as a face of the future.

His first mentor, a 'face' called Tony, called Lincoln over to his table in a boozer just off Jamaica Road in Bermondsey. Lincoln walked over and said that he was too busy to sit and take a pint with Tony. Tony smiled and, offering a £20 note, asked Lincoln to nip outside and check that his black Mercedes still had its wheels. Lincoln took the money and walked out with no intention of doing the job he had been paid for. As he took the first left, at speed, he walked into a cracking right hander. He went down and was immediately picked back up. His head was banged against a brick wall and his hands and feet were stamped on. He passed out. When he came to he was sat next to Tony in the same boozer. The place was full but nobody seemed to notice his presence or condition. Tony slapped him on the back, thanked him for checking the car and told him he was hired. Lincoln never crossed Tony again.

For Lincoln, the perfect Saturday involved getting up late, rolling enough joints for the day and going to Manzies pie and eel shop on Peckham Hill Street for lunch. He would have a small bowl of hot eels followed by double pie mash and liquor. His mates would usually meet him there and then they would make their way to Cold Blow Lane to see Millwall play. If Millwall were playing away then the afternoon would be spent in the King's Arms pub opposite Peckham Rye.

The best part about going to watch Millwall was the planning involved. Lincoln would spend hours on the phone, speaking to mates about their knowledge of the visiting supporters. No home match would be complete without a well-planned ambush as the visiting fans made their way to New Cross railway station. The afternoon was considered to be a failure if at least two of the unfortunate visitors didn't end up in King's College Hospital. If one made it to the intensive care unit, Lincoln would be on the piss through the night. If one died then festivities would continue until Monday morning. Lincoln didn't see himself as a thug and a hooligan, he saw himself as an ambassador for |South London and a guardian of his beloved Millwall Football Club.

Although he tolerated school, legitimate work was never going to play a part in the life of Brian Lincoln. From his early teens he earned a respectable income dealing just about anything that his customers wanted. Puff was the only product that he personally enjoyed. He considered everything else to be a mug's game. He had extensive contacts across London and was not precious about dealing with Londoners who were black or who lived on the other side of the river. Mates and customers saw him as an intense but humorous man who looked after those he liked but who would not tolerate those whom he considered to be lowlife and nonces.

After Lincoln met Tony he had contacts in levels of the underworld that he thought would be forever closed to him.

The players and 'faces' liked him because he was trustworthy and could deal out 'lessons' without a thought for the victim. They tolerated his Saturday afternoon 'fun' and justified it as training sessions. Other people went to the gym, Lincoln went to Cold Blow Lane. The possibility that he might, one day, fall victim to a few serious slaps never crossed Lincoln's mind. Who on earth would have the nerve to take him on? He didn't include Tony in his thinking because that 'event' had been a lesson and not a beating.

With support from Tony, Lincoln put together his own crew. A couple were Millwall fun boys but the others were more serious students who wanted to make serious money and not have the festivities interrupted by forced absences. His best mate was a strikingly good looking youth called Jed Simmonds, who was born and raised on a vast estate in Peckham and had a reputation as a piece of work. Simmonds could pull the birds with an ease that was staggering. Lincoln liked to think of himself as a ladies' man but, being around Simmonds made life so much easier in that department. When the crew met for pie and mash on Saturdays, that was when business was generally discussed. After business it was off to the match and, hopefully, to change the lives of a few mugs.

Lincoln and Simmonds were clearly the inner circle of the crew. The content of the business discussed over pie and mash had usually been put together over joints shared by Lincoln and Simmonds. The idea of a robbery first struggled to the surface during one of these drug-fuelled discussions between the two. The idea was simple in its outline and, if properly executed, would produce excellent wages for the crew with the lion's share going to Lincoln, closely followed by Simmonds.

A massive computer, audio/visual outlet was due to open on a new industrial estate situated between Lee and Lewisham, on the first Saturday in June. The backers had spent hundreds of thousands of pounds on advertising, both locally and nationally. Good quality laptops were to be sold for under £200. Plasma screen televisions would be going for a song.

Mobile phones would be going on sale with free 12 month call plans as part of the incentive to buy.

What had particularly attracted Lincoln was the promise of a further 20% off the already low prices if the punters paid cash. Cheques and debit cards would not attract the discount. Pound notes would. A simple concept but profitable to both parties. The offer would last for the duration of the opening day only. Opening hours were to be 9am through to 9 pm. The advertising assured future customers that there would be unlimited stocks of all the products on sale. There would not be the usual excuses, after the initial rush, of no more cheap goods but a surfeit of the expensive gear. Those who knew the market were predicting the biggest one-day sale in the past 20 years, with the cash-only discount predicted to be a runaway success. Lincoln and his crew were planning to run away with the cash.

There was a little under two months to get everything together. One of the crew, Dave Stein, managed to get his son, Alex, who was on his gap year, into the place as a sweeper up. Alex had told the person who interviewed him that he was computer mad and wanted the chance to get one of the cheap ones. The man said that he could have one in lieu of wages. Alex had jumped at the offer, so had the man.

Alex had sat down with Dad every evening and recounted everything he had seen and heard. Lincoln had no problem with Alex, because the lad been given a few serious slaps by a black and white team of filth because he had told them to fuck off when he'd been stopped late one night. The beating had left him with a drippy mouth and a hatred for authority. He had not complained, nor had his dad. When dad explained why he hadn't complained, Alex understood. If another team had picked on him, Alex knew that dad would have made them disappear.

So far, so good. Lincoln had learned from Tony that the less complicated a plan was, the more chance of success. Alex had learned to be almost invisible as he moved around the vast shop. He dribbled more than he needed to and was either patted on the back or completely ignored. People rarely spoke to him, why would they? If they did he would slowly reply but not make eye contact. No one realised that he was as sharp as a tack and had a rapidly developing photographic memory. These gifts served him well.

'Why do you want a laptop when you're a fucking knob?' asked the computer area supervisor, attracting the laughter of two delivery boys.

'Answer me, knob head,'

'I want a laptop to learn,' Alex slurred.

'Don't be a cheeky tosser or you're in line for a slap.'

'Sorry.'

'So you fucking should be, now fuck off.'

When Alex recounted the day's events to his dad he saw a look in his dad's eyes that he had seen only once before. Alex carefully described the computer area supervisor until dad was satisfied. They went out and had fish and chips.

Two weeks before the grand opening Lincoln asked Tony for a meet. Having made the mistake, once before, of showing a lack of respect he wouldn't be repeating the exercise. They met in the Printer's Devil, a pub near Fetter Lane in Holborn. The usual lunchtime crowd were in and conversations couldn't be heard over the boom, boom, boom music.

'Problem?'

'No, Tony, just a plan I've got and maybe you might want in.'

'I'm in whatever you're up to. No?'

'Sorry, Tony, yea of course.'

'Tell me.'

Lincoln spent the next half hour telling Tony about his planning so far. Lincoln was not interrupted and carried on, careful not to leave any detail out. He finished speaking and went to the bar for another tonic water and a pint of lager. After a lifetime, probably five minutes and a phone call, Tony spoke.

'It might work, with some serious tinkering from me and mine.'

'No problem, of course.'

'I'll provide the tools.'

'Of course.'

'My take will be fifty per cent.' It clearly wasn't a question but a statement of fact.

Lincoln couldn't speak and just nodded.

'Only joking son, thirty per cent will do unless I change my mind. OK?'

'Sure, Tony, a deal.'

'Job done.'

Two days after the meet with Tony the tools arrived in a car driven by a huge Rasta called Ben. What Ben didn't know about guns and ammunition wasn't worth knowing. Lincoln had got his crew together and, with Ben following, drove to a disused airfield in Kent which was owned by Tony. The huge hangar was ideal for the task in hand and just under two miles from the nearest main road.

Ben laid the tools out on wallpaper paste tables. There were six sawn-off shotguns, six handguns, two flare pistols, eight stun grenades, eight high velocity grenades, six K-Bar U.S. Marine knives and six pepper sprays. On the last two tables were piles of black, police-style overalls, rubber soled boots and ski-masks. Lincoln and his five crew members fussed over the clothes until each was satisfied that their choices fitted perfectly.

Once Ben was satisfied, the master class in weaponry began. Each crew member was instructed how to fire and care for the sawn-offs and handguns. They learned how to shoot standing up, seated and laying down. Simmonds and Stein were shown how to use the flare pistols. Although some of the crew had used knives before they quickly understood just how little they really knew. As they were having a tea break, Ben walked towards them wearing a gas mask and ear protectors. Lincoln was puzzled and was about to laugh when Ben lobbed a grenade in the middle of the seated group. The sound was deafening and the group lay on the ground holding their ears. Stein was sick and the others were heaving.

Ben took off the gas mask and ear protectors and sparked up a Marlboro Light.

His mobile rang.

'Hello Darling...what, sorry boss I thought it was the old lady. No of course I don't think you sound like me old lady. Yea, things are going well. They now know how to shoot and cut and how a stun grenade can mess up your day. Catch up with you in the Temple Bar about eight. Yea I'll bring Brian with me.'

For the life of him, Lincoln could not see the funny side. Stein had a murderous look in his eyes but realised that if he went for Ben it would probably be the last thing he would ever do. After about twenty minutes everyone was feeling better and getting back to normal. The training continued until just after five. Ben said that, although they were a sad bunch of wankers, he was reasonably happy with the collective performance. He never mentioned the grenade.

Lincoln dropped the lads off by New Cross railway station and parked the transit. Ben was waiting for him and they made their way through heavy traffic to Walworth Road and the Temple Bar pub. Visiting that particular boozer always gave Lincoln the creeps because it was two doors away from Carter Street police station.

Tony sat at the back of the big bar nursing a glass of red wine. Ben went to the bar and got a round of drinks. Lincoln sat down. Ben returned with two pints of lager and said that he had tried to get a grenade and soda for Lincoln but the barman didn't have any. Tony and Ben laughed, Lincoln didn't.

'Ben said you have the makings of a solid crew.'

'Thanks. A grenade does have a way of bringing people together.'

'Enough,' Tony said, 'Get over it, Ben acted on my orders, I wanted to see if you could handle a drama. It would appear that you can.'

'Is the training over?' Lincoln asked, wondering what was coming next.

'Yes, but there is one change which I want made.'

'Which is?'

'Ben is your number two on the day.'

'Why?'

'I'm protecting my investments and it's not up for discussion.'

'What will I tell Jed?'

'Your crew, your problem, deal with it,' Tony answered.

Simmonds took the news remarkably well especially when he found out that Ben would be getting his wages from Tony's thirty per cent. Stein was less happy but kept his thoughts to himself.

The crew returned to the hangar twice more before the big day. Each member was assigned a specific task as well as a policing role when it came to managing the customers. Stein had a very specific role. He would travel to the home of the computer area supervisor and hold the family hostage. The supervisor was crucial to the plan and would lead Lincoln and Simmonds to the cash. The other team members would make noise and issue threats only as a last resort. The black outfits and hardware would be a suitable deterrent. If it was necessary to shoot somebody then so be it. The raid would take place at approximately 8.45pm.

Staff at the outlet would be tired and the number of customers should have reduced to a trickle. There was parking for a thousand plus cars on the estate and it was projected that all spaces would be taken. There was a regular bus service, close by, and Lewisham Council had promised additional services on the day. Mini cab firms as far afield as Battersea and Hampstead were predicting huge profits. Many other large outlets selling similar products were giving staff the day off. Lincoln was banking on all predictions coming true.

Seven days before the raid, Stein's son Alex left work early saying he felt unwell. Dad was waiting for him and was amazed at the news. The managing director of the outlet was going on national and local television, at 6 o'clock that evening to announce that, for a cash deposit of ten per cent, customers could reserve the goods they were after as long as they collected their goods on the day and paid the balance in cash. The M.D. promised that all orders would be filled.

Stein called Lincoln and gave him the news. Lincoln calculated that, although the deposits would be banked on a daily basis before the opening, increased volume in sales would more than compensate. He phoned Tony, who said that he was going to increase the crew to ten. He would use players known to Lincoln and they would join him on Sunday afternoon. Tony silenced Lincoln's objections by saying that the additional wages would come from his cut. Lincoln thanked him and, for the first time, wondered what he had got himself into.

The outlet had opened six smaller units, across the Capital, to take cash deposits and there were queues from 9am till closing time at 9pm. On Wednesday, Thursday and Friday the units stayed open until 11pm. Conservative estimates said that profits of between seven and ten million pounds were predicted.

Lincoln had spent all week rehearsing for, he hoped, every eventuality. He called the crew together at the hangar late Thursday afternoon. The new additions had slotted in well and were known and trusted men.

'Are there any final questions?' Lincoln asked, confident that there would be at least one.

'What do we do if armed old bill turn up?' Simmonds asked, still secretly miffed about being replaced as number two.

'Don't allow yourself to be captured, if they start shooting return enough shots to stop them.'

The silence in the vast hangar was deafening and there were no further questions.

Lincoln informed the crew that they would be collected from pre-arranged pick-up points between 6.30 and 7.00 on Saturday evening. He also told them not to take any booze or drugs from that moment on until they were well clear of the outlet on Saturday evening. Surprisingly, there were no objections and Lincoln knew that he could trust them.

Saturday arrived and it was pouring down with rain. Lincoln visited the outlet at 8.30am and was staggered at the length of the queues. Burger and doughnut vans were doing brisk business as was a Pakistani lad who was selling metre square sheets of clear plastic for £1.50 each. Lincoln waited patiently in line, bought his plastic and entered the vast outlet about forty minutes after the doors opened. He carefully noted the twenty collection points and had seen fifty articulated lorries parked out back waiting to be unloaded.

He also noted twenty security guards spaced randomly across the store. He wasn't unduly concerned because they were, to a man, fat and obviously out of condition. He left the store at 11 o'clock and returned at 3.30. Business was frantic but orderly. The same security guards were still in the same positions and most were now sat down. One even appeared to be asleep. Lincoln couldn't wait to get started.

He knew that if things went well he would be able to retire on his cut. He was planning to buy an apartment on Spain's northern Costa Blanca and visit it several times a year. He fancied buying in a village called Orba which was a few kilometres from the coast. He'd been there once and was impressed because most of the residents were ex-pats and the restaurants catered to his South London tastes. He couldn't imagine mixing with the locals or eating foreign muck. He fancied a regular little home from home. Not for him the Costa Del Sol because he was always reading about how well known 'faces' were getting their collars felt by the Spanish old bill and being shipped back to the UK. That was not going to happen to him. Certainly not.

By 7.15pm the crew were safely hidden in the back of a large van which had been stolen a couple of hours before from the back of a shopping mall in Leytonstone. At 7.30 Stein called to say that he had the computer area supervisor's family safely bound and gagged and was waiting for further instructions. Lincoln told him to be patient.

Lincoln and the crew entered the outlet through five fire-escape doors at exactly 8.45. Business was still brisk but the staff looked tired and disinterested. There were now only four security guards visible so, no problem there. Lincoln, now heavily made up and doing his best to impersonate Lily Savage, walked up to the computer supervisor and asked if he could speak with him privately because he was nervous when other people were around. Would he mind because he was shy? The supervisor raised his eyes, looked at a male assistant serving close by and mouthed the words 'fucking poof'. The assistant laughed and took a handful of notes from a black guy who was obviously in a hurry. The supervisor led Lincoln to a small office next to the entrance to one of the unloading bays.

'What can I do for you sir?' The supervisor sneered.

'Actually it's more what I can do for you,' Lincoln whispered, no longer lisping his words as he had done a couple of minutes before.

'Just over an hour ago a friend of mine entered your home in Forest Hill and is presently admiring your wife who is tied up and crying. Nice tits but a fat arse. Your kids are with her and safe. I am now going to ring your wife's mobile and you will hear her voice for exactly ten seconds.

You will not speak. Once the call has been made we will speak again. If you try to speak to your wife my friend will kill her. He will make your children watch because he is a family-orientated man who likes to get everyone involved. Do you understand?'

The supervisor tried to speak but couldn't. Bile was rising into his throat.

'I said do you fucking understand?'

The supervisor started to vomit and Lincoln quickly moved out of the way. When the man finished Lincoln punched him lightly on the side of the face.

'Now do you fucking well understand?'

The man nodded, said yes and vomited again. Lincoln rewarded him with a slap on the back of the head and waited for him to recover. Five minutes had passed.

'If you want to see your fat arsed wife with the nice tits again, you will now do exactly as I say. Do you understand?'

The man quickly answered yes and sat, trembling, with vomit drying on his white shirt.

'What will happen to all the cash collected today? Don't give me any bollocks or I phone my friend and it's goodbye wife.'

'Staff are presently counting and verifying the amounts. We may stay open a bit longer because of the number of customers still in store,' he answered trying to suppress a sob.

'What time do Securicor arrive to collect it?'

'I don't know.'

Lincoln punched and kicked him, repeatedly. The man rolled into a ball.

'Let's try again, what time do Securicor arrive to collect the cash?'

'At 10.30, two vans will arrive and take the money to their depot at Tower Bridge.'

'Who's in overall charge?'

'It's Mr Carter and he's in Administration up on the first floor. He can look down on the sales floor from there. Please don't hurt my wife.'

'If you've lied to me, my friend will kill your wife and shag one of your kids. He's not bothered which one, any port in a storm.'

The supervisor started to dry vomit but a smack to the side of the head shocked him into silence. Ten minutes had passed.

The crew waited patiently by the fire escape doors. Lincoln pressed the speed dial button on his mobile and sent the pre-recorded message to the pagers held by each crew member. As they walked casually into the rapidly emptying outlet they pulled their ski masks down over their faces.

Lincoln walked behind the supervisor with his handgun jammed into the man's lower back. They walked up a short flight of stairs and through a door into the administration department.

Mr Carter turned and was about to shout at the supervisor when he saw Lincoln pointing a handgun at him. As he reached across his desk, Lincoln fired and the telephone disintegrated, inches from his hand. As if on cue there were several loud bangs as flares were fired at the high ceiling of the sales area. One of the security guards lunged at Simmonds and was pistol whipped to the ground. It took a couple of minutes for all staff and the few customers left in the outlet to be bound and gagged.

In administration the supervisor was slowly reading the prepared statement which he had been given by Lincoln. The statement described, in graphic detail, what would happen to the man's family if the instructions were not followed to the letter.

Lincoln was scanning the large office and did not see a small balding man slowly reach under his desk. His shaking hand found the button and pressed it.

The audible alarm silenced the chatter in the control room at Lewisham police station. The duty inspector rang the chief superintendent. C.S. Bird entered the control room and announced that he was activating Operation Laptop.

The room sprang back to life and contact was made with surrounding police stations and, in particular, the superintendent in charge for the armed response units. Because of the size of the outlet, and the possible millions of pounds at risk, six armed response units were deployed with an ETA of nine minutes.

Lincoln was blissfully unaware of the coming problems and had summoned three of the crew to join him in administration and, in particular, the secure room where the day's takings were kept. It had taken several blows to Carter's face and shotgun blasts to the hinges of the door to gain entry to the secure room. The sight that greeted Lincoln was incredible, stunning. There was money, literally everywhere. Piles of notes of every denomination and small sacks of coins.

After the chief cashier had been punched and kicked in the face, he rapidly offered the information that, so far, the money counted was just over £6 million. There were still loads to be counted. He also said that they had discovered four thousand in counterfeit notes. Lincoln said that there was no honesty left in the world. This had the crew members in fits of giggles with Lincoln failing to understand what was so funny.

Lincoln ordered the staff to start loading the notes into the four-wheeled trolley's which Securicor had delivered the day before. Because Lincoln had failed to post lookouts no one saw the armed and unarmed police surround the outlet. An exclusion zone of five hundred yards had been established and the place was eerily quiet.

The crew on the sales floor were getting agitated because time was passing and they were stood there like spare parts. Then it happened.

'We are armed police. The area is completely surrounded. My name is Inspector Main and, in one minute, I will be placing a telephone call to a Mr Brian Lincoln. I have your mobile number, Mr Lincoln, and I urge you to take my call before this situation deteriorates any further.'

Lincoln was stunned as were the other crew members. His first reaction was to ring Stein. He tried, three times, but got no answer. What the hell was going on?

Lincoln's mobile rang and he answered it.

'Is that Mr Brian Lincoln?'

'You know the fuck that it is.'

'Mr Lincoln, firstly I want you to know that your colleague Mr Dave Stein is presently enjoying a late supper, with wine, at a police station some miles from here. After he was arrested at a house in Forest Hill he seemed anxious to bring this sad situation to an end. A sensible man is Mr Stein. Now, I want you to be equally as sensible and order your team, on my command, to leave the store in a single file after placing all weapons they are carrying on the ground. Do you understand, Mr Lincoln?'

Lincoln was lost for words for the first time in his life.

'Cat got your tongue Mr Lincoln?'

'If I could get at your tongue I'd rip it out of your head and shove it up your arse.'

'Mr Lincoln, I have a complete knowledge of the whereabouts of your colleagues, staff and customers. I have armed police in the store and weapons are presently trained on your team. If, in a few moments, you do not do exactly as I say I will take further action. If you or your colleagues use your weapons, my officers have instructions to forcibly control the situation. You will not hear the usual warnings because I am giving them to you now. Your call Mr Lincoln.'

Lincoln had been well and truly stitched up. Stein was going to be pig food at the earliest opportunity but that didn't help right now. He looked at the crew who were with him. They were good lads and didn't deserve this. When he told them what the filth had said, he asked them what they thought. They offered the opinions that prison was a better option than Honor Oak Cemetery.

Lincoln felt empty, betrayed and powerless. He'd never felt like that before. The thought of doing bird didn't bother him but the possible length of the sentence did. Had his life really amounted to this? He looked at the pistol in his hand and, for a moment, considered doing the deed. But he knew that wasn't the way.

'Alright, your call, I'll do it.'

It ended as easy as that.

'Foreman of the jury, have you reached a verdict on all the charges against Mr Brian Lincoln,' intoned the clerk of the court. He had worked in Court 10 of the Old Bailey for eight years. This particular case had been interesting because it had all the ingredients of a good thriller.

'Yes we have,' replied the jury foreman. He was chuffed at getting the foreman's job but didn't like the way that Lincoln had looked at him for the duration of the three week trial. The clerk took the folded piece of paper and handed it to Lord Justice Arnold Cray. After reading the paper the Judge nodded at his Clerk.

'Will the defendant Mr Brian Lincoln please stand?'

Lincoln stood and stared at the judge as he read out the verdicts on the three charges against him. Guilty, guilty and guilty.

'Mr Brian Lincoln, do you have anything to say before I sentence you?'

'Only that I have really enjoyed being here for the past three weeks and that I hope you die of cancer before your next birthday. Be lucky.'

The judge then read out the prison terms awarded for each charge, 'Each of the six year terms of imprisonment will run consecutively, therefore you will serve a total of eighteen years in prison. Take him down.'

As he turned, one of the escorting staff grabbed him by the right arm. Lincoln smiled at the guard and head butted him. The guard fell holding his nose, trying to stop the blood.

Lincoln turned again and bowed to his mates in the gallery.

'Nice one Brian, see you soon. Don't forget the visiting order.'

With that, Lincoln was dragged to the cells and taken back to Belmarsh Prison.

What had begun as a means to an end had developed into something that Lincoln really enjoyed. He looked forward to their 'sessions', as he called them. It certainly beat the endless talk of sex and past jobs which many of the other long-termers seemed to enjoy. When Philips was on a day off, or working elsewhere in the prison, he found himself feeling annoyed and frustrated and couldn't understand why.

Some weeks into the sessions rumours had started to circulate that a lock-down search was imminent. One of the orderlies, who worked in the officers' mess, had overheard a conversation where staff had been discussing how the use of illegal drugs was about to be addressed and massively reduced. The orderly had put two and two together and come up with a lock-down.

The prisoners knew that a lock-down would involve every part of the prison being searched. The search teams would pay particular attention to the cells and personal belongings. The majority of staff could be relied upon to be fair in how they conducted a search, but as one con put it, there would be a small number who would be like pigs at a trough.

The rumours proved to be correct and the lock-down began at 6.30 on a Tuesday morning. Teams of staff moved onto the wings whilst others began to search the other places where a prisoner was able to go. Auxiliary staff were positioned on the yards and paths outside the wings, watching for items being thrown out of windows. Lincoln wasn't overly bothered about the prospect of being searched. He knew that it would happen and had carefully hidden the three joints which he had purchased from a con on C wing. His turn came later that afternoon.

A big, overweight officer with 'D. Ashworth' on his name badge entered the cell, slipped the lock and stared at Lincoln. Two more came in and positioned themselves either side of Ashworth. Lincoln thought he recognised Ashworth but couldn't place the other two.

'We're here to search your cell. Do you have anything in your possession which you are not entitled to have?' Ashworth wheezed, his puffy face struggling not to envelope his shirt collar.

'Nothing,' Lincoln replied, adopting an air of indifference.

'Sure?' the one on the right asked.

'Positive,' Lincoln answered, now stood with his hands on his hips.

Ashworth leaned forward, 'Have you fucked Miss Philips yet?'

'What?' Lincoln spluttered.

'Simple question. Have you fucked Miss Philips yet?'

'Eh?' the word sounding like a cough.

'Are you fucking deaf or what? Everyone knows that she puts it about. Rumour has it that she can suck a bowling ball up a hosepipe. So, for the last time of asking, have you fucked her yet?'

Lincoln felt his face turning red and a rushing noise was starting to fill his head. What the hell was going on? This wasn't part of any cell search he'd had before. As he was about to speak...

'I'll take it as a yes, then, by the colour of your ugly face. That makes you number five, by my reckoning. Was she good? Did she moan with her mouth full? Did you...'

Lincoln lunged at Ashworth and pushed him back against the door. As he tried to follow it with a kick, the other two grabbed him. They pushed him to the floor and started to punch and kick him. As Ashworth joined in, Lincoln managed to roll himself into a ball.

All of a sudden it stopped. Whilst the other two held him in wrist locks, Lincoln watched in horror as Ashworth went straight to the wooden cross which was hanging on the wall over the end of his bed. He ripped it from the wall, turned it over and removed the sheet of toilet paper which was stuck on the back.

'Well, well, well, who's a naughty boy then?' Ashworth shouted as he removed the three joints from the hollow space in the back of the cross. 'Illegal drugs and shagging a screw. Not good news for you, eh? Take him to the Seg.'

After the adjudication and a period of cellular confinement, Lincoln was returned to his cell. He wasn't surprised to find that his radio was in pieces and his photos ripped to shreds. Despite making discreet inquiries, he couldn't find out anything about Esme Philips. He never saw her again.

Two weeks later he was informed that he would be making the long journey to a new prison in the North West, to begin the next stage of his sentence.

Chapter Seven

It's a cold and windy Saturday. The big tree on the hill in the distance is blowing and bending like mad. Terence 'Cutler' Grove treats the seasons like a personal challenge, something to look forward to as each season arrives.

If the yard is clear of shit parcels then he will run. He will run, flat out, for the whole 60 minutes. There will be no point in stopping for 15 minutes worth of sunbathing because the wind has definitely got the better of Mr Sunshine today.

'I'm getting bored on my landing on D wing with just Raymond fucking Butterworth for company. He's doing his life sentence the hard way. Always winding the screws up over nothing, which can be a laugh if done properly. That stupid smile he carries about with him don't fool anybody. Most of the chaps think he's a right knob but somebody to be watched. He made a tidy mess of that lad's face in the showers on C wing before they moved him over here. It's amazing what two razor blades in a toothbrush handle can do. It wasn't possible to stitch the kids face back properly so he's waiting for a bit of plastic surgery. Butterworth got two years concurrent for that piece of mischief, so doing a life does have some advantages.'

'Been in this shit-hole of a prison for five months now and I've had no visits. Phone calls are OK but you can't stay on long enough. I suppose the distance is a factor but to plead poverty when you've got a five bedroom drum in Sevenoaks is a bit steep. Still, Pete knows what it's like to be captured and do bird. He knows and he won't forget me.'

'When I've had me run I'll be off to the gym. Getting the orderly's job was a stroke of luck. The gym screw is a half decent muppet and showed me how to lift weights when I was on remand in Belmarsh. Nice tickle, for me, when he was transferred to this dump. I suppose I was lucky not to get Durham or Frankland and end up doing me bird with those Geordie bastards.'

'No, this place will do for now. I'm getting me perks and a bit of relaxation is easy to come by. I'm not a silly cunt, I don't do 'H' or rock, just a bit of blow and the odd pill. No harm in that is there? Rumour has it that next week's intake of new boys could be interesting. I'll ask Smith when I get to the gym.'

'Smith's not bad for a screw and I don't really hold it against him because he's black. I mean it's not his fault is it? Always Mr Reasonable me, live and let live. What is a bit dodgy, though, is that he's an arse mechanic, a bum boy. He thinks nobody knows but I do because I've got a nose for these things. I've seen the way he looks at the wing boss, Watts. Mentally strips him, dirty bastard. But I suppose any port in a storm does it for some people. Still, some new arrivals would cheer me up. Butterworth thought he'd got the chaplain on his side when he started walking out on exercise with a bible under his arm. Silly bastard. That smiley face slipped when he didn't get the chapel orderly's job. I suppose it was right when old Motty got it, what with him doing a five and being a church warden on the out. Must have really pissed Butterworth off but that smile was soon back in place. Motty's a nice geezer but I don't like the way he stares at you when you've got your gym kit on. Roll on next Tuesday, Smith will tell me who's coming.'

With that, Grove rang his cell bell and, after a couple of minutes, Officer Hilary Brand came onto the spur to let him out. As she reached his cell door she heard Grove singing, 'I just can't get enough, I just can't get enough, I just can't get enough of your love.'

As she opened the door he looked up and frowned.

'What a shame I thought it was Mr Smith.'

Brand ignored him, but as he walked past her he smirked and blew her a kiss.

'I could place you on report for that, Grove.'

'I know you could but you won't because the other screws would piss themselves when you read the evidence out. On second thoughts, do it.'

Brand said nothing and knew that he was right, she couldn't make herself a laughing stock. It had been difficult enough getting herself accepted as one of only twelve female officers on the staff.

'Get moving Grove.'

As he walked along the landing Grove started to sing again, 'I won't let your son go down on me, I won't let your son go down.' What do you think Miss, my words better than Nik Kershaw's?

As she stared at his back she couldn't stop the blush covering her face. How the fuck did Grove know that she had a four year old lad?

Grove was deep in thought as he made his way to the gym. That Brand screw wasn't a bad looker and she knew that he had her sussed. Was it worth a go? Screw a screw? Sleep on it.

That night his dreams were cluttered with the reasons for his present predicament. Just before five in the morning he covered his face with the duvet and sobbed.

Terence 'Cutler' Grove is as skinny as a rake and his mates are fond of saying that he could be flushed down a toilet without blocking the S bend. When his first million is safely off shore he intends to sort the acne scars on his face. It is said that he could charm the birds out of the trees and charm them back in again. At his fourth appearance at Bromley Magistrates Court he'd got his mates in stitches by trying to teach one rather attractive solicitor how to milk a flea. He might have got away with it but he went too far when he invited her to join him and his mates in a group get-to-know-you session. On his way back to jail Grove had a feeling that his next court appearance, at the Old Bailey, would not be a pleasant one.

The events leading up to his appearance at the Old Bailey shocked some of his more normal friends. By normal I mean friends who had spent less than half of their lives in prison. On the day in question Grove's usual outward appearance of court jester/loveable rogue seemed to have been consigned to a cupboard. Grove had turned into a vicious, gun-wielding thug. He'd got up at 9.30am and was due to meet two mates at New

Cross station at 11 o'clock. The object of their days work was to rob a building society at the bottom of Peckham Hill Street near Manzies pie and mash emporium.

It was a Friday and they had planned to hit the place just after three o'clock. They reckoned that the lunch time trade would have passed and the staff would not be alert as their minds would be on five o'clock and the start of the weekend. The problem was how to fill the four hours before the raid. They decided to go for a drink.

Their first port of call was the Apples & Pears pub, just off the Old Kent Road. Grove had parked the stolen silver grey Astra two streets away and was leading the way up the steps when a particularly nasty piece of work called Detective Sergeant Plowman came out of the front door. 'Well, well, well if it isn't Mr Grove and his band of low-life scumbags.'

'Come on Mr Plowman, that's no way to be addressing law abiding citizens.'

'Grove, the last time you were a law abiding citizen was one second before you were born.'

Plowman snarled. 'Maybe you take after your father, but that would be difficult to prove because your mother must have been shagged by most of the lowlife in the Bromley and Lewisham telephone directory.'

Grove felt in his pocket for the blade he always carried. Enough was enough. He didn't have to take that kind of disrespect from filth like Plowman. Grove's best mate, Robert Austin, guessed what might be coming and tried to defuse the situation.

'Come on Mr Plowman, Mrs Grove was the salt of the earth and devoted to his dad, everybody on the patch knows that.'

'Austin, you are as big a shit bag as Grove and that goes for Penn and Shapiro who are trying to look invisible.'

'Can we go now Mr Plowman,' muttered Austin.

'What's the rush, are we off to rob a bank or take an old age pensioner's last few quid?'

'Nothing like that Mr Plowman?, just a few pints at the end of a busy week.'

'Busy week, my arse. Now fuck off and don't let me lay eyes on you around here again.'

The four about turned and walked back in the direction of the Astra. Grove took his hand out of his pocket and realised that he had been squeezing the knife so hard that the blade had sliced into the palm of his hand.

When they got back to the car they jumped in and headed off in the opposite direction, anxious to avoid any further contact with D.S. Plowman. Grove needed to shed the anger that was consuming him. He reached under the seat and found the small plastic bag he was looking for. Cocaine. That would do. Just a couple of toots would burn off the stress and help him to chill. His mates needed to see him calm. They headed towards the Rotherhythe tunnel and, once through, turned left on to Commercial Road. A quick left turn found them at the back of a block of flats. Grove found the Astra owner's manual and cut four lines of coke on the back cover. As he was leaning forward with the rolled-up tenner to his nose, Penn sneezed and blew the coke over Austin. Grove reacted by punching Penn in the chest and the face.

Everyone froze. Penn didn't react. This was definitely not how things should be. The silence seemed to go on forever but had only lasted just over a minute.

'We don't need this, that bastard Plowman is to blame. Send the bill for your nose to Peckham Police Station.'

Penn laughed at Grove and winked at Austin. Drama over.

Grove parked the car in Neville Close behind a row of shops on Peckham Hill Street. The plan was for Austin to stay with the car because he was the best driver. This would have to change because Penn couldn't go into the building society with a nose like Rudolph. Penn would stay with the car. Grove took the bag out of the boot and carefully unwrapped the sawn-off.

This nice piece had cost Grove two grand because the contact had assured him that it had never been used on business before. Grove had no reason to doubt him because he was an armourer with a good reputation.

A close friend of Grove's, Danny Sollis, had been into the building society two weeks before and had provided a detailed plan of the shop, from memory, after being promised a nice drink. Sollis was no fool and knew where his interests lay. His immediate future held the promise of being the proud owner of a ten year old BMW which he had put a deposit on. He also knew where the cash would come from to pay the balance.

Three o'clock arrived and Grove, Austin and Shapiro casually strolled along the pavement opposite the building society. A mini-cab was parked outside. Nothing could happen until the cab left. A minute later the Asian driver came out of the building society and, turning, informed an invisible employee that he would be moving his money somewhere else where he could withdraw it. He also advised the invisible person that she was a useless fat slag.

Grove decided to let the situation chill for a while because the staff would be hyped and may have called the old bill. It would just be his luck that D.S. Plowman responded to a call from the building society and would find you-know-who giving grief to the staff. He was also aware that Peckham Police Station was less than half a mile from the building society. Grove was confident that he had covered all bases despite the hassle that Plowman had laid on them. He had also promised himself that, by placing a bit of cash around, he would find out where Plowman lived. He would then pay to have Plowman killed. He wouldn't do it himself although he knew that he could, without a second thought. He wouldn't do it because it would ruin his hard-earned reputation as a harmless blagger. Plus the fact it would be difficult to pursue the ladies if he was doing a life at the pleasure of Her Majesty.

It was just after 3.30 when Shapiro crossed the road and entered the building society. He was dressed in a leather jacket, blue jeans and trainers. He didn't appear to attract much attention but he was acutely aware of the CCTV in the top, right corner of the room. His role was to assure himself that everything was normal. When he was happy that everything was cool he would act as if he had forgotten something and, mouthing 'sorry' he would walk out the way he came in.

He looked around and joined the small queue of customers waiting to be served. Everything appeared fine so after waiting a respectable ten minutes, as rehearsed, he mouthed 'sorry' and headed towards the door. When he was out on the pavement he gave a slight nod towards Grove and Austin and headed towards Peckham High Street. The plan was that he would jog along the High Street and wait for the others by the school in Sumner Avenue.

Grove and Austin crossed the road and walked up to the entrance of the building society. Both donned black ski masks and Grove pulled the sawn-off from an old sports bag. Grove opened the glass-fronted door, turned to the right and fired one round at the CCTV camera, which immediately disintegrated in a shower of glass and metal. As he turned left to face the people behind the glass screens everything seemed to slip.

'We are armed police, drop the weapon and lay down on the ground with your arms out in front of you. Do it now, do it now.'

Grove froze and Austin barged into his back sending him stumbling forward. The sawn-off slipped from his hand and clattered to the ground. All of a sudden the room seemed to be filled with black-clad figures pointing rifles and handguns at them. Grove couldn't move and Austin was making a noise which sounded like sobbing.

With his hands pinned behind his back, and secured with plastic cuffs, the ski-mask was pulled back over Grove's head.

'Well, well, well so this is where you go for a quiet drink after a busy week. Would you like to accompany me to Peckham Police Station where we can play bar billiards and have a quiet pint while we discuss what changes are going to take place in prison over the next twenty or so years.'

Grove looked up into the smiling face of Detective Sergeant Plowman. As he was about to scream at Plowman, a black man stepped forward and cautioned him. Grove knew the caution off by heart, hawked and spat on Plowmans' shoes. He waited for the kick but nothing happened. Shit, shit, shit.

Parked in Neville Close, Penn started the engine and noticed a shadow pass behind the car.

'We are armed police, step out of the vehicle and lay down on the ground with your arms out in front of you. Do it now, do it now.'

As Penn tried to force the car into reverse, the driver and front passenger doors flew open and he found himself facing two black-clad figures pointing handguns at him. Shit, shit, shit.

Shapiro reached Sumner Avenue sweating and seriously out of breath. The sweat was running into his eyes and the t-shirt under his jacket stuck to his skin. As he was trying to take the jacket off...

'We are armed police, kneel on the ground with your hands behind your head. Do it now, do it now.'

Shapiro was confused and for a long second thought that the voice was not talking to him. As he wiped the sweat from his eyes the instruction was repeated. He looked up to see three black-clad figures pointing handguns at him. He slowly dropped to his knees and placed his hands behind his head. What really pissed him off was that the voice that had issued the instruction was female. Shit, shit, shit.

Grove and Austin were taken the short distance to Peckham Police Station. Penn was taken to Camberwell Green Police Station and Shapiro to Brixton Police Station. It was some days before they were to see each other again. Later that day, in the pubs and clubs frequented by the faces and players it was generally agreed that Cutler was not the cheeky-chappy-blagger that everyone thought but was, in fact, a grade one tosser who should not be allowed out without parental control.

Early the following afternoon, in a wine bar in Fleet Street, Danny Sollis took a call on his mobile. The call lasted barely a minute. Sollis ordered another glass of red and a slice of chicken and ham pie. After a further glass of red he phoned his girlfriend Wendy to tell her that he would be home later than expected because he had to meet a mate in a boozer in Eltham and then collect his beloved BMW from the dealer on the Old Kent Road.

Seven months later the four stood trial at the Central Criminal Court, more commonly known as The Old Bailey. The preceding months had seen Grove placed in the segregation unit in Belmarsh Prison after the unprovoked attack on a prison officer during a routine cell search. The officer had sustained serious facial injuries and the matter had been passed to the police. Grove's reputation as the cheeky-chappy, Ronnie Wood of the underworld had finally been laid to rest. Penn had turned Queens Evidence and was presently ensconced in a Witness Protection Programme unit in a prison in the Midlands. The price on his head had been posted, not because a serious player felt aggrieved that Grove, Austin and Shapiro had been grassed up, but more as a deterrent to others in the future.

Two days into the trial found Detective Sergeant Plowman sworn in and preparing to give evidence. As he started to speak Grove shouted at him. He said that he knew he would spend his future banged up but that the screws were going to have some seriously bad days. He promised Plowman that he would use every last penny he had to track the bastard down and have him killed. He said that if Plowman had a wife and kids he would do for them as well. Grove was dragged off to the cells but not before he had managed to head-butt one of the custody staff. The judge ordered that he would be handcuffed for his future appearances in the dock unless he promised that there would be no repeat of the violence and threats. He told the judge to go fuck himself. He stayed handcuffed for the remainder of the trial.

Plowman described his meeting with Grove, Austin, Penn and Shapiro on the steps of the Apples & Pears. He said that he had joked with them and had even enquired about the health of Grove's mother. When challenged by the defence council that he had threatened Grove and had verbally abused his mother, he totally denied the accusations. Defence counsel did not pursue the matter. Plowman described the unease that he had felt when seeing the four together and how Grove had looked edgy and uptight. He said that his instincts told him that something wasn't right about the situation so he decided to follow the four. It had proved difficult so he had called to the station and requested support, in an unmarked car.

The car arrived, quickly, with two detective constables on board. They spotted the silver grey Astra as the four were walking up to it. As Grove unlocked the driver's door Plowman called in the registration number to be checked on the Police National Computer. The response confirmed the vehicle had been stolen in Hampstead, north west London, two days before. It was quickly agreed, at detective superintendent level, to continue surveillance but to take no further action at that time.

Plowman described how the Astra had been followed down Willowbrook Road and onto Peckham Hill Street. The vehicle had taken a left turn into Goldsmith Road and then a further left turn into Neville Close. The police car had parked in Wentworth Crescent and the officers had followed the Astra on foot. Plowman described seeing Grove open the boot of the Astra and unwrap a package to reveal a modified, sawn-off shotgun. Plowman identified the gun when it was produced as evidence. He also confirmed that it was the same weapon that had been confiscated when Grove had been arrested.

Plowman said that he had immediately contacted the duty superintendent and had requested that armed response units be placed on standby. This had been agreed. More officers had joined the surveillance team from Peckham police station, which was less than a quarter of a mile away. Grove, Austin and Shapiro had been followed and had been observed watching the building society from across the busy road. Because the only other shops were a pie and eel shop, an estate agents and a dry-cleaning outlet, it was decided that if there was a target it would be the building society. A call was made to the building society and armed police gained entry to the building from an access road at the rear. Armed police then replaced the surveillance team who were watching the parked Astra. Further armed officers were ordered to follow Shapiro as he left the building society. As the attempted robbery began, officers were ordered to intervene and arrest Penn and Shapiro.

When asked for his opinion, by prosecuting counsel, Plowman said that he considered the attempted robbery to be the most inept and poorly planned raid that he had investigated in over 20 years as a police officer. His comments attracted derisive laughter from the gallery and sent Grove in to a screaming fit of temper. Plowman merely smiled as Grove was dragged down to the cells.

Grove was sentenced in his absence, to ten and seven years to run consecutively, and returned to Belmarsh prison. Austin and Shapiro received eight years each and were transferred to other prisons. Penn received a five year sentence in recognition of the help he had given the Crown Prosecution Service. He was serving his sentence in segregation and, to date, no one had managed to collect the price on his head.

On his return to Belmarsh Prison, Grove was still ranting and raving and was placed under restraint whilst the handcuffs were removed. As he was being escorted to a special cell in the segregation unit, he took the opportunity to grab a female officer around the throat and tried, unsuccessfully, to bite her left ear off. The officer collapsed and, after a struggle, Grove was placed in a body-belt. He remained in the belt for three days, the only respite being when one hand was released to allow him to eat and use the toilet.

At the end of the third day, Grove was released from the belt and located in a normal cell in the segregation unit. He remained in the unit for a further two months. During that time he took the opportunity to consider his options and decided that, as he couldn't beat the system, he would turn as much of it as possible to his advantage.

Chapter Eight

Raymond Butterworth is white and aged 57. He's overweight and most of his hair has left for pastures new. When he looks in the mirror he sees a man who is hard and not to be messed with. He is serving life sentences for the murder of his wife and her lover and has a 30 year tariff. He does not expect to be released. He was born in Liverpool. Staff know Raymond as a smiling, vicious manipulator. Butterworth classes himself as a 'senior prisoner', a person to be reckoned with. Although he couldn't care less he has, publicly, embraced religion.

Growing up in Liverpool in the 50s and 60s was pure education. He was born just off the Scotland Road in a small terraced house, which faced a bomb site. Butterworth played on the bomb site and had his own secret place which he'd carefully built behind the remains of the side wall of a house. He filled the special place with a paraffin lamp, an old bed frame and cups, saucers and eating irons. All had been taken from a tip or stolen from his grandmother's maisonette. His latest 'purchases' were a sheet, pillow and eiderdown once again courtesy of granny's cupboard. He spent most of his spare time there but had not yet dared to stay overnight. His dad had been a docker but had got the sack for being too greedy. His best mate had told him that there was plenty to go round but Butterworth senior took more than his share. The dock foremen had received a tipoff and caught him with bags of the stuff. He was sacked on the spot.

Dad was now Billy-no-mates, which was not good in the Liverpool of 1962. He ended up collecting glasses in a local pub and doing a few hours as a bookies runner. Suddenly he vanished. He was never seen or heard of again. Rumour had it that he had topped himself by hanging. That raised a few laughs and was soon forgotten, as was Raymond's dad.

With dad gone and his mum holding down two cleaning jobs and a bit of pub work, Butterworth came to rely on his own company and resources. His special place became his real home for about a year. One Thursday, he stayed there overnight and his mum never appeared to notice. Or if she did she never mentioned it. He went to school when he felt like it. Nobody told him off. He was a loner and couldn't give a damn about anyone or anything.

At 14 he was a big lad for his age and could pass for being a lot older. He used this to his advantage as he would wait behind a bank of trees opposite the girls' school in Crosby. Over a couple of days he would carefully select his new 'friend'. The latest was called Priscilla and he followed her to a terraced house about a mile away. He guessed that she couldn't be older than ten. She wasn't a pretty girl, in fact she was plain. She was a bit fat, and didn't seem to have any friends, always appearing to be on her own. A loner. A bit like himself. Perfect.

The following afternoon he followed her as usual. As she turned the corner into her road he caught up with her. He asked her if she could direct him to the nearest paper shop because he wanted to buy cigarettes. She carefully gave him directions and, with the biggest smile he could manage, he thanked her and went off in the direction of the shop. The following afternoon, a Friday, he watched her leave the school gates and start her journey home. As she turned into her road, he called 'hello' and waved. She looked in his direction and waved back. He smiled, turned and walked away.

The following Monday afternoon was going to be the big day. After he'd carefully washed, dressed and brushed his teeth for the second time, he waited in his usual spot behind the trees. As she came out of the school gates he waited for a couple of minutes and then he followed her.

'Hello, I wanted to say thank you for helping me the other day but I don't know your name?'

'Priscilla,' she answered nervously.

'Thank you Priscilla, I don't know around here very well so it's nice to have a new friend,' and he gave her one of his big smiles. She smiled back.

'Because you were so helpful I've bought you some flying saucers, red liquorice sticks and a bar of Cadburys milk as a thank you present. I hope you don't mind?'

Priscilla's dad had always banged on about not taking gifts from strangers but this man seemed so nice that she didn't want to upset him by saying no. She was feeling very grown up because it was nice for someone to speak to her without making fun of her glasses.

'No I don't mind, saucers are one of my favourites. Thank you very much.'

'It's my pleasure, but we won't tell anybody or else all of your friends will want to help me and I won't have any money left.'

Priscilla nodded, she wouldn't tell anyone because she didn't have anyone to tell and she certainly wouldn't tell her dad because he would get angry and slap her. Dad had changed since mum had died and didn't really speak much other than to tell her off. No, this would be her little secret.

'What's your name?' a now very confident Priscilla asked.

'My name's Robert.' Butterworth replied, barely able to conceal his happiness at how well this was going.

'Thank you Robert.'

'It's my pleasure, but I have to be going now.'

The look of disappointment on her face told Butterworth that he was well on the way but there was the need not to rush things.

'I'll see you in the week and, hopefully, you can help me again.'

Two days later he was ready and confident. As she crossed the road he walked up to her. The look of pure joy she gave him almost stopped him. Almost.

'Hello, how are you today?'

'Hello, Robert, I'm fine.'

'I've got you some more saucers and some Maltesers. I hope you like Maltesers because they are my favourite.'

'Yes I love Maltesers as much as I love saucers.'

'That's good then. Are you in a hurry to get home or shall we do something?'

Priscilla knew that she should be going home to do her homework but she would do it later. Her dad was going to the pub to play darts straight from work, and wouldn't be home until late. She had the coins in her pocket for her tea from the fish shop and she could pick that up later.

'Yes, what shall we do?'

'I'd like to take you to my special place. You'll like it there. We can walk there in a few minutes. I've got loads of our favourite sweets and a bottle of Tizer. Do you like Tizer?'

'Yes I love Tizer. Will we be long?'

'No not long, I just want to show.'

'OK.'

They walked to the bomb site but Butterworth took her in through the hole in the back fence just in case his mum had come home early from work and might see him. He knew that his grandmother was at bingo so he felt safe. He had spent the past two days adding things to the place. His new prized possession was a battery transistor radio which he had stolen from Woolworths in town.

'What do you think then?' he asked as he moved the sheet of corrugated iron away from the entrance.

'I don't know, I've never been anywhere like this before.'

He managed to hide his disappointment and set about putting the sweets on plates and pouring Tizer into two cups.

After eating and drinking Priscilla visibly started to relax. She said that she really liked the place and would he invite her to come again. She added that she could visit again tomorrow, but it would have to be earlier because school finished at 2 o'clock. Butterworth said she could. He was secretly over the moon. Priscilla left and made her way, happily, to the fish and chip shop.

Priscilla's dad got home from the pub well after closing time. He was seriously drunk and fell, fully clothed, into bed. When he woke in the morning, Priscilla had already gone to school. He felt absolutely dreadful so he phoned the building site, where he was a store man, and said that he wouldn't be in because he had woken up with a dreadful migraine. He added that he hoped he would be in the following day. The foreman sounded satisfied and wished him a speedy recovery.

As he lay in bed he began to really feel sorry for himself. He was 39, worked on a building site and had a young daughter whom he barely knew. Life had been bad since Linda had died and he hadn't really had the heart or interest in women since. Surely there had to be more to life than his pathetic existence.

He fell into a deep sleep and when he woke he felt a lot better. He decided it was time for changes to be made, and he was the only person who could make the changes. He decided that his number one priority was to become a proper dad for Priscilla. He would really get to know her. Do something about those dreadful glasses and spend some money on some nice clothes for her and himself. He knew that she would finish school early and decided to meet her and take her to the Wimpy Bar in town. He got up, had a shave and a bath, dressed and made his way to surprise her at the school gates.

Butterworth had added some candles, in milk bottles, and had stolen some more sweets. Today was really was going to be the day. Priscilla was going to make her own way to him and meet him at the hole in the back fence. He couldn't wait.

Priscilla couldn't concentrate during lessons. To finally have a friend who didn't take the mickey was really nice. She really hoped that she could take him to meet dad, one day, but not yet. Dad would probably blow a fuse. Mum would have liked him. She started to cry and the teacher asked her if she was alright. She told the teacher that she had a tummy ache and the teacher said that, as it was only half an hour to the end of classes, she could leave early. Priscilla thanked her, picked up her books and made her way to collect her coat. Going through the gates she wondered what new sweets Robert would have for her today.

Priscilla's dad arrived at the school gates feeling better than he had for ages. He was on time and couldn't wait to see her face. He knew that she would wonder what she had done wrong. He would quickly put her mind at rest and tell her that things were going to change. Big time. They would catch a bus into town, go and look at the clothes shops and end up in the Wimpy Bar.

The school was rapidly emptying and there was no sign of Priscilla. He walked into the yard and approached the one teacher that he knew. She told him that Priscilla had complained of being unwell and had left over half an hour before.

He thanked the teacher and made his way home. He would surprise her and then they would head off into town.

On her way to meet Robert, Priscilla suddenly felt unwell. She really did have a tummy ache. She knew that she really needed to use the toilet as soon as possible. She remembered that Robert's special place didn't have one so she decided to go home. She knew that dad wouldn't be there so she could use the toilet, wash her hands and go off to meet Robert. She decided to run because her tummy was really aching.

She got home just in time. After she had washed her hands she dropped her books on her bed and left the house.

As he turned the corner her dad saw Priscilla skipping down the steps and heading towards the paper shop on the corner. He called out to her but his voice was drowned out by a passing bus. He called again but she had turned the corner. He was determined that he was going to enjoy the afternoon so he decided to follow and surprise her. She was moving along at a fair rate and he was struggling to keep up. Priscilla reached the hole in the fence and called Robert's name.

'I didn't think you were coming,' Butterworth said, angry that he had been made to wait. He guided her past the sheet of corrugated iron.

'I'm sorry, Robert, but I had to go home because I had a tummy ache.'

'OK, OK, are you alright now?'

'Yes I think so.'

Butterworth put his arms around her and kissed her on the cheek. Priscilla stiffened, but relaxed when he asked her if she really was OK.

Dad was just turning the corner when he saw his daughter walking through a hole in a fence bordering a bomb site. What on earth was she doing here? He didn't know anyone on this road so how could she?

Butterworth was starting to get confused. He didn't know what to do next. He wanted more than sweets and Tizer. He'd had enough of being on his own. Other boys could pull the birds. Why did they laugh at him when he tried to chat them up? He decided that enough was enough. This girl was an ugly cow but she would do for now.

'Come here Priscilla, there's a mark on your cheek.'

Priscilla walked, smiling, towards him.

He grabbed her around the back of her head. He pulled her face towards him and kissed her on the lips. Priscilla was confused. What was he doing? Where were the sweets and Tizer? He was hurting her. He seemed to be grunting.

His hands were pulling at her school blouse. Dad would go mad if it got torn. When he put his hands under her grey school skirt she started to panic. She asked him to stop but he didn't seem to hear her. She shouted at him to stop. He didn't. She couldn't stop herself screaming.

He heard her screams and ran through the hole in the fence. He pushed the sheet of corrugated iron aside and screamed with anger when he saw a lad trying to get up his daughter's skirt.

Butterworth knew that things were going badly wrong when he heard the scream behind him. He let go of Priscilla, and was turning, when he felt the blow to the back of his head He felt himself falling to the floor. The man pushed past him and grabbed at Priscilla. Who was this man? How dare he touch Priscilla and why wasn't Priscilla pushing him away?

As he struggled to his feet, he looked at the man who was cuddling his Priscilla, and felt himself starting to get hot. He started feeling sensations which he didn't understand. He reached for the hammer that he'd stolen from his grandmother's shed. As he moved forward he felt a great relief when he struck the first blow. The feelings started to intensify the more he hit the unknown man. The hot blood splashed on his face but that made it even better. Some got in his mouth and it felt as though he was chewing on tin foil. It made his mouth water.

He only stopped when there wasn't anything else worth hitting. God, he felt good. He was panting when he heard a strange sound like a cross between crying and screaming. The sound was similar to the racket next-door's cat had made when he'd strangled it. It was Priscilla. She had wet herself and was staring at what remained of the man's head.

Butterworth walked forward and hit her around the side of her face with the hammer. Those strange feelings were consuming him and he loved it. He had to stop that strange noise she was making so he hit her again and again and again. He only stopped when he had run out of face to hit. That lovely warm feeling was still with him and he felt wonderful. The front of his trousers were wet, but not with blood.

Butterworth stood back and surveyed the carnage laid out in front of him. There was blood, skin and bone everywhere. The cold reality was starting to dawn on him. He didn't feel afraid, more an intense curiosity. He knew he couldn't leave the situation as it was. He had to clean up and make a proper job of it. He had to wash and change his clothes. He walked out and carefully replaced the sheet of corrugated iron.

There was nobody that he could see as he crossed the road, so he went up the steps and let himself in. Mum wouldn't be home for hours so he knew that he had the place to himself. He went to his bedroom and took a pillow case off the bed. He undressed and placed his blood-stained clothes in to the pillow case. He went into the bathroom and, taking his time, carefully washed himself from head to toe. He even washed his hair. He dried himself and dressed in blue jeans and a check shirt.

After checking himself in the mirror, he picked up the pillowcase and made his way down to the kitchen. He felt a little light headed and, realising that he hadn't eaten since breakfast, turned on the grill above the oven and made his favourite meal of cheese on toast with a scrape of Marmite on the top.

He sat at the table and was determined to enjoy every mouthful. It was like a celebration meal. He was sad that he was having to celebrate on his own but that was Priscilla's fault. Stupid bitch. All she had to do was let him touch her, that was all. A portion of finger pie. No big deal. She didn't seem to object when that man put his arms around her. Still, he wouldn't be doing that again.

He washed the knife, fork and plate and put them away. There was a place for everything and everything had its place. He looked around the room and, satisfied, picked up the pillowcase and locked the front door on his way out. He crossed the road and decided to enter the place through the hole in the fence. There was little chance of being seen. He pulled the sheet of corrugated iron aside and went in. The metallic smell of blood was almost overpowering. There were other smells but he didn't know what they were. He seemed to spend ages looking around and then it dawned on him what he had to do.

He left, and after putting the corrugated sheet back in place, made his way to his grandmother's house. The street was quiet apart from the sound of a baby crying. He opened the wooden gate, crossed the small front garden, and looked in through the crack in the curtains. His grandmother was sat in her favourite chair fast asleep. The radio was on and he heard the closing credits of The Archers. He hadn't realised how late it was, where the time had gone. He let himself in and moved quietly through the house to the back door. He let himself out of the door and down the garden path to the small garden shed. As he had cut the grass the previous Sunday he knew that the lawn mower was nearly full of petrol. After almost swallowing a mouthful, he siphoned the petrol from the mower into a watering can. There was the spare can of petrol under the bench. He calculated that it contained about a gallon and a half. That would be more than enough.

On his way back through the house he found his grandmother's purse where she always kept it. He took the note but decided that it would be foolish to take more. After checking the she was still fast asleep, he let himself out and made his way back to the bomb site. It was now dark and he was pleased that some of the street lights had been smashed. He moved the corrugated iron and stared at the remains of Priscilla and the man. He felt the bile rising in his throat and was sick over the man's feet. When he had stopped heaving he carefully checked himself and was relieved that he was clean. As he polished his shoes on the man's trousers he noticed that the man's wallet was on the floor.

He picked it up and found two notes and some coins. This really was his lucky day. The only other thing in the wallet was a small black and white photograph. It showed the dead man, a tasty looking woman and a little girl. The little girl was Priscilla, so the man must have been her dad. So he had met her dad. Such a shame that they hadn't got to know each other. Bit late for that now. He should have said something instead of bursting in and acting like a maniac. It was his fault that this had happened.

After stroking Priscilla's hair he set to work. After pouring petrol over Priscilla and her dad and over the floor, he checked and rechecked. He was certain that there was nothing left which could identify him so stepped outside and tossed a lighted match back in through the entrance. Nothing happened. He tossed another lighted match in and, again, nothing seemed to happen. As he was about to go back in to check, he heard a crackle and saw smoke and flames. He picked up a pile of old newspapers and threw them onto the bodies. Jesus, it was starting to get hot.

He backed away, put the corrugated iron back in place and went out through the hole in the fence. He checked himself and was satisfied that he looked OK. He walked towards the bus stop and, after waiting for 15 minutes, was on his way into town. As the bus was turning the corner a fire engine was clanging its way past. Butterworth couldn't help but smile. He got off near McDonalds and treated himself to a Big Mac without fries. After drifting around the city centre he eventually went to the pictures. Years afterwards he still couldn't remember what film he'd seen.

When he eventually got home just before 11 o'clock, the fire engine was still there. Two police cars were parked across the road from the bomb site. As he walked towards his house he was stopped by a policemen and asked who he was. He said that he was Raymond Butterworth and that he lived at number 20. When asked where he'd been, he said that he'd been in town and had gone to the pictures. He reached into his trouser pocket and produced the cinema ticket stub. The policeman smiled and thanked him. Butterworth asked what had happened and was told that there had been a fire on the bomb site and that two bodies had been found. The policemen wished him goodnight and turned away.

Butterworth unlocked his front door and, seeing his mum in the kitchen, called out hello. His mother turned and gave him one of her silly smiles. He climbed the stairs and went into his bedroom. After undressing he put on pyjamas, got into bed and closed his eyes. He could still see Priscilla and her dad and he could still smell them. As he was drifting off he felt that lovely warm feeling starting to fill his head.

Over the coming years, Butterworth surprised those who knew him by getting and holding down a job in a rapidly expanding printing company. As the sixties moved into the seventies, he prospered as the company grew. He was a technical manager with his name on his office door. Every other year he took a small amount of shares instead of the annual pay rise. By the early nineteen eighties he was financially comfortable. In fact more than comfortable. He lived alone in his mortgage-free house which backed on to Aintree race course.

He often thought back to that day on the bomb site and, reaching into his imagination, he could summon up that wonderful, warm feeling. He often visited the girls who walked the streets of Toxteth but he could never recapture the emotions he had experienced, that day, on the bomb site. Deep down he knew that what had happened that day would happen again. He dreamed about it, he craved it. Being a patient man, he knew his time would come.

In 1985 he met Annie and fell in love. They met when they were attending the same printing conference in Harrogate. Butterworth was midway into his presentation on the need to combine the old processes with the new computer-generated programmes when she raised her hand.

'Why are you so stuck in the past, Mr Butterworth?'

Butterworth looked down and saw a slim, blond woman who was probably in her early thirties. She wasn't conventionally pretty but she definitely had something about her.

'I beg your pardon.'

'Were there too many words in the question?' A smattering of laughter drifted up from the delegates.

'I beg your pardon,' he repeated, not used to being challenged in a public forum especially as this woman was getting a laugh at his expense.

'I'm trying to get you to answer my question.'

'Bear with me and I will,' Butterworth answered, trying to control his anger. He took a deep breath and as he began to answer he felt that wonderful, warm feeling starting. He spoke, without a pause, for nearly 11 minutes. His response was wide-ranging, full of technical data and the occasional humorous aside. He didn't know he had it in him. The audience, although modest in size, clapped when he sat down.

'What about that then, Annie?' shouted a fat, pin-striped Londoner from the back row.

Annie knew when it was expedient to keep her mouth shut and this was definitely one of those times. She just smiled. Butterworth finished his presentation with the usual thanks and endorsements. As he was leaving the room Annie approached him.

'Fancy a drink Mr Butterworth?'

'Why would I want to have a drink with you?'

'Because I want you to.'

'Really.'

'Yes.'

'Convince me.'

'I don't have to. I'll be in the main bar in about twenty minutes. I'll wait for as long as it takes for me to drink a gin and tonic. As I like G & T's it won't take long.'

Butterworth nodded and went to his room. He was in the main bar 16 minutes later.

Annie was born in the tiny village of South Witham, which straddled the Leicestershire/Lincolnshire border. Annie's family were liberal in style and attitude. Living was easy and there was never a shortage of money. Life was centred on four and a half days of frantic activity in the city, the two and a half hour drive out of London and then a weekend of doing just about anything anyone wanted to do.

Annie loved sex and made no secret of the fact. Sex had played a significant part in her life since a relatively early age. Uncle Reg, Auntie Eva and second cousin Dennis had all enjoyed Annie's more than ample charms. Her father did have a sniff after a particularly heavy Sunday lunch, but her mother had already beaten him to the punch. Annie didn't see any harm in the goings on and the family were certainly not going to rock the boat. To Annie, sex was like eating a packet of crisps. She preferred ready salted but was happy with any flavour. When she challenged Raymond Butterworth on that fateful day in Harrogate she thought that she just might have made the right choice for once in her short life.

'So you turned up then.'

'I fancied a drink before dinner,' Butterworth answered, fully aware that she was mentally undressing him. Strangely he didn't mind.

'What can I get you?'

'Thanks, but I'll get my own. Top up for you?'

'Large G & T please, more G than T,' she giggled.

Butterworth turned, waved to the bartender and ordered Annie's drink.

'What would Sir like?' the lad sneered.

'I'll have a lager top please,' he answered, completely unaware that the lad was being sarcastic

Butterworth took his glass and guided Annie to an empty table near the cigarette machine.

'So, Annie, why are you here?'

'To learn from the master,' she replied, careful not to spill her drink.

'What have you learned?'

'Nothing, he never turned up.'

Butterworth laughed and stared into her eyes. She stared back. Her eyes were intense.

'Are you going in for dinner?'

'Are you?'

'Is this a fucking are-you, are-you contest?'

Annie laughed, a deep full laugh which was obviously well used. Secretly she was surprised at his use of the 'fuck' word. It just didn't sound right coming from him. From anyone else that she knew, yes, but from him, no.

She decided not to make an issue out of it as she had probably taken the piss enough for one day.

'There's an Indian about fifteen minutes' walk from here. Fancy it?'

'It has to be better than this mausoleum.'

They finished their drinks and left the hotel. They arrived at the restaurant to find that other delegates had decided that hotel food was not on the menu for them this evening. They were shown to a table and ordered poppadoms, chicken tikka masala and wine. The food turned out to be overpriced and under cooked. The wine would have given a bottle of mouthwash a close run for its money. But they didn't seem to notice. They just talked and talked.

When they got back to the hotel it was just a case of deciding which room they were going to. Annie could sense how nervous Butterworth was and decided, rather uncharacteristically, to be quiet and sensitive and not use the raving nympho routine which was normally right for these circumstances.

After slowly undressing, in the dark, they climbed in to his bed. They kissed which, instantly, had the effect of making him rock hard but he didn't know how to take the next step.

Although he couldn't see her face he sensed that she was staring at him. As he was about to kiss her she patted him on the shoulder and whispered that he must be as tired as she was. With a sigh of relief he turned over and drifted off in to a dreamless sleep.

Annie was happy just to rest. Her managing director had taken his share two nights before, and his secretary had been like a rutting stag the night before so, yes, the rest was good. Maybe this Raymond Butterworth would be a welcome diversion from her usual 'friends'.

'Do you take Annabel Pauline Street to be your lawful wedded wife?'

Butterworth lay in bed in the hotel recalling the events of the day. Annie had looked gorgeous, as had the bridesmaids. That wonderful warm feeling had started when he caught one of the bridesmaids adjusting her stockings but he had quickly shut it down. Maybe later but this was definitely not the place to be indulging himself.

He looked over at Annie and sighed. She was drunk, sleeping the sleep of the dead. Still, he loved her to bits and she loved him to bits. He knew it was still early days and was confident that he would get the sex thing right. Annie said she didn't mind and that all good things came to she who waited. He loved to hear her say those words. His day would come. He knew it would.

Children were never an option and were rarely discussed. They enjoyed having nieces and nephews to stay for the weekend but were happy when the parents arrived to collect them. There was one niece, in particular, who interested him. She was the same age as his beloved Priscilla and had the same overweight body. He knew that he couldn't indulge himself but it didn't stop that lovely warm feeling arriving. He'd searched far and wide until he'd found an old fashioned sweet shop where he bought a quarter of flying saucers. To his great delight his niece loved them. At every opportunity he would hug her and stroke her hair, But he knew that he had to be so careful.

Annie had changed jobs and moved into the music business as a P.A. It suited her personality. The up and coming groups and solo artists loved her because they could never embarrass her with their language and jokes. If plied with the right amount of booze she was a true athlete. Permanently drunk bass players, coked-up drummers or prima donna female vocalists were all the same to Annie. She was careful to keep distance between her work and home life. It helped that Butterworth had absolutely no interest in, or knowledge of, popular music.

Butterworth continued to amass his shares and his savings grew. His in-built caution had stopped him revealing, to Annie, the truth about his finances. His frugal nature did not stretch to being tight when it came to spending money on her. She was earning a good salary so money was rarely discussed.

His infrequent couplings with Annie were satisfactory but short lived. She always made the right noises, or at least he thought she did, but he was never absolutely certain. She always seemed so tired when she got home from work and was absolutely exhausted when she had been on the road doing her P.A. duties for a rock band. Trips away seemed to be on the increase but he wasn't concerned as long as Annie was happy and proud to be his wife. She always said that she was proud of him and he loved to hear her say those words.

They would spend their holidays in nice villas on mainland Spain and the Canary Islands. He particularly liked the Costa Blanca and had friends who lived in a villa near a village called Pedreguer. They drove a Mercedes sports car which he had driven, once, himself. He knew that he could easily afford one, but if he did treat himself then Annie might start asking questions. Better to leave things as they were. Their days on holiday were spent sunbathing and reading trashy novels. Evenings were spent eating and drinking, mostly at overpriced bars and restaurants. If he could get Annie back to their villa before she was too drunk then nice moments might happen but, invariably she was staggering alongside him muttering words he couldn't understand.

Annie's travels stretched to weeks in America, which was where she met Germaine. Annie was sat in a bar in Brooklyn waiting for a record producer to arrive. Drinks and dinner were a possibility and, after that, anything might happen. The guy should have arrived at 8 o'clock but still hadn't shown at 8.30. As Annie was about to leave, the door flew open and a very harassed young woman almost fell into the place. She was early twenties, slim, brunette and absolutely stunning. Her tight-fitting black skirt accentuated her long legs. She straightened herself, adjusted her long hair and looked around the room. She looked at Annie, nodded and walked over to her.

'Mrs Butterworth?'

'Yes.'

I've come on behalf of David Shaw. He's still at the studio. Things are going really slowly.

He said that he thinks he will be lucky if he's away by midnight. I'm so sorry that I've kept you waiting but the bridge was a nightmare. My name's Germaine.'

Annie looked at the vision in front of her and smiled.

'Please call me Annie and I'm sorry that David can't make it.'

'I'll be off now Mrs Butterworth. Once again, I'm sorry to have kept you waiting.'

Annie knew that this one would slip away if she didn't control the situation.

'Please, please call me Annie, I insist.'

'Thank you, Annie'

'The only way that you can make this right is by having dinner with me. My treat.'

Germaine wasn't expecting that. She had planned to see her partner Kate for an early dinner and an even earlier night. Still, needs must.

'Thanks Annie, I would love to, I just need to make a quick call.'

'Fine, I'll finish my drink. Make your call.'

Germaine phoned Kate and said that she was stuck at work and didn't know what time she would be home. Kate reacted, as usual, by calling her a useless fucking dyke and slammed the phone down. Germaine knew that their relationship was slowly coming to an end but, obviously, Kate didn't. Still, tonight could be interesting and certainly wouldn't do her any harm. David would be pleased that she had sorted the problem. If she had any sexual feelings for a man then David would have been very lucky. Annie obviously had connections so she could be a useful lady to know. Not bad looking either. Nice clothes and very little make-up. Germaine hated wearing make-up but knew that it was a part of her work uniform. She had perfected her way of deflecting the advances of the male musicians and was comfortable in her own skin.

As she turned away from the payphone, Germaine saw that Annie was staring at her. She recognised the look in Annie's eyes. That was how it started.

In 1995, Butterworth was promoted to production manager. As the business was thriving there was plenty of overtime to be had for the shop floor workers. Although on a salary, Butterworth was expected to work the occasional Saturday. He didn't mind because with Annie away so much, particularly the endless trips to New York, he had plenty of time on his hands. He didn't have any hobbies apart from a real addiction to Radio 4. He liked good wine but never over indulged when Annie was home because it wouldn't have been right if they were both drunk.

Annie had fallen head-over-heels in love with Germaine and the feeling was reciprocated. After the relationship with Kate had ended Germaine had found a very expensive loft conversion in Greenwich Village. To her delight Annie immediately offered to pay half of all the expenses, which included the mortgage. The only downside was that Annie could only visit for a few days each month but at least they had their mobiles. Their love and passion was so intense that neither could see a future without the other. They often discussed the future and Annie knew, increasingly, that Raymond would play no part in it.

In the February of 1997, Annie paid for Germaine to fly, business class, to London. She then took an internal flight to Liverpool where she was met by Annie. Annie had booked them into a suite in a five star hotel on the outskirts of the city. Her record company had stumped up for a nice hire car so everything was good.

They sat in bed on the following morning, Saturday, and discussed how Annie was going to tell Raymond that she was leaving him. Annie had already arranged for a transfer, at her own expense, to the record company's New York office. She couldn't wait. She wanted a little money from him but wasn't interested in his shares portfolio. He didn't know that Annie knew about the shares and if he got awkward about providing some cash then the shares would become part of the divorce settlement.

Annie had no concerns about Raymond. He wasn't a violent man and Annie knew that he was in awe of her. So, just the telling to do. Better late than never. She rang the house and got no reply. She rang his mobile and it went straight to answer phone. She didn't leave a message. She didn't bother ringing the factory because he didn't normally work on weekends. She decided to drive to the house and Germaine insisted on going with her. If he was out they would wait for him. It would also give them the opportunity of loading up the hire car with Annie's clothes. She wanted nothing else from the house.

Butterworth hadn't intended to go into work but then he decided to make a surprise inspection. He loved doing that because it upset the floor workers.

During the visit he found a supervisor asleep behind a photocopying machine and a pretty cleaner giving one of the security officers a blow job in one of the many, empty offices. After he'd watched the couple, through a glass partition, he burst into the room. After informing them that they had, instantly, become unemployed he returned to the sleeping supervisor and gave him the same news.

He'd arranged to drop his car off at the garage, on his way home, because it was due its 10,000 mile service. The garage staff were good because they worked Saturdays and, more importantly, didn't rip him off. He turned down their offer of a courtesy car because he wasn't going anywhere over the weekend but he did ask them to book him a taxi to take him home after dropping the car off. He would collect the car on his way to work on Monday morning.

Annie and Germaine arrived at the house just after lunch and left the hire car on the drive. She let them in. The house smelled of a place that she didn't know any more. She needed to get this over with as soon as possible and get on with her life. As she stood in the lounge Germaine came up behind her and kissed the back of her neck. Annie turned and kissed her on the lips, searching her mouth with her tongue.

Butterworth paid the taxi driver and, as he got out, noticed the hire car on the drive. It couldn't be Annie because her company always paid for taxis from Manchester Airport. He hated the unexpected and was instantly on his guard. He walked quietly down the drive and remembered that he hadn't opened the curtains before leaving for work. Something made him look through the small gap where the curtains didn't quite meet. He wished he hadn't.

He saw Annie kissing a woman in a way that she had never kissed him. She was massaging the other woman's breasts and the other woman was clearly enjoying it. Fucking bitch. He moved away from the crack in the curtains as the women parted but still held hands.

'Are you sure you want to tell him, I don't mind if you think it's too soon,' Germaine said, her face flushed.

'I've never been so sure of anything in my life. I love you so much I think I'm going to explode.'

'Will he get violent, you know, try to slap you around a bit?'

'You must be fucking joking. If he tried anything like that he'd be dead meat. He's a fucking wimp.'

'I love you.'

'And I love you, my little Brooklyn bird.'

Butterworth could just about hear the conversation and was stunned. He was trying to make sense of it and looked through the crack in the curtains again. Annie had her tongue down the other woman's throat again and the cow was grinding against her. He'd seen and heard enough. As he turned he started to feel warm. Not sweaty warm but bomb site warm. His mind flashed back to Priscilla and that man, her dad. If he hadn't intervened then they would have become friends. Good friends. Butterworth was sure of that and it made him sad. He turned back to the window and the sight made him shiver. His mind seemed to fog but cleared when he found himself opening his garden shed door.

Two doors down the road, Mrs Beach was conducting her usual vigil by her front window. She never missed a thing. Since hubby had died she had nothing else to do and it filled the long, lonely hours.

He lifted the old sweatshirt he kept in the cupboard, for gardening, and picked up the hammer. Grandmother's hammer. It was the only souvenir he'd kept from his special place. It felt good to hold, like an old friend. He'd frequently gone to the shed, when Annie was away, and thought back to those magic times in his special place, raising the hammer and crashing it down in a chopping motion as he had done all those years ago. The lovely warm feeling was all over him now and he didn't really want it to go away. Deep inside his head he knew what would happen next.

Mrs Beach was intrigued. Why was Mr Butterworth peeking through his own front window, especially as Mrs Butterworth was already home with that woman in the red leggings.

Butterworth opened the back door and stepped into the kitchen . None of the doors or stairs in the house creaked. He'd spent a lot of money stopping the creaks. He look into the lounge, through the partly open door, and saw Annie and the woman lying on his settee with their hands all over each other. The woman started to kiss Annie and they were moaning like dogs on heat.

As he walked into the room it all became clear. This was so like Priscilla and her father it was uncanny. So unfair.

As Annie looked past Germaine's left shoulder, he hit her on the top of her head with the hammer. It felt good, so good. As she started to scream he hit her again and again. Germaine felt the blood splash on to her face and, after a moment, started to scream. Butterworth started to hit her and was soon in a frenzy and, as far as he could fathom, loving it. It was like playing the drums. One to the other, one to the other.

Mrs Beach couldn't contain her curiosity so she decided to go out to her front garden and do some weeding. She might get a better look at what was happening at Mr Butterworth's. When she heard the awful screams she ran back inside. After three failed attempts she finally managed to dial 999.

The operator managed to calm her down after almost a minute. She was babbling but the operator sensed that something serious had happened. Between deep gasps for breath, Mrs Beach told the operator of the awful, awful screams. The operator double checked the address and alerted the duty inspector.

Butterworth was starting to tire. He'd used his hammer well and Annie and the other woman were now almost fused into one soft, almost unrecognisable thing. Still, a little bit more wouldn't hurt. He was concentrating so hard that he never heard his front door splinter and crash inwards. As the policemen were trying to subdue him he was laughing his head off. He was laughing so hard he wet himself.

He never did collect his car from the garage.

Butterworth pleaded guilty, to both murders, and after months of examinations by eminent psychiatrists, the consensus was that he was bad not mad. The judge accepted the findings and sentenced him to two life sentences for the murder of Annie and Germaine. The Judge said that he must serve a minimum of 30 years before he would be eligible to be considered for parole. Butterworth smiled at the Judge and thanked him.

Part Two

HM PRISON RAYMAR

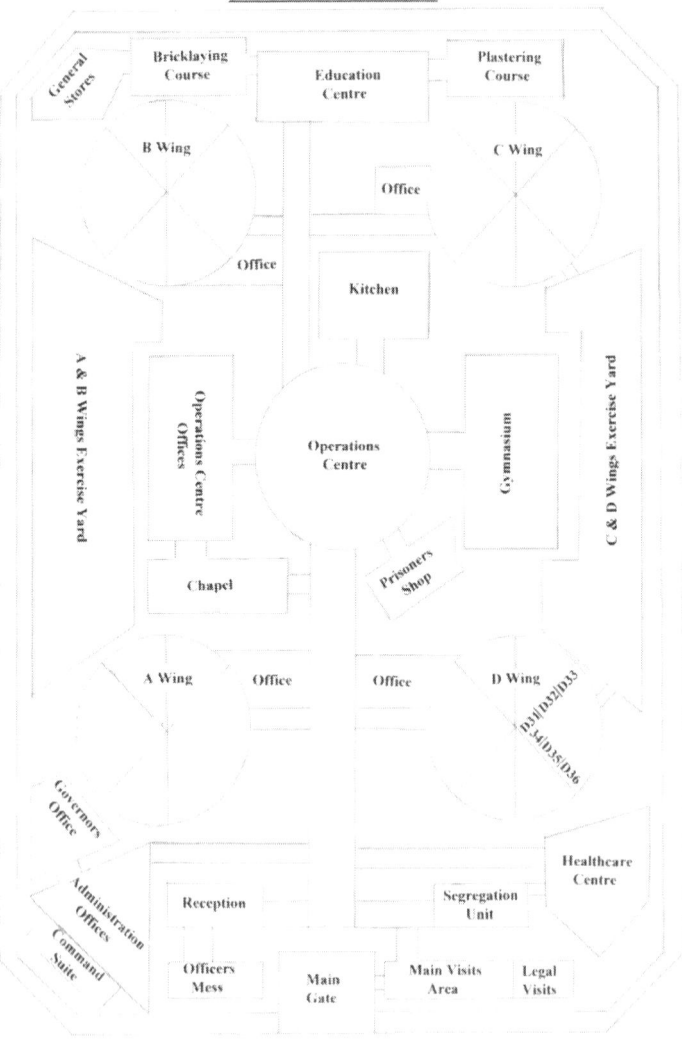

- General Stores
- Bricklaying Course
- Education Centre
- Plastering Course
- B Wing
- C Wing
- Office
- Office
- Kitchen
- A & B Wings Exercise Yard
- Operations Centre Offices
- Operations Centre
- Gymnasium
- C & D Wings Exercise Yard
- Chapel
- Prisoners Shop
- A Wing
- Office
- Office
- D Wing
- D31/D32/D33
- D34/D35/D36
- Governors Office
- Administration Offices
- Command Suite
- Reception
- Segregation Unit
- Healthcare Centre
- Officers Mess
- Main Gate
- Main Visits Area
- Legal Visits

Chapter Nine

HM Prison Raymar is situated two and a half miles north of the village of Whittingham in the North West of England and opened for business in 2003. It sits on the top of a small hill and is surrounded by a mix of oak and beech trees and a tributary of the River Mar. The wall is of standard design and does not blend in with the surrounding countryside, much to the annoyance of the two gentleman farmers who own the land which surrounds the prison. Both regulars at the centuries-old village pub, they happily embellish the rumours of ghosts living on the site from the days of Rosmere prison.

The prison is rectangular with the corners cut off. There is an operations centre, mid-way between the four wings, and all movement is controlled from the centre. The segregation unit (seg) is considered to be a short-term option for prisoners seeking protection. Adjudications take place in the seg. The healthcare centre is managed by a senior nurse who, it must be said, is about as popular as a chocolate fire-guard. Healthcare is fund-managed by a local Care Trust. Inpatient occupation is not encouraged.

Prisoners located on the third levels, or spurs, of the wings can see over the wall and are rewarded by the splendid vista of the gradually changing seasons. Those incarcerated pilgrims with patience and sharp eyes can witness, most Saturday evenings, sexual shenanigans played out in a car park between two particularly splendid oak trees a little under a quarter of a mile north of the prison. One gay prisoner was about to complain about the lack of equal opportunities, view wise, until he was advised that any such complaint would be followed by a sound beating with the sharpened end of a mop handle. Needless to say, the complaint never found its way to the wing principal officer.

The rattle of the chain and the key in the lock told Grove that it was morning unlock. Tuesday morning in cell D32. Who thought up a stupid name like Raymar? Some knob who'd never been in jail.

Grove threw back his duvet, stretched and swung his legs off the bed. The floor was cold so he sat back down and put his socks on. He went behind the modesty partition and used the toilet. Still, there was one good thing about being banged up in 2004. No more slopping out. Grove used to hate that, especially as the officers used to laugh when you were half asleep and banged into the con in front of you with your pot, urine going everywhere. Not nice at all.

Two thousand and four. The seventh of April to be exact. Twenty minutes to eight to be even more exact. Grove stretched again and pulled the curtains open. He looked out of the window. It was pouring down. It was always pouring down. The tree in the distance was hidden by mist. He felt depressed just looking out of the window. As he wasn't going down for breakfast and didn't have to be at the gym until 10 o'clock, he closed the curtains and got back into bed.

In cell D35, Raymond Butterworth was up, dressed and sat on his bed. He was going over 'the dream'. He called it 'the dream' because it happened every night. Same one, never varied. A bit frustrating, but then life was frustrating.

As he started to enter her throat with the tip of his blade, Raymond Butterworth whispered, 'Mother, I've been so looking forward to this.'

The blade was shaking in his hand but he ploughed on, ever the diligent son. Mother was being particularly awkward. Her right hand was trying to tear at the waist band of his jeans and her nails were starting to break. Kneeling on her back to pin her to the kitchen floor wasn't ideal but, life was never ideal.

The blood was thick, viscous like oil. Mother was bucking and shivering at the same time. She couldn't seem to make up her mind. Raymond wasn't bothered because he had a job to do and do it he would.

Finally he found the spot he was searching for and got stuck in. It shouldn't have taken long, but he slipped on his knees and fell into the rapidly spreading pool of blood. As he tried to regain his balance he seemed to lose his way. Noise, like doors being banged. Banging doors were not right. Voices were not right. As he opened his eyes reality hit him like a hammer. He was in prison in the shit hole laughingly described as his room. A poxy cell. Ten by four. Rust and grey. Pants and socks. Piss and sweat. He was a lifer. He couldn't even kill Mother in his dreams.

He'd heard the officer walking along the landing and called to him as he was unlocking the door.

'Morning Mr Jones.'

'Morning, Butterworth, how are you on this beautiful morning?'

'Not feeling that great. Can you put me down for the doctor?'

'Will do. Are you coming down for breakfast?'

'No, I'll give it a miss today.'

'Right, I'll come back for you just after 9.30.'

With that, Jones walked out slamming the door behind him. Butterworth hated the door being banged but he never complained because that would show weakness and he knew that the officers and cons saw him as a hard bastard. Someone not to be messed with. Someone who deserved respect.

He lay back on his bed thinking about what he was going to say to the doctor. Of course, there was nothing wrong with him. For a man of 57 he was as fit as a butcher's dog. No, the reason for the trip to healthcare was to see Tim the orderly. Tim had got a message to him saying that he had the two joints that he'd asked for. Excellent. Tim would also place a bet for him with the bookie on A wing.

He opened the drawer at the bottom of his cupboard and took out the blue biro pen. After he carefully withdrew the ink barrel he unwound the two five pound notes. He folded each note into squares not much bigger than large postage stamps. He took his bible from the small shelf under the television and pressed the notes into the small space he had created at the bottom of the spine. He knew that some of the officers were suspicious and this had proved to be the case when he had been cell-searched twice the previous week. Despite making a mess, as they searched, nothing was found. The best place to hide stuff was right under their noses.

Just after 9.30, he was escorted to healthcare. It was a relatively short walk and didn't involve going outside because it was still pouring down. As he walked along the corridor leading to the iron gate and wooden door that was the entrance into healthcare he heard something kicking off in the Seg.

'Some poor bastard getting a kicking for asking for two sheets of bog roll. Would that be right Mr Jones?'

'No need for that Butterworth, no need at all.'

'Of course you're right Mr Jones, probably slipped in the showers,' Butterworth laughed.

'What's your problem Butterworth, always taking the piss, always got an opinion. Never satisfied are you? Maybe a transfer to Long Lartin might be more to your taste.'

'I've heard that they are looking for senior screws at Long Lartin. Would that be right Mr Jones? Get yourself promoted and we can go together. I'd like that. My own senior officer to look after me.'

'You're coming very close to getting yourself placed on report Butterworth, so watch your mouth.'

'I certainly will Mr Jones. But you know as well as I do that you will never come with me to Long Lartin, will you? Got to get promoted first haven't you? Shame.'

Before Jones could answer, Butterworth was rattling the iron gate outside healthcare.

'I retire in eight years, Butterworth, on a nice pension off the backs of people like you. Prison will then be a memory for me. Prison will always be with you. It will probably be the last memory you will have.'

Butterworth turned, looked Jones up and down, and laughed.

'Whatever.'

Jones ushered Butterworth into healthcare and saw senior nurse Nelson.

'One on Matron.'

'Thank you, Mr Jones,' Margaret Nelson shouted. She hated the Welsh bastard. He thought he was the bee's knees.

'Good morning, Mr Butterworth, and what can we do for you today?'

Butterworth liked coming to healthcare because they always called him Mr.

'Hello Maggie, I've got a massive hard on and I need nursing to help me walk properly.'

'Don't call me Maggie, Mr Butterworth. My name is Nurse Nelson to you. Understand?'

'Whatever.'

'Why do you want to see the doctor today?'

'I'll tell the doctor when I see him.'

'Tell me now.'

'Why should I, you're not a doctor are you?'

'Go and sit in the waiting room Mr Butterworth, there are people in front of you this morning.'

'Nil problemo Matron,' Butterworth said, winking at Tim who was drinking a mug of tea in what passed for a small kitchen.

Bryce Jones was angry as he walked back to D wing. That bastard Butterworth had really got to him. Staff should not talk in front of the cons. That must have been how Butterworth knew about his latest promotion failure. His darling wife Anwyn never stopped bleating about his failures and now he was getting it from a convict. Mustn't use the word convict. Must use the word prisoner. One of the many criticisms on his last failed attempt at promotion. The use of proper words. Political correctness was the current thing. What a load of old bollocks.

Butterworth was the last one left in the waiting room. It suited him. He knew they would keep him waiting, they always did. When he was finally called he asked Tim to look after his bible while he was in with the doctor. Nurse Nelson was stood behind Dr Hall who was seated at the desk.

'Good morning Mr Butterworth, what can I do for you today?'

'Does Nurse Death have to be in the room while I'm discussing my medical shortcomings?'

'It is part of Nurse Nelson's duties to assist me as and when necessary. Now, how can I help you?'

'My knob dropped off and I can't find it. As I...'

'I beg your pardon,' Hall spluttered. He'd spoken to Butterworth before but this time he really had crossed the line. 'I'm going to have to ask you to leave my office.'

'If you let me finish, I was about to tell you that my knob has dropped off my television and as I was bending down looking for it I pulled something in my back.' He smiled at the doctor and winked at the nurse.

'You obviously don't want to help me so I'll petition to have another doctor look after me. I'm sure that you'll support my request won't you Maggie?' Butterworth laughed, saluted, turned and left the room.

Hall looked up at Nelson and shook his head. Neither spoke.

As Butterworth walked back to the waiting room Tim handed him his bible. He examined the spine with his fingertips, knowing that the money was gone and two thin joints had taken their place. Nice one Tim.

Butterworth was surprised when Jones came to take him back to D wing because he was accompanied by principal officer Richard Watts. Watts was the D wing boss and wasn't usually seen unless there was a problem, and certainly not to escort a con back to the wing. Butterworth stood as the pair walked in to the waiting room.

'Sit down, Butterworth, we need to have a little chat.'

Ominous, especially as Watts normally addressed the D wing cons by their Christian names.

'What about Mr Watts?'

'About your attitude. We don't mind the jokes, as well you know, but your piss taking has risen to an unacceptable level.'

'Who's got it in for me?'

'No one has got anything in for you, we don't operate like that as well you know.'

'So what happens now?'

'If you don't convince me, in the next few minutes, that you are planning to improve your attitude towards staff, then I will have you placed in segregation and you will be transferred to Wormwood Scrubs later today. Convince me that I won't have to set up the escort.'

Butterworth looked past Watts and saw that three more officers had arrived.

He considered his options and knew that his nuts were in a vice. Watts would do it. No doubts on that score. He also knew that Watts liked to captain a quiet ship. If he kicked off there was every likelihood that a few slaps would come his way courtesy of the Seg screws.

'Looks like there's been a big misunderstanding Mr Watts. I love the wing screws and the wonderful doctors and nurses.'

'So we agree that changes are starting to happen, do we Butterworth?'

'I think you could say that was an accurate assessment, principal officer.'

'Excellent, so I won't have you placed on report for the two joints hidden in the spine of your bible. Obviously, some villain has placed them there to get you into trouble. You just can't trust people, can you?'

Butterworth was stunned and didn't trust himself to speak. Watts reached over and took the bible out of his hand. He went straight to the hiding place and removed the joints.

'Take Butterworth back to the wing, Mr Jones. I'm staying in healthcare to help them choose a new orderly.

On his way back to the wing Butterworth reflected that he had just had a very close shave. He'd lost two joints and ten pounds. Not a major setback but something not to be repeated. What would have been a disaster was a transfer. He had made a nice niche for himself at Raymar and a move to Wormwood

Scrubs was definitely not on his radar. He decided to keep his head down for a few days. No harm in that. Poor old Tim. Nice lad but a loser. Leave it a few days and he would contact that spade on C wing who, apparently, scored good stuff. Patience was the word. Patience.

Grove woke up with a start to see the physical education officer Harland Smith standing in the doorway.

'Come on Grove, the gym isn't going to clean itself. Let's get going.'

'Sorry Mr Smith, I was having a lovely dream about being back ended by a gym screw.'

'Anybody I know?' Smith glared.

'A black gym screw at Belmarsh.'

Smith thought for a long minute.

'There aren't any black gym staff at Belmarsh.'

'Must have been a poof at another jail then.' Grove smiled. He knew that he'd pressed the right buttons but couldn't take it too far in case he lost his gym job. He left the wing, escorted by Smith. Not a word passed between them. Cutler wondered if he really had gone too far. Whatever.

Deputy governor Liam McGill was sitting in his office in the administration block. The rain had stopped so he hadn't needed to use his umbrella when crossing the car park. He had a pile of paperwork to do, not least some senior staff appraisals. He was duty governor, call-sign Victor One, until 09.00 the following morning which meant carrying the radio everywhere and being on call overnight. A quiet night in then, no wine bars tonight. The minute hand of his desk clock had just hit 14.29.

'Attention all stations, general alarm, main visits area.'

'Attention all stations, general alarm, main visits area.'

'Acknowledge Oscar One, over.'

'Oscar One received.'

'Acknowledge Victor One, over.'

'Victor One received,' McGill answered.

'All stations, Romeo Mike November standing by.'

McGill stood and put his suit jacket on. No need to rush. It wouldn't do to arrive in visits before the staff got there.

In the main visits area it was pandemonium. There were four staff on duty and the place wasn't particularly busy for a Tuesday afternoon. The senior officer in charge had decided that caution was the watch word for today particularly as Wolf and his wife, whom he called Mother, were the main attraction. No prizes for heroes today.

Principal officer Watts was Oscar One and arrived as eight other staff were arriving at the visits gates. As he let himself through, he saw Wolf, first and then his wife.

Wolf was a biker down to his socks. He was average height and slightly overweight. His beard was long and unkempt but he was scrupulously clean. It wouldn't do to see his darling Mother and not be as clean as a new pin. Plus the fact that if she caught the slightest whiff of BO he would be letting himself in for a public bollocking. So, he had put on his best shirt and jeans and had even run a comb through his beard. He was doing seven years for biting the ear off another biker who had not shown the required amount of respect to his wife. He adored his wife. She was his life. She was slim and of average height. She looked like butter wouldn't melt until she opened her mouth.

Wolf was rarely a problem to C wing staff. The only thing that really pissed him off was when he didn't get his biker and music magazines on the day he was expecting them. He rarely engaged staff in conversation and they were happy with the arrangement.

Mother was sat astride a young, petite brunette, punching her alternately in the stomach and face. The woman was putting up no resistance. Her husband, a con known as Noddy, was not able to help his wife. Wolf had Noddy by the throat and was slapping him around the face. Real slow but with a certain rhythm. There was no blood but Noddy would certainly remember this afternoon for a few days to come.

Watts quickly issued his instructions to the staff. They entered the room and split into two teams. Team one went for Mother. Officer Hilary Brand was part of the team. Mother was quickly restrained and taken, forcibly, into legal visits. Her shouts and screams could be heard all over the place. Team two went for Wolf. He dropped Noddy, casually kicked him in the face and sat down. Team two now numbered six. No other con had attempted to intervene. No point in ending up on closed visits was there! Wolf would definitely be on closed visits for at least six months.

Wolf was taken to the segregation unit. He wasn't under restraint because he hadn't resisted. He had done exactly as he had been told. Mother could still be heard although Wolf made no mention of hearing his wife's salty language. Staff took Wolf into a special cell and strip searched him. They found nothing. He dressed and was taken to another cell.

'What was all that about then?' Watts asked. McGill stood in the background saying nothing.

'Nothing for you to worry about, Mr Watts,' Wolf answered.

'I'll be the best judge of what to worry about, now tell me what it was about.'

Wolf said nothing but thought about his options. He couldn't help Mother. Her temper really was a problem. She flew off the handle when there wasn't even a handle. There was no point in lying to the screws because there were cameras everywhere in visits.

'I'd rather not say, Mr Watts.'

'I'm trying to help you Wolf, I really am. Surely you don't want to see your wife on closed visits for the next six months. Do you?'

'We'll get over it.'

'The police will be coming for your wife, you do know that don't you?'

'We'll get over it.'

That was the last that Wolf would say on the matter. Noddy and his wife were interviewed by both police and prison staff. Neither said a word. But the incident was not forgotten.

After visiting Wolf in Segregation, McGill ordered that he be returned to his wing. He had been placed on report and he would be dealt with on adjudication the following morning. The Seg staff were not pleased that Wolf was being returned to his wing so soon. They felt that he should have stayed with them overnight in readiness for the adjudication the following morning. Wolf smiled at them as he left the unit.

Just as McGill reached his office his phone rang. The ringing tone told him that it was not an internal call.

'McGill, deputy governor.'

'Liam, it's Angela. How are you today?'

'I'm well.' McGill grimaced. What did the bitch want? Probably checking up on him. She couldn't take a day off without phoning in at least once.

Angela Painter was 34 and married to Steve. She was a product of the accelerated promotion scheme, having joined the Service in 1998. She had graduated with honours from Durham University. This was her first in-charge posting as a governor and she intended to make a success of it. She had discussed her career plan with Mitchell Hagen, the North West area manager. He had confirmed that she had a very promising career ahead of her as long as she avoided any major errors of judgement. Her last performance appraisal had been very encouraging and she was due the next one in a couple of weeks' time.

Hagen had warned Painter that her deputy could be a handful and had come up through the ranks. He said that her management and personnel skills would be tested to the limit but that he would always be at the end of the phone for advice. His next visit to Raymar was scheduled for the middle of May. In the short time that she'd been at Raymar she had come to hate Liam McGill. She guessed, correctly, that he felt the same about her. He never tired of banging on about his years in uniform before he moved into a suit. He particularly seemed to enjoy reminding her that he had been the deputy governor when Raymar had opened and what a great bloke her predecessor, Dick Anthony had been. Bastard.

A secret which she had not shared with Hagen or any of her senior staff was that her career plan included getting pregnant before the end of the year. She intended returning to the job after taking the maximum maternity leave entitlement. She would drop that bombshell when she was absolutely certain that she was pregnant. She fancied a stint at head office and, returning from maternity leave might just offer the opportunity. Child minding would not pose a problem because her doting parents lived a 30 minute drive away.

'Any problems I need to be aware of?' she asked, trying to sound pleasant and confident. McGill recounted the incident with Wolf and that it had been resolved without injury to staff. When she asked how Noddy was he told her that he had been taken to Healthcare and admitted for observation. He told her that he intended to visit Noddy during his rounds that evening. He ended the call by telling her that four new receptions were on their way and were expected at about 6 o'clock. He said that he would be seeing them on arrival. The prisoners were named Masters, Lincoln, Perry and Scapes. They were serving a lot of bird between them, two being lifer. The Security PO had been faxed the relevant sections of their files and there had been no reason to take any special measures. The Reception staff had been told to allocate them to C and D wings as the rest of the jail was virtually full. Painter said she would see him the following day before the morning meeting.

Just after 6.pm, the Group 4 cellular vehicle pulled up outside the main gate. After checking the registration number, staff opened the big outer gates. The vehicle drove slowly into the vehicle lock and the gates closed. The driver jumped down from the cab and walked over to the office window.

'I've got four for you this evening,' he said handing over the transfer documents. The gate officer checked the paperwork and was satisfied.

'Any problems en route?'

'None.'

'Have you been to Raymar before?' he asked the driver.

'No, it's my first time,' replied the driver.

'Restart your engine when the inner gates are fully open. Drive forward and then take the first left. Reception is 150 yards on the right. Staff are expecting you.'

'Thanks, any chance of a cuppa and a bite to eat?'

'No problem, the Mess is opposite Reception and it's open until 7.30'

Although it was getting dark the rain had held off. The vehicle stopped outside Reception and the iron gate opened.

'Four on,' shouted the Group 4 officer to the reception senior officer.

'Any problems on the way?' grumbled the senior officer. He had planned to see Preston North End that evening, with his eldest boy, and go for an Indian afterwards. Not much chance of that happening now was there? Still, he would pick up a take-away in the village on his way home. He was off tomorrow so he intended to sink a few pints of Stella with the curry.

Masters was the first to be unlocked. He stepped down off the vehicle and walked the short distance in to Reception.

'Name?'

'Masters.'

'Number?' asked the reception officer, not looking up.

'You know my fucking number. Why the fuck do we have to go through this stupid routine every time I have a move?'

'Moved a lot have you?'

'What the fuck do you think? You've got my record in front of you, read it.' The reception senior officer stood next to Masters.

'What's with the attitude then, Masters?'

'The screws got the attitude, not me.'

'We don't like the word screw here and we punish any prisoner who insists on using it.'

'Really?'

'Yes, really.'

Masters nodded, leaned forward and sent the papers and a cup of tea flying. One of the officers stepped back, turned and pressed a button set in a brass plate on the wall. This activated a general alarm in the communications centre.

'Attention all stations, general alarm Reception.'
'Attention all stations, general alarm Reception.'
'Acknowledge Oscar One, over.'
'Oscar One received.'
'Acknowledge Victor One, over.'
'Victor One received.'
'All stations, Romeo Mike November standing by.'

Staff responding to the alarm found Masters being restrained on the floor He was bleeding from his mouth and the flesh around his right eye was starting to swell.

'Hotel from Romeo Mike November, acknowledge over.'
'Hotel received.'
'Hotel, a nurse is required in Reception, over.'
'Received.'
'All stations, Romeo Mike November standing by.'

When McGill arrived in reception, Masters was still on the ground.

'Hello, Tony, still keeping your ear to the ground,' McGill said, smiling at the laughter from the staff restraining Masters.

'Fuck off, McGill. About now I get a boot in the face, don't I? Old habits die hard for an old cunt like you, don't they?'

McGill couldn't stop his face going bright red. Staff noticed but kept quiet. He thought back to when he was an officer at Pentonville. He'd been proud of his nickname but, unfortunately, it had travelled with him. Bootsy. Quick with the kick. That had been his way. Back then nobody complained. Certainly not the cons. The staff had their own code. The governor was in charge but the chief officer was God. When the chief officer grade was abolished in1987, as part of the 'Fresh Start' initiative, many considered it to be a massive mistake from which the Service would struggle recover.

'Take him to Segregation and make sure there are no more surprises.'

Lincoln, Perry and Scapes were kept waiting in the van while Masters was taken, under restraint, to the Segregation Unit. McGill walked with the staff to ensure that no mishaps occurred. He wanted a quiet word with Masters and would have that word when he had been processed in the Seg. 'Right Masters, shall we start again?' McGill tried to sound as though he cared but he wasn't sure if it worked.

'As I said before, when does the kicking start?'

'This jail already has a reputation for fairness so don't start your fun and games here.'

'Your reputation for giving out a good kicking still follows you around McGill. I don't suppose the young screws are aware of it, eh?'

'As usual you're talking through your arse, Masters, but I will give you one piece of advice. Shut your mouth with your stupid allegations and rumours or I will make life extremely unpleasant for you. I run the fucking place.' McGill sneered, the spittle collecting at the corners of his mouth.

'You can't do fuck all to me, you cunt,' Masters growled.

McGill smiled. 'For a start, I will keep you in Segregation for a month. Let's call it assessment shall we?' McGill smiled again. 'Once the assessment period is over I will place you on a particular spur on B wing where the sensitive prisoners live.'

'What the fuck is a sensitive prisoner?' Masters said.

'The more common term is nonce.' McGill patted Masters on the shoulder.

'When you fail on B wing, as I know you will, I will move you back to the Seg. After a further month I will move you back to B wing. Anything to say?'

Masters said nothing.

'When I've had enough of moving you between the Seg and B wing I'll transfer you to Frankland. My friend is the Deputy Governor and he owes me favours. How does that sound, good?'

Masters, again, said nothing.

'I'm off on my rounds and I will see you before your adjudication in the morning. You will have reflected, overnight, on our little chat and you will be happy to assure me that you will no longer be a problem to me or my staff during the rest of your stay here. Is that clear?'

'Fuck off, you cunt,' Masters whispered.

'Sleep well and we'll talk again in the morning.'

Scapes was next off the vehicle and, after being fast-tracked through reception, he was taken to C wing. The speed of his arrival and location caused some discussion amongst the prisoners working in reception but the subject was soon forgotten.

Lincoln and Perry were hungry and irritable when they were finally escorted off the vehicle and into Reception. Lincoln overheard the orderlies talking about how a con called Masters had kicked off in Reception and how the Deputy Governor had sorted him out. Lincoln guessed, correctly, that Masters must have been the fourth con on the van. Poor bastard. Lincoln and Perry were given a meal in reception, which had been microwaved into oblivion.

Perry managed a snatched conversation with a black con who was one of the orderlies. The lad, Robbie, said that although Raymar was a shit hole it was a lot better than most of the other places he had done bird in. That sounded good to Perry. He was also pleased to see a brother working in reception. Apart from the gym, reception was a prime job and usually reserved for the high profile white cons. Robbie said that both Lincoln and Perry would be going to D wing. Robbie was also on D wing so that also seemed like a result. Both suffered the reception procedure in silence, only speaking when spoken to.

Just after 20.30 hours they were escorted to D wing and taken up to the third floor. Perry quickly realised that the place was clean and there were only two other cell cards outside the doors. Cosy.

As Lincoln walked towards his cell he experienced a strange sensation which made him shiver. It had first happened when he was in short trousers. When he'd asked his mum about it she had said that somebody had walked over his grave. She'd laughed at the look of confusion on his face and had tried to explain. He had listened, patiently, but had gone out to play none the wiser and with the sound of her laughter ringing in his ears.

Over the years he'd experienced the same strange sensation a few times, mostly when he was stressed or was in a place he didn't want to be. As he was let into his cell he thought hard about his mum but couldn't see her face in his head. As hard as he tried he couldn't see her face. The door slammed behind him and, after a moment he burst into tears. What the fuck was going on? Shit. He hoped that he was going to feel better after he had met the other cons on the wing and had got himself into a routine. First day nerves. New jail, new screws and four new walls to stare at. He was a hard man and wouldn't let anything fuck with his head. Who the fuck would dare to walk over his grave? Silly idea.

Chapter Ten

CJ and Tot ran a garden centre about a mile west of the village of Whittingham. They had moved up from the Midlands in 2002 having heard that a new prison was being built nearby. They knew they had really arrived when they bid for, and were awarded, the franchise to provide the prison, and prisoners with plants and flowers. Twice a week Tot would drive to the prison with completed orders. The prisoners loved to give their partners a bunch of flowers in visits and CJ made sure that the flowers looked great. Tot would also provide, free of charge, flowers to decorate the visitors centre. He didn't go over the top but provided enough to make himself popular with the prisoners and staff. A friend in the administration department was happy to provide the birth dates of the partners of staff members and Tot ensured that a single rose was delivered to the lucky person.

Tot would go through the search procedures, the same as everybody else, and the staff always laughed when he asked if they were going to search the flowers. He always got the biggest laugh when he mentioned searching the pot plants for pot. Silly bugger!

They lived a comfortable but careful lifestyle. On their twice yearly visits to Benidorm they always took considerable amounts of Euro notes to add to their Spanish bank accounts. They had considered buying a place on the Costa Blanca but decided not to because it might draw attention to them. Not a good idea. The garden centre provided them with a comfortable living because there was no competition within a 15 mile radius. However, their biggest source of income was the cash accrued from providing their hungry clients in Raymar with a wonderland of illegal drugs.

They were in partnership with a prison officer named Terry Ferguson and business was good. A delivery of grass, speed and cocaine arrived from London every Friday afternoon. Not to the garden centre but to a pub car park two miles from the M6 slip road. Drugs and cash changed hands and no conversation was required. Business was conducted from public telephones at pre-arranged times. Getting the gear into Raymar was easy. Pot plants indeed!

Prisoners paid for the gear by arranging for amounts of money to be transferred, electronically, into a Jersey bank account. When CJ, or Tot, received a silly text message, which confirmed that money had arrived in Jersey, they would forward the text message to Ferguson and he would arrange for the deal to be completed. When Tim had been sacked as healthcare orderly supply had slowed down but the new orderly was quickly on board. A constant cause of concern was the presence of senior nurse Nelson. Ferguson knew that he would have to do something about her but, unless the situation became critical, he would just monitor the situation.

Ferguson understood that he was on dodgy ground but was confident that he had all the bases covered. He was happy with his arrangements with CJ and Tot and the one prisoner he had recruited to work for him was a devious little bastard who knew that he was on good wages and wouldn't rock the boat. The man had committed a serious sexual attack on a four year old black child years before and Ferguson had stumbled on the information purely by chance. He had shared his newly acquired knowledge with the prisoner and a deal had been struck. Ferguson had arranged for the prisoner, Stan Smith, to get the healthcare cleaner's job and everything was back on track.

The following morning was a typical one, it was pissing down. Masters was woken by the segregation senior officer and given his notice of report. He was charged with attempted assault on the reception senior officer. He was told that the governor-in-charge, Mrs Painter, would be conducting the adjudication which was scheduled for 10.00 hours.

At 09.30 hours, his door opened and a small man in a check suit stepped into the cell.

'Good morning Mr Masters, my name is Nigel Crossland and I'm chairman of the Independent Monitoring Board at Raymar. How are you today?'

'How the fuck do you think I am? Is it part of arriving here that you get beaten up and threatened by Bootsy McGill?'

'I beg your pardon!' Crossland spluttered.

As Masters was about to answer, McGill walked into the cell.

'Well well, how are you this morning Mr Governor Bootsy?'

'Good morning Mr Crossland, is prisoner Masters causing problems again?'

'No Mr McGill, but he has alleged that he was assaulted and, why is he calling you Bootsy?'

'I have never encountered prisoner Masters before, he is obviously confusing me with somebody else,' McGill answered, managing to control his temper.

'Are you confused, Mr Masters?'

Masters thought about his options. He knew that he would have to be as devious as McGill if he was to survive at Raymar.

'I might be confused, Mr Crossland, but I'll be happy to clear my head when I go to D wing after my adjudication. Is there a problem with that, Mr McGill?'

McGill realised that he had been backed into a corner. He also knew that Crossland was inclined to take the side of a prisoner in any dispute, and was not popular with staff.

'Of course not, Masters, as long as you pose no more problems.'

Masters winked at Crossland.

'Can I speak to you privately, Mr Crossland?'

'Yes, Mr Masters, now?'

'Yes please.'

McGill was about to speak but, biting his lip, he turned and left the cell.

'How can I help you, Mr Masters?'

'I was out of order in reception and I'll put my hands up to that. I do know Mr McGill from some time ago but that is all

I'm prepared to say. All I ask of you is that you keep an eye out for me and ensure that I do go to D wing. A certain person said that I would be moving between B wing and the Seg and that, when I failed, I was on my bike to Geordie land.'

Crossland puffed his chest out. 'I can assure you that I will be keeping a very close eye on your stay in segregation and your move to D wing.'

'Thank you sir,' Masters whispered.

McGill was standing close enough to the cell door to hear the exchange. He left the Seg and made his way back to his office. Deep in thought, he ignored greetings from two members of staff. When he arrived at his office he closed the door and reached for the telephone.

'Hi Angela, how are you?'

'I'm well Liam.'

'I need to take some urgent leave, family problems. If it's OK with you, I can get myself on tomorrow afternoon's flight to Belfast.'

'Any work issues I need to be aware of?'

'Not really but I'll email you a briefing note.'

'No problem then, tell the orderly officer that I will take over as duty governor but I will be staying at home.'

'Thanks.' McGill put the phone down. Stupid bitch. Best to put some distance between that bastard Masters and himself. Crossland was a wanker but could be managed. A bit of sick leave might also be necessary; a week or so. Something to think about.

After an incident-free night, Painter arrived at work and, after checking her emails she went to the segregation unit to conduct the adjudications.

'I find you guilty as charged, Mr Masters. Is there anything further you wish to say?'

'Nothing, Governor.'

'As you have cooperated, completely, with this adjudication I am going to award you one hundred per cent loss of earnings for two weeks but the award is suspended for two months. In other words if you stay out of trouble for the next two months nothing further will happen. Do you understand Mr Masters?'

'I understand Governor.'

'This adjudication is now finished, but one last question for you. Do you wish me to take any further actions with regard to the injuries you sustained in reception yesterday evening?'

'No Governor, the injuries were my fault. I just want to get on with my sentence and go to normal location.'

'You will be moved to D wing later this morning Mr Masters. Good day.'

Masters was taken back to his cell. When the door closed he sat on the bed and put his head in his hands. He knew that the screw was looking through the spy hole. He was not upset but was trying to stop the tears of laughter running down his cheeks.

McGill was enjoying a late breakfast and the Telegraph crossword when his mobile rang. 'Mr McGill, it's Tony in the Seg.'

'Hello Tony, what can I do for you?'

'I thought you would be interested to know that Masters virtually got away with his stunt in reception.'

'What happened?'

'Butter wouldn't melt during the adjudication. Masters said that everything was his fault, including his injuries. The governor swallowed the lot and gave him loss of earnings suspended for two months. He's being moved to D wing just before lunch.'

'Thanks Tony, good of you to call. By the way, when does your fixed post in the Seg finish?'

'Not until October, I'm sorry to say.'

'If a vacancy were to occur in the gate, next month, would you be interested?'

'Mr McGill, I would bite your hand off. Thanks.'

'No need to do that Tony.' McGill laughed, 'Just keep on being my eyes and ears. OK?'

'No problem Mr McGill.'

'Excellent and, of course, we never had this conversation.'
'What conversation?'

As he ended the call, and returned to the crossword, he knew that he would have to fix Masters before he got too settled on D wing. That bitch Painter would need to be watched. Still, he would enjoy his leave and then decide if it needed to be extended.

Just before lunch Masters was told that, due to a burst pipe on D wing, he would not be moved until the following morning. He nodded and asked for a book and a newspaper. When he was asked if he wanted to watch television with the other Seg residents, during the evening, he declined. He took his one hour exercise even though it was still pouring down. He said he didn't mind the rain and spent the time jogging and sprinting as much as was possible in the confines of the yard. The tea meal of mystery pie and chips was reasonable and he ate the lot. He was given a shower and told the evening duty staff that he required nothing further until the morning. He overheard one of the officers say that Masters wasn't half as bad as the deputy governor had said. The officer also added that they would sort him if he ever had the misfortune to return to the Seg.

Masters lay back on his bunk and smiled. He knew that his time would come. This place was no match for an experienced player. They had treated him like two-bit bag snatcher and that was unforgivable. McGill had treated him like a second rate idiot and that was also unforgivable. Raymar would always remember Tony Masters.

'We've had two new arrivals over the past couple of days with a third who will be arriving from the Seg at 9 o'clock. Because of that bloody burst pipe and the usual problem of staff shortages we will only now start their induction process. The new arrivals are Masters, from the Seg, Lincoln and Perry. As you know they will all be on D3. With Grove and Butterworth that will make five on D3. I've purposely decided to leave D3.6 empty in case of management problems on the spur.'

There were nods of agreement because it made sense and it meant that there was one less moaning prisoner to have to listen to.

'OK. Masters, Tony, comes to us via the Seg because he kicked off in reception on Tuesday evening. Somehow he managed to convince Governor Painter that he was a good boy but don't be misled by that little performance. Also, he has the ear of the IMB chairman Crossland, and we know that Crossland is all for the prisoners, not the staff. So be cautious on both fronts. Masters is aged 32 and comes from Peckham, South London. He's been in and out of juvenile, young offender and adult jails. He is serving seven years for assault and robbery. He has a poor disciplinary record. Read his F2050 (record).'

Nods all round.

'Our second new arrival is Lincoln, Brian who is 27. Lincoln is doing 18 years for armed robbery. He comes from Deptford, South London so there may be some links with Masters. He is a known druggie so be aware when searching his cell.'

Again, nods all round.

'Last, but by no means least, is Perry, Roman. Aged 34, Perry is doing life for a gang-related murder and has a tariff of 20 years. So far, he has done two years. He was born in Stockwell, South London so there may be links with both Masters and Lincoln, although their security files don't point in that direction. But, as we know, security files are rarely correct.' His last comment raised some genuine laughter.

'So, read the 2050s and submit SIRs when you have any concerns or suspicions. Any questions?'

'Can I have the next year off as annual leave PO?' Jones said.

Watts laughed along with the rest of his team.

'OK. All three to healthcare and then start induction. I know that we have lost a day but I want the process finished by end of play on Friday. Any more questions?'

There were no questions and the staff drifted off for cups of tea and to prepare for unlock at 08.00 hours.

Because of the burst pipe, and staff shortages, Lincoln and Perry had spent most of the previous day locked in their cells. Both were playing it cool. No need to start to complain yet. Plenty of time for that in the days to come. They had heard the sounds of other prisoners, coming and going, but no one had actually spoken to them. Plenty of time for that as well.

Masters had slept remarkably well considering that there had been thunder and lightning most of the night. He declined breakfast and was escorted to D wing just after 09.00 hours. He was met at the wing gates by principal officer Watts.

'Hello Masters, my name's principal officer Watts, welcome to D wing.'

'Whatever,' muttered Masters, trying to put on his most bored expression.

'Whatever indeed, we'll speak later. Mr Ferguson, take Masters to cell D3.3 please.'

'Yes Mr Watts,' Ferguson answered and led Masters up the six short flights of stairs.

'I'll be back for you in one hour and then we're off to healthcare,' Ferguson said as he let Masters into the cell.

Masters said nothing as he dumped his kit on the bunk. A single cell with a television. Not bad when he could have been spending the next couple of months bouncing back and forwards between the Seg and the nonces wing. Not bad at all.

True to his word, Ferguson was back one hour later and they made their way to the healthcare centre. They entered and Ferguson let Masters in to the waiting room. The only other occupants were Brian Lincoln and Roman Perry. There were nods and muttered "alrights".

'Rumour has it that you interfered with the reception process the other evening,' Lincoln said with no trace of a smile.

'Rumour has it that you are a nosy bastard,' Masters said, also with no trace of a smile.

'Rumour has it that you two are shagging each other,' Perry said, staring at the wall.

Nothing was said for a few seconds and then all three burst out laughing. Hands were shook and introductions made.

After seeing the doctor and being refused sleeping tablets the three were escorted back to D wing.

'So, who else is on the spur then?' Masters asked Ferguson as they were approaching the gates.

'Only two others, so it's nice and cosy like.'

'Do these two have names then?'

'Yes of course. One is an old lifer called Raymond Butterworth and the other is a gym orderly called Grove.'

The hairs on Perry's neck stood to attention.

'Does this Grove have a first name then?' Perry asked.

'I'm not sure of the real one but everybody knows him as Cutler. Plenty of time for formal introductions on association this evening,' Ferguson answered, oblivious to the look on Perry's face.

Both Masters and Lincoln saw the look on Perry's face but said nothing. Both were thinking how interesting the evening association was going to be.

As he was making his way back to his cell after the day in the gym, Grove slowed down to read the cell cards. When he got to D3.4 he read the name 'Perry' on the cell card. Life. Shit, shit, shit. He'd read Perry's trial in the paper and knew that it was the same man. With a name like Roman who else could it be? Did Perry think that it was Grove who had shopped him? He would have to sort the situation straight after unlock for association.

'Unlock for association,' shouted the senior officer. He was covering D wing for the evening as he normally worked back to back with another senior officer, on B wing, unless their duties clashed. The evening duty staff on the three levels of the four main residential wings unlocked the cell doors and the prisoners made their way slowly down to the association areas on the ground floors. Only those prisoners excluded from association would remain in their cells. All the prisoners on D wing were unlocked.

The list was up by the telephones indicating who would be allowed to make their calls during the association period. As there was no gym or education on that particular Thursday evening, due to staff shortages, all prisoners were restricted to the wing.

Four of the prisoners on D3 were aware of the possible drama about to unfold but the others, and staff, had no idea.

'So we meet again do we, Cutler you cunt?' Perry whispered as he followed Grove on to the association area. Butterworth overheard the exchange and stood well back.

'I'm Raymond Butterworth,' he said as he walked towards Masters and Lincoln.

'Tony Masters.'

'Brian Lincoln.'

'Something about to go down then, is there?' Butterworth whispered. Ferguson and Brand were the two D3 officers on association and tended to watch the prisoners from their spur more closely than the rest.

'Quite possibly,' said Masters and Lincoln nodded agreement.

'Listen Roman, there are things you need to know,' Grove stuttered.

'Really?'

'Yea really.'

'Well start your little speech before I get round to cutting you a second mouth. Might help you to speak a bit faster,' Perry said as he reached into his right hand pocket. Grove followed Perry's hand and caught a glimpse of a small blade. How the fuck had he managed to get tooled up so quickly? No point in worrying about that now was there? Grove walked into the small TV room followed by Perry.

'Fuck off, I need this room for a meeting. Keep Ferguson and Brand away for 10 minutes and there's a nice drink in it for you,' Grove said to a pasty-faced man who was on his own watching BBC2. The prisoner didn't look at Grove or Perry and quickly left the room.

'Spit it out, you cunt, I'm doing a minimum of 20 and that's just for starters. I've never been a boy to keep my nose clean so I'm expecting more. I've got nothing to lose.'

Grove thought about his options, which he quickly realised were virtually nil. He had no tool and a seriously pissed off black man stood in front of him. Suddenly the answer came to him but he had to present it in the right way.

'The reason I backed out was because I was told to take a walk. Take a holiday. In other words piss off.'

Perry laughed and pulled the blade out of his pocket.

'Convince me, shit head, or my tariff will last forever.'

'A mutual friend said that I would cause him further offence if I stayed on your firm.'

'And who the fuck could that possibly be, eh?'

'Tony,' Grove said. The name seemed to hang in the air, almost filling the small room, almost suffocating Roman Perry, doing life with a minimum of 20 years. Grove went for it.

'He said that because I had a good rep with him he would put my behaviour down to a lapse of judgement. His words not mine. Brief and to the point. He ended his warning by saying that he had eyes and ears on the operation and that I would end up as pig food if anything got back to you or any members of the crew. So, man, I walked. No, in fact I ran. I went to Margate and disappeared into the woodwork for a month, I think. When I surfaced I heard that you had been captured and I was sorry, really sorry. I liked you, liked working with you. That's the truth man, I swear.'

Perry had seriously considered informing Tony of his impending piece of business but was not about to give up a minimum of 30 per cent of any wages for very little input. Tony was a greedy cunt but Perry realised that for the loss of 30 per cent he would almost certainly now be expanding his business across South London. Big mistake, in fact a fucking massive mistake.

Perry was stunned and Grove could see the confusion on his face. He also noticed that the blade had vanished, much to his relief.

'How do I know you're telling the truth?' Perry said, also aware that an officer could enter the room at any moment.

'The reason I'm here, and not fucking porker food is because I'm telling you the truth. It's a simple as that. Now, I'm leaving this room and going for a smoke. As I said, I liked you, and this place appears to be a fucking joke. Gonna join me?'

Perry thought about it and nodded. As they left the room Ferguson walked up to them.

'Educating ourselves with BBC2 are we?'

'No, I'm studying for a degree in being ugly, small minded and fucking incompetent just like you Mr Ferguson,' Grove said, causing Perry to burst out laughing.

'I'm placing you on report for that, Grove,' Ferguson answered, his faced flushed with embarrassment.

'Whatever,' Grove growled.

Masters was still with Lincoln and Butterworth when Perry and Grove left the TV room. They heard Grove's exchange with Ferguson and joined in the laughter. Perry and Grove walked over to Butterworth and the introductions were made. Officer Brand had witnessed the exchange between Grove and Ferguson but had not intervened because there had been no need to. In fact, she had stopped herself laughing because, secretly, she agreed with Grove's comments. She had also witnessed the coming together of Masters, Grove, Lincoln, Perry and Butterworth and decided to submit a security information report, SIR, at the end of her shift. Although it was probably of little significance, she would do it anyway. Unfortunately, a general alarm had sounded on C wing, at lock-up, and Brand had responded. A planned cell extraction had meant that she had not returned to D wing until just before 8.45 and she completely forgot about the SIR.

Friday was busy for the three new arrivals with a tour of the jail and a meeting with the governor grade responsible for D wing. The governor had told them that he had big plans for work opportunities at Raymar but, with the unemployment problems in the North West, bringing work into the prison was proving difficult. 'Thank god for that,' was the unspoken comment. For now, the new arrivals would be on full-time education. But all was not lost because they had been made aware of the ability to get drugs from the healthcare orderly. Butterworth had been the source of that particularly tasty morsel of information. Butterworth considered himself to be a player. The others considered him to be a grade one wanker but one who would have his uses.

'Here, Ray.'

'It's Raymond.'

'What?'

'What?'

'Why do you carry that bible with you all the time?'

'It helps me to concentrate on the positive aspects of my life. My humility, my love for those who are experiencing similar circumstances to mine and my ability to mind my own fucking business!'

'What?'

'Whatever.'

Chapter Eleven

It happened on Saturday morning at ten minutes past eight on D wing.

'Unlock D2 before you go up to your spur, Mr Jones.'

'Yes PO,' Bryce Jones answered. He hated weekends particularly when they were as short staffed as they were today. He went up on to D2 landing and unlocked all the occupied cells. As he was about to go up to D3, Watts called for him to return to the ground floor.

'I'll need you down here to supervise breakfast so we'll have to stagger the unlock, Bryce.'

'No problem,' Jones answered but his face couldn't disguise his feelings. He hated any change to his routine and this, he was sure, had contributed to his failure to gain promotion to senior officer. Plus the fact that he hated Raymar but couldn't afford to pay for his own transfer back to Wales. Cardiff prison to be exact. He knew there were officer vacancies but not at public expense.

Jones stood by the hotplate as the prisoners drifted down to collect breakfast. They always made the effort on weekends because the kitchen turned out a half decent fry up. The first prisoner to arrive at the hotplate was a lifer called Brian Waller. He was a trouble maker and concerns had recently been raised about his mental health.

'Morning, Mr Jones,' Waller said with a beaming smile on his face. Jones started to relax, maybe today wouldn't be too bad after all.

'Morning, Waller,' Jones answered and turned his attention to the other prisoners arriving at the hotplate.

'Can I change my knife, Mr Jones, this one won't cut butter?' Waller laughed.

'Give him a sharper knife, Minky, otherwise we'll be here all day.'

Minky Mather was serving six years for his not-insignificant role in a scam which offered cheap-rate internet access to clients in the UK and Europe. The company fronting the scam was called WyServe. Clients paid 450 Euros for a one year contract/connection. Access to the internet was excellent for the first two months but then abruptly stopped. Clients were unable to reach anybody at the WyServe office from that day onwards. The Guardia Civil, in Alicante, had informed the Home Office of their wish to provide Mather with a long, free holiday when he had completed his six year sentence. Mather was in his early fifties and a confident salesman. His frequent boast was that he could sell guitar lessons to Eric Clapton. He fancied himself as a disc jockey but those who knew him well said that his knowledge of music was about as shallow as a puddle. Nice bloke, though, and good orderly material.

Mather tested the knives in the box and, when satisfied, handed the sharpest one to Waller.

'Thanks Mr Jones. Oh, just one more thing,' Waller whispered.

Jones frowned and stepped to the side of the hotplate because he couldn't really hear what Waller was saying. As he turned and started to ask what his problem was, Waller plunged the knife into Jones' neck just above his shirt collar. The blade clipped his collar bone and came to a halt at the start of the handle. Mather almost choked on the bacon, egg and sausage triple-decker which he'd just started on.

After a couple of seconds, blood started to exit the wound. Jones looked at Waller, frowned and felt himself falling into a tray of fried eggs. A prisoner, it was never ascertained exactly who, pressed the alarm bell which was sited next to the light switch near the door to the stairs.

'Attention all stations, general alarm, D wing servery.'
'Attention all stations, general alarm, D wing servery.'
'Acknowledge Oscar One, over.'
'Oscar One received.'
'Acknowledge Victor One, over.'
'Victor One received.'

'All stations, Romeo Mike November standing by.'

Jones was now laying half on, half off the hotplate. Brand ran down from the first floor as the servery room was starting to fill with prisoners. She could see Watts trying to reach Jones.

'Romeo Mike November from Delta One over,' she screamed into her radio.

'Romeo Mike November receiving over.'

'Romeo Mike November, urgent assistance required on D wing over.'

'I repeat, urgent assistance required on D wing over.'

'Received. All stations, urgent assistance required on D wing. I repeat, urgent assistance required on D wing. Romeo Mike November standing by.'

Staff from the other wings immediately started to run to D wing. Nurse Simmons, who was sorting through the Kardex on the medication trolley in the healthcare centre, grabbed the emergency bag and started her run to D wing.

The orderly officer, principal officer Dennis Walker, call sign Oscar One, was first through the wing gates. About a dozen prisoners were in the servery room but were stood against the walls. One was eating a bacon sandwich and laughing at something the prisoner next to him had said.

Richard Watts was leaning over an officer, who was slumped on the floor, but Walker couldn't see who it was. He did, however, notice prisoner Waller who was sat with his back to the hot plate holding his head. Brand was stood over him with her extended baton in her hand. Her face had a deathly white pallor and she was shaking.

Other staff quickly followed Walker through the wing gates and he detailed the first six to start returning the prisoners in the servery room to their cells. Nurse Simmons was the last to arrive and she forced her way through the crowded area to reach Jones. By now, Jones was lying on his side with a pool of blood starting to spread away from his neck. A mess of fried eggs and grilled tomatoes was making it difficult to stop from slipping over.

As Simmons reached Jones she heard a raised voice.

'What about Waller then? The screwess smacked him. He needs treatment first.' The voice belonged to Butterworth.

'And I ain't going nowhere until I've had me breakfast.' This time it was Masters.

The room went silent and staff took a step back from the prisoners. Just then, the duty governor, Roger Mason, call sign Victor 1, entered the room.

'What about Waller, what about breakfast?' four of the prisoners started to shout. More staff started to arrive including three physical education instructors. The shouting stopped.

'Romeo Mike November from Victor One, over.'

'Romeo Mike November receiving over.'

'Romeo Mike November, instruct Hotel One to send two more nurses to D wing immediately, over.'

'Received. Hotel One from Romeo Mike November, over,'

'Hotel One, receiving over.'

'Hotel One, send two more nurses to D wing immediately over.

'Received, over.'

'All stations, Romeo Mike November standing by.'

'PO Walker, telephone the kitchen and tell the senior officer that I want enough additional breakfast meals brought to D wing immediately.'

'Yes, Governor.'

Walker phoned the kitchen and had to order the senior officer to provide the additional meals because he said that he was too busy preparing the lunch meal.

'Just fucking do it and that's an order,' Walker said and slammed the phone down.

'Right, you will now return to your cells. Waller will receive treatment and you will receive your breakfast meals in your cells.'

The prisoners were now outnumbered by staff and Butterworth certainly didn't fancy doing a tango with that big black PEI.

'I'm going to return to my en-suite and wait for room service. Anybody care to join me?' Butterworth sneered.

The others laughed and started to shuffle towards the stairs.

'Oh, just one more thing. Give Mr Jones our best wishes and tell him that we hope he fucking dies, the Welsh cunt,' shouted Masters. The other prisoners started jeering but did not resist as staff moved them towards and up the stairs. The wing was locked up in 15 minutes. The kitchen staff eventually arrived and breakfast was served in the cells.

One hour later Bryce Jones was in an ambulance and on his way to Accident & Emergency in Carlisle. His condition had stabilised after Nurse Simmons had put an intravenous line into the back of his hand. When he left the prison the knife was still sticking out of his neck.

Waller had been strapped to a stretcher and located in a special cell in the healthcare centre. His head wound had required two sutures but staff were not unduly concerned because he had not lost consciousness. When asked why he had stabbed Jones he said that he was bored and wanted to see if a prison knife would snap if used to stab somebody. He said that he was glad that it hadn't.

So, that's about the sum of it, Angela, you're right up to speed,' said Roger Mason. He felt as though he'd been at work all day but it was just after 10 o'clock.

'Thanks Roger, and for your excellent work this morning. Ring me when you've got more news on Mr Jones. I'll visit him in hospital this evening. I'm going to ring the area manager and appraise him of the incident. If anything comes from the call I'll let you know. Bye for now.'

'Bye Angela.'

'Morning, Mitchell, it's Angela. Sorry to disturb your Sunday morning.'

'No problem, it's always nice to hear from you. How can I help?'

Painter then went into a brief but concise description of the incident on D wing.

'Well, Raymar certainly has been busy this morning. Has Roger Mason organised a staff debrief yet?'

'Knowing Roger he will conduct it towards the end of today's main shift. He will want to get the staff off on time.'

'Absolutely right, as well, but I have a better suggestion. This is the first really serious incident at Raymar since it opened and it deserves to be recognised as such. As you know, I was planning to pay a scheduled visit next Thursday. I intend to move my visit forward to Monday. It will be a normal business day but schedule the staff debrief for 10 o'clock. I will be present but you will chair it. Give my regards to the POA Chairman particularly if staff rest days have to be moved. Ask Roger to email me a copy of the incident report that will be going to headquarters. If there's nothing else I'll see you on Monday at eight sharp.'

'Nothing else but I may ring you tomorrow with an update on Mr Jones's condition.'

'Thanks, see you Monday.'

'So, end the afternoon early and brief the staff about the area managers visit on Monday. Stress the importance that he is placing on the incident and the debrief and that he intends to visit Mr Jones late Monday afternoon. Ring round the senior management team and tell them that I expect a one hundred per cent attendance on Monday. The only exceptions will be if they are out of the country. Any questions?'

'None, Angela, leave all the arrangements to me.'

'Thanks Roger you've done really well today. By the way, will you be going for the deputy governor's job when it eventually becomes vacant?'

'I certainly will. I see my future in the North West and I really enjoy working here.'

'Excellent. One more thing. Can I trust you to hold a confidence?'

'Absolutely, of course.'

'Good. I don't want you to ring Liam McGill because I don't want him in the establishment on Monday. His negativity will hinder progress at Raymar particularly after today's incident. I don't have to spell it out do I?'

'No, Angela, you don't. I fully understand and I won't let you down. You can trust me completely.'

'I know I can Roger that's why I have confided in you. Oh, don't forget to email the incident report to the area manager and copy me in as well.'

'Will do. Would you like me to accompany you when you visit Mr Jones this evening?'

'Excellent idea, pick me up at 5.30.'

'See you then. Bye.'

Roger Mason sat back in his chair and replayed the conversation in his head. He savoured every word of it. He was 35 and felt that his career was slowing down. He was a graduate of the Accelerated Promotion Scheme, as was Angela Painter and they had often spoken about it. His performance today would do him absolutely no harm. He knew that the area manager, Mitchell Hagen, rated him and saw him to be a safe pair of hands. From today he was going to become more than a safe pair of hands. As head of residence he had responsibility for the wings, kitchen and segregation unit and had been working on ideas to improve performance and staff involvement. Tonight's car journey to Carlisle might be just the right moment to start the ball rolling. He had tried out a couple of ideas on the deputy governor but had always received negative feed-back. He had let the matters drop because McGill was his reporting officer and could damage his career. It was not what McGill put in staff appraisals, it was what he left out.

Painter was the countersigning officer and had asked him if he was happy with his last appraisal. He had said that he was because he couldn't say anything else, could he? Still, after this morning's conversation he felt that change was on the way. Big change. If McGill ever asked him why he hadn't been contacted he would counter by saying that he was aware that McGill was going to Ireland on family business. Perfect. If he hadn't yet left for Ireland it was no business of Roger's. Perfect.

Back on D wing tensions were running higher than normal but were manageable. The morning gymnasium sessions had been cancelled and two of the physical education officers had been sent to work on D wing, one being Harland Smith. Smith went up on to D3 and checked the cells. When he reached Grove's, he unlocked the door and went in.

'Yo Mr Smith, bad scene this morning or what.'

'It certainly was, Mr Jones is seriously ill.'

'He's not everybody's favourite screw but what Waller did was totally OTT.'

'Any thoughts on why he did it?'

'Nah, Mr Smith, if I had any ideas on the matter I would tell you, honest I would.'

'I believe you, thousands wouldn't.'

'Honest Mr Smith....'

'Only joking Cutler, don't go all soft on me.'

'Yea, right Mr Smith, right.'

'There is one thing that you can do to, let's say, improve staff/prisoner relations.'

'Anything, Mr Smith, anything,' Grove whispered, knowing full well what was coming.

'Let the other residents of this spur know that the comments that were made in the severy room this morning were not, and I repeat not, appreciated. Catch my drift Cutler?'

'Absolutely Mr Smith.'

'Good, because I know how much you enjoy working in the gym. Would that be a fair assessment?'

'Absolutely fair Mr Smith. Consider it done.'

'Sound. Be ready for work at 1.30 and I'll come for you.'

Smith left Grove's cell, slamming the door. It was the slamming that every con hated. Grove would have to pick his moment to pass on the good news to the others but it certainly wouldn't be today. Not having association on weekend evenings did, sometimes, have its advantages. Monday morning would be soon enough.

Sunday passed without incident and gave Roger Mason ample opportunity to ruminate on the conversation which he had enjoyed with Angela Painter the evening before. She had given him plenty to think about. Plenty.

Hagen enjoyed visiting Raymar. Angela Painter was developing into a good governing governor and never asked for anything that was over and above the job. Her deputy, Liam McGill, was old school and was hanging on. If she asked for McGill to be transferred then Hagen would move him but she would have to ask and have good reasons for the move. Roger Mason was part of the new order and a product of the Accelerated Promotion Scheme (APS), as was Angela. Although relatively young in service he had a promising future and had defused a potentially very serious situation two days before. The principal officer grade, the backbone of the prison, were a good bunch and deserved to be looked after. There was the problem of drugs getting into Raymar and his 'eyes and ears' had indicated that a prison officer might be involved. He wouldn't share his intelligence with Painter, yet, because he wanted her to solve the problem and bring the answer to him. He would be patient, but not for too long.

As he pulled into the staff car park at Raymar he was looking forward to a productive business day and, in particular, the debrief of the incident on the previous Saturday morning.

'Morning, Sir, how are you today?' the gate officer asked.

'Good and glad to be dry. Whose keys will I use today?'

'The deputy governor's, Sir. He's on leave.'

'Fine,' replied Hagen. Normally he would have had his own set of keys to use but, at Raymar, he had not yet insisted on this accommodation. In time he would but not yet. It was always useful to see who was not in the jail at difficult times, such as today. Obviously, McGill's spies had let him down. Hagen wondered if Painter had engineered McGill's absence. He would soon find out.

Painter was deep into a stack of emails when her secretary introduced Hagen. She stood and shook his hand. Her secretary rushed off to get the decent coffee on the go and to warm the Danish pastries she'd remembered to buy on her way in.

'So, how is my youngest governor this fine morning?' Hagen asked, as he settled into one of the leather couches which fitted nicely into the not overly-large office.

'I'm fine thank you and glad you were able to join us today.'

'How was Mr Jones when you last saw him?'

'Better than I thought he would be, he's a tough one.'

'I know it's probably too early to say, but do you think he'll return to work?'

'My initial thinking is no.'

'My thinking as well,' Hagen ventured and then decided to go for it. 'No deputy governor today I see.'

'No, he has family problems in Ireland so I gave him leave.'

'Does he fly or take his car on the ferry?'

'Always takes his car. Says that he wouldn't pay the high rental prices in Belfast.' Painter answered, wondering where the conversation was headed. 'Why do you ask?'

'I drove past his place on the way here and his car was still on the drive.'

'Sure it was his?'

'Who else do we know who drives a black Audi TT?'

'Only McGill to my knowledge,' she answered and, realising her mistake, she knew what was coming.

'Unlike you to call your staff by their surnames, especially your deputy,' Hagen said, with just the hint of a smile.

'Slip of the tongue, sorry,' she countered, trying to regain her composure.

'Obviously, his spies have let him down this time,' Hagen ventured.

'Pardon?'

'You heard me,' Hagen laughed, conscious that he couldn't back her too far into a corner.

'Every jail he's worked in he's had, let's say, people watching his back, Raymar probably being his last.'

'His last? I'm sorry Mitchell but I'm confused.'

'There is always someone in every prison who's happy to ring the area manager with gossip and, sometimes, the truth. I have pretty solid intelligence that McGill threatened a prisoner in reception during the evening of Tuesday 7 April. A lad called Masters. A bad boy but one who was severely provoked. I can't prove it, of course, but there are some advantages in being area manager.'

'I still don't really follow, believe me, but I'm trying,' she said in quiet desperation.

'McGill is quietly undermining your authority. He's old school and is trying to attract a following. I know this because you have a loyal following from staff who want to continue to move Raymar forward. You might be surprised who some of them are.'

'You know you want to ask me.'

'Ask you what?'

'The sixty four thousand dollar question.'

Painter knew that if there was ever the right time to ask the question, it was now.

'Yes.'

'Yes, what?' Hagen smiled, knowing that she had reached the point of no return.

'I want McGill moved away from Raymar. He's a constant thorn in my side and his negativity is starting to be felt amongst some of the younger, more impressionable staff,' she replied, breathing a sigh of relief.

'Okay, we'll discuss the specifics after the debrief. Also, think of whom you will want as acting deputy governor until we can convene a selection board.

As she started to answer, the coffee and Danish arrived. They ate and drank in contented silence.

The debrief lasted nearly two hours and almost everyone left the boardroom reasonably satisfied. The catering senior officer received a verbal dressing down but it had been decided to take the matter no further. The officer started to shout at Painter and was told, by the branch chairman of the Prison Officers' Association, to shut up, sit down and grow up.

Nothing further was said but Painter noticed an exchange of nods between the chairman and Hagen. Painter and Hagen returned to her office.

'Right, get McGill on the phone and tell him to be here at 12.30 sharp. If he asks why tell him I have some news for senior managers.'

Painter phoned McGill on his mobile.

'Liam, it's Angela, I thought you would be in Ireland by now.'

McGill stared at his mobile. How the fuck did the bitch know that he wasn't?

'Problems with the TT which I've sorted so I'm on my way when I can get off the phone.'

Painter ignored the slight. 'The area manager's here and wants to see all senior managers with some important news. Be here at 12.30 sharp, casual attire acceptable.'

'But...'

'Don't be late,' Painter said and broke the connection.

McGill immediately rang the prison and asked to be put through to the Segregation Unit.

Luckily, the officer he was trying to contact answered.

'It's the deputy governor, what the fuck is going on?' McGill roared.

The officer flinched and then told him about the incident and the debrief which had ended less than an hour before.

'Why didn't you ring me?' McGill demanded.

'I was told that you'd gone to Ireland on family business so I didn't think it was important enough to bother you. Did I do wrong?'

'No, the TT was playing up but I've sorted it. No problem, speak soon,' and McGill ended the call.

At a little after 12.30 McGill walked into Painter's secretary's office.

'Is she in?'

'Go right in Liam.'

McGill knocked and walked in.

'Morning Angela, morning Sir,' McGill muttered barely managing to conceal the irritation in his voice, 'Are we meeting in the boardroom?'

'No Liam,' Angela answered. 'The meeting is here, just the three of us.'

McGill was starting to smell a rat. 'I've got urgent family business in Ireland and I don't need this aggravation.'

'Shut up and sit down, now man,' Hagen growled.

McGill was stunned at being spoken to in such a manner and did as he was told.

'What's going on, Sir?' McGill whispered.

'Tell us what you have contributed to Raymar since it opened?' Hagen said, a tightness in his voice.

McGill was nonplussed, knew that he'd missed a pointer but couldn't guess what. 'I've been here since it opened and supported the previous governor, my contribution being my wealth of experience,' he answered.

'Being here from the start and your 'wealth of experience', is not a contribution, it's what you were paid for. Tell me how you have supported your present boss Angela Painter?' Hagen asked.

The penny was starting to drop and McGill knew that he was in trouble.

'I've always supported her new ideas and have defended her against staff who thought that the Service was going to pot.'

'Tell me about the new ideas that you have introduced, I'm sure there have been many.'

'I helped design and introduced the new attendance system before Angela arrived, which has been extremely successful,' McGill answered, hoping that he was moving onto solid ground.

'Are you certain of your facts?' Hagen said, with a sarcastic edge to his voice.

'Yes, of course,' McGill spluttered, wondering where the hell this was leading.

'You will remember when we first met, or I hope you do. I made my usual address to my senior managers, with the emphasis on the need for honesty between yourselves and in particular in your dealings with me. Remember?'

'Yes, Sir, I do,' McGill whispered.

'The attendance system, in question, was designed by Roger Mason and two members of our very efficient POA committee. The previous governor introduced it at a staff meeting whilst you were on one of your many visits to Ireland. He did it in your absence after taking advice from influential officer grades and senior managers. It has, you will agree, been a great success. Care to comment?'

'I had urgent family business in Ireland and...'

'Just like today?' Hagen said, his tone indicating that he was running out of patience.

'What are you accusing me of?' McGill shouted, jumping to his feet.

'I'm accusing you of being a liar, Mr McGill, and of exerting a negative effect on a new prison which is trying to move forward. I have enough written information about you and your 'spies' which I'm happy to make public. Your time is up at Raymar and this is what is going to happen. Initially, when your leave is over you will report to area office where I will review your performance and the future direction of your career. Before coming here today I discussed the reasons for my visit with the director general and he listened with great interest. He is a great believer in Raymar, its governor and her staff. Unfortunately, he never mentioned you in a positive light. So, spend the next few minutes collecting your personal belongings and leave the establishment. Be sure to leave your ID card at the gate. The gate senior officer has been told to ring this office as you leave. He is not aware of anything else. Hurry along now.'

McGill was stunned, speechless. It took him what felt like hours to regain his composure.

'It will take me some time to clear my office,' he said, speaking to Hagen but glaring at Painter.

'Wrong,' said Painter. 'You're belongings are in two boxes in my secretary's office. Take them and go.'

McGill turned and, yanking open the door, almost walked into Roger Mason who was stood there. As McGill started to speak he heard Painter.

'Come in Roger, the area manager and I have something to discuss with you. Close the door behind you.'

McGill stood there and thought that his head would explode. He felt completely humiliated. Painter's secretary wouldn't look him in the eye. He collected his boxes and struggled to carry them to the gate. He passed staff but all seemed to avoid him, or was he being paranoid? Surely they couldn't know about what had just happened? Surely not.

At the gate he handed his pass through the key hatch. The officer accepted it without a word. He saw the senior officer look at him and pick up the phone. As he walked through the gate lock he was sure that he heard 'good riddance you bastard' but knew that he must be mistaken. The staff respected him. They respected the old ways, even the young ones who never seemed to laugh at his jokes. He would sort the whole mess out when he got to area office. A public expense move might be on offer. It occurred to him that Hagen might be shagging Painter. Jesus, he must be desperate. It would all be sorted next Monday.

'I do not want to go to the Standards Audit Unit,' moaned Liam McGill, his head in his hands.

Mitchell Hagen listened but said nothing. He had carefully considered McGill's future, realising very quickly that there was no future at area office for the deposed Raymar deputy governor. Hagen had discussed the problem with his staff officer and valued his opinions. The word 'wanker' was not one that Hagen used but it was a regular part of his staff officer's vocabulary. For once, he was forced to agree. Maybe he should have done something about McGill earlier but, still, better late than never.

'You are going to the Standards Audit Unit with effect from next Monday. You will be on full subsistence and the secondment will be for six months initially.'

'Why can't I stay in area office?' McGill whined, not realising how pathetic he sounded.

'Because my office is sharp, progressive and doesn't need old fashioned thinking to make it work,' Hagen said, fixing McGill with a stare.

McGill knew that he had run out of options. He had thought long and hard about what had happened and realised that he was not to blame. He was convinced that the staff loved and respected him and that Painter had fucked him over. Fucked him over big time. Retirement was not a million miles away and he had to make sure that his pension was safe. He would go to the graveyard which was Standards Audit Unit and he would excel. He would say all the right words and kiss arse when necessary. He would be a great auditor and others would realise what a loss he was to Raymar prison. He would have his time in the sun and the sun would burn Hagen and Painter. He would have his revenge and would return to Raymar in triumph. He knew he would.

The three south-bound lanes of the M1 were closed for the best part of five hours between junctions 20 and 21. An eyewitness told police that the Audi TT was probably travelling in excess of 100 miles an hour in the outside lane. A articulated lorry, with Spanish registration plates, was in the middle lane and had ventured into the outside lane to avoid a Ford which had swerved in front of it. The lorry clipped the TT, which then started to cartwheel across the lanes and ended upside down in a ditch next to the hard shoulder. Paramedics and police were on the scene quickly but the driver of the TT was beyond help and declared dead in the Accident & Emergency Department of the Leicester Royal Infirmary soon afterwards. Police ascertained that the registered owner of the Audi TT was one Liam Eamon McGill.

The funeral was held in the small church of a village 15 miles from Raymar. Angela Painter represented the prison, no other staff asked to attend. Four months later a board was convened to select a suitable candidate to fill the vacant position of deputy governor at Raymar. It came as no surprise when Roger Mason was selected. The three person board had consisted of Mitchell Hagen, Angela Painter and the Governor of a North East prison who was a friend of both. Informed opinion had noted that the selection of Mason was as predictable as day following night.

Seven months later staff were disgusted to hear that Waller had been given an additional five years to run concurrently with his life sentence. Officer Bryce Jones never did get promoted or achieve a transfer to Cardiff. A little over four months after he was attacked, Jones was found hanging from a beam in the double garage of the detached house he shared with his wife Jean.

Chapter Twelve

Rod and Alan basked in the reputation of being a vicious pair of thugs. They had known each other for more than 30 years and, a little over 20 years ago realised that their relationship went far beyond mere friendship. They had both originated from the South Coast and had gravitated to the Wanstead and Leytonstone areas of East London. They had shown the required amount of respect to the gangs who ruled at that time and were given enough space to develop their own 'business'. This business generally involved vice, in its many forms, and a light dusting of drugs.

In the May of 1994 they were well established on the edge of the 'real' East End. They were making a tidy packet and always sorted out any problems personally. They didn't employ muscle as they found those boys rough and too flash. Rod was known for his expertise with a lump hammer and Alan excelled with an old fashioned cut-throat razor. It was said that Alan could shave you to within an inch of your life. Scary stuff.

Early in the June of 94 they were taking a short break in a caravan near Skegness. Their friends thought that holidaying on a caravan park was common but would never have dared to say as much.

It was known, by a select few, that the 'light dusting of drugs' had developed in to quite a heavy fall of the white stuff, as Michael Fish might have said. The majority of their expanding fortunes was coming from their careful supply of a range of drugs to a number of prison establishments in the north of England. They were meticulous in their supply arrangements and were confident that, apart from a massive collection of unexpected problems, all bases were covered.

They had spent a very nice evening in Skegness town centre, having enjoyed a really above-average Indian meal followed by a nice few drinks. Just after 11 o'clock they had taken a taxi back to the caravan site and had decided, on impulse, to have a last drink in the site club.

'Can I have a G & T with ice and lemon and a large brandy with ice please?' Rod said, ever the polite customer. He had realised many years before that being aggressive, in public, could be a recipe for disaster. Keeping one's cool was definitely the ticket. The bartender, a nice looking but not overly intelligent youth, nodded and started to prepare the drinks.

'Have we run out of fucking birds on this poxy site then, eh Davy?' slurred a fat, red-faced blond youth.

The bartender turned round, looking for the person using his name. He spotted the youth.

'What on earth are you on about, Richard?'

'I said, have we run out of birds?'

'Where are you coming from, Richard?'

'Well, we must be out of birds because you've now started allowing poofs into our club.'

'Eh?'

'The G & T and large brandy pair. What the fuck is this place coming to? It's Benidorm for me, next year. Why the fuck should I waste my money in a fucking pink palace like this?'

Davy was confused. What did he do? Scare off his regular trade or serve a couple of gay boys? No contest.

'Are you club members? he asked Rod.

'Didn't know we had to be members? First time on this site and the booking agent said that all the amenities were included.'

'No, sorry, membership is a must and the book is full for this year.'

Rod looked around the empty bar and smiled.

'So, no drinks for us then?'

'Sorry mate, no,' Davy said, growing in confidence. He didn't know much about gay people but he did know that he couldn't afford to lose the trade that the "Richards", who came here all through the summer, provided.

'Looks like it's early to bed for us then,' said Rod and, with that, they both left. They paused outside the door to listen to the comments coming from the bar.

The following day was pandemonium. Police everywhere. Every caravan received a knock on the door. Rod and Alan were up and dressed. They offered the young, harassed police woman a cup of tea which she refused. Yes, they had been on the site the evening before but had not used the club because they weren't members. They had spent the early evening enjoying a nice Indian meal. Rod showed her the till receipt and she left satisfied.

The following morning's national newspapers described the brutal murders of two men on a caravan site near Skegness. One of the men had been beaten to death with a blunt instrument but the other, a blond man, had been castrated. His penis and testicles were found in a pint glass decorated with a twist of lemon. The police had been forced to admit that they had no suspects at the time of going to press.

'So, no more Skegness for us then?' Rod said, as they were enjoying a leisurely drive back to London.

'Oh, I don't know, give it a year or so,' Alan said, always the optimistic one of the pair.

'I always thought it was a cut above the other places,' Rod said.

'I bet that blond fucker wished that he had been a cut above us, eh?'

'He was such a rude boy so, no loss.'

They both smiled, laughed and decided to visit their local when they were comfortably back in London.

By 2004, Rod and Alan were well respected and feared across London. There had been no further 'Skegness' incidents and they had become accepted by the wider criminal fraternity. They had their own turf which they guarded with ferocious care. They were not greedy and had amassed a considerable fortune. They owned a villa on the Spanish Costa Blanca and a series of properties on the south coast of England.

'We've never given a line of credit before and I don't see why we should start now,' argued Alan and Rod knew that he would take some convincing.

'CJ and Tot have been good customers down the years and this is the first time that they have failed to come up with the agreed price. Tot said that the officers are really clamping down and he has to be extremely careful. Apparently Raymar have got a new deputy governor who is a fucking pest, sticking his nose into everything.'

'Maybe so, but it's not our problem is it? If word gets out that we are going soft we'll have every sooty and spic on our backs trying to take a piece of our pie,' Alan growled.

'OK, this is what we'll do. I'll contact Tot and tell him he's got seven days to make up the balance plus an additional fifteen per cent. I'll also tell him that we'll be driving up to the North West to collect in person. How does that sit with you?'

'Better, much better, but what will we do if they can't or won't toe the line?' Alan said.

'Easy. Should that unlikely event become a reality then CJ will have to learn to run their garden centre from a wheelchair.'

'Yes but its Tot who's letting us down.'

'I know, I know, but we will still need Tot to continue business in the prison and to look after CJ as she recovers from her terrible injuries,' Rod said, smoothing a crease from his perfectly tailored chinos.

'You know, that's why I love you so much. You keep our businesses on track but never forget to consider the welfare of our customers. Shall we toss a coin to see who gets to change CJ's walking habits should it become necessary?'

'Not necessary, I know you like to add the personal touch so it's yours.'

'Great, something nice to look forward to,' giggled Alan as he caressed the back of Rod's neck.

'How the fuck am I going to come up with the money in seven days, they're just not being reasonable,' cried Tot.

CJ was starting to worry, really worry. She'd heard stories about Rod and Alan and did not want to upset them.

'Get hold of Ferguson and tell him to come and see us tonight. Don't take no for an answer.

That cunt has made a healthy living off us and it's about time that he put himself out for us. If you won't ring him I will,' fumed CJ as she stroked one of the many cats which roamed the garden centre.

'Alright, alright, don't fucking go on, I'll ring him,' stormed Tot as he reached for the phone.

'I can't give you what I haven't got,' ventured Terry Ferguson, clearly bored and regretting his decision to make the journey to the garden centre.

'You don't understand how serious this is, do you?' shouted Tot.

'Not my problem, I can only do what I can do,' muttered Ferguson as he tried to brush the cat hair off of his uniform trousers.

'This problem is of your making and you really do not want to upset our contacts in London,' shouted CJ.

'Don't be a fucking two-bit drama queen, you daft cow,' shouted Ferguson, 'I'm really not about to be bothered by two fucking cartoon gangsters from the Smoke.'

CJ frowned, stepped forward and slapped Ferguson hard across the right side of his face. Ferguson staggered back, regained his balance and moved towards CJ. Tot stepped between them and pushed Ferguson away.

'This is getting us nowhere, nowhere at all,' screamed Tot, 'These 'cartoon gangsters' are serious players and are not to be fucked with.'

CJ and Ferguson were staring at each other, oblivious of Tot. Ferguson knew that he had to regain control of the situation.

'OK, let's all calm down, there's no point in us falling out cause it's only us who can make sense of this fucking mess.'

The tension started to evaporate although CJ was still staring at Ferguson like he was a piece of shit.

'We've got seven days so we need to make a decision now on how to make up the shortfall,' Tot muttered, as if he was talking to himself.

'Don't start going soft on me now Tot, for fuck sake,' stormed CJ, still not taking her eyes off of Ferguson.

Tot was staring into the distance, deep in thought. Ferguson started to speak but CJ held up her hands to tell him to be quiet. The silence stretched to nearly four minutes.

'I think I might have the answer,' Tot said, and slowly outlined his thoughts to the other two. Hostilities ceased and they listened.

Tot finished describing his survival plan and Ferguson was impressed. CJ fixed a round of drinks but said nothing.

'So, the con's visitors are going to take the gear in for us. It's as simple as that is it?' Ferguson asked

'All the best plans are simple,' stated Tot, clearly feeling like the top dog.

Ferguson thought long and hard about his options which were, he had to admit to himself, extremely limited. In fact almost fucking non-existent.

So, it was agreed. CJ decided to e-mail Rod and Alan to tell them that they were going to need a further two weeks to get the money which was owed.

Tot also agreed with her that their inconvenience money would be increased to twenty per cent. They were sure that the pair would agree to the increase because they were getting the money for doing absolutely nothing. More than fair. Ferguson still considered Rod and Alan to be a pair of low-grade gangsters but decided to keep his opinions to himself.

'Didn't I make myself clear?' growled Rod.

'Yes of course you did. Crystal. Don't get yourself all upset, we'll sort it,' Alan said, trying to soothe Rod. He hated to see Rod upset and knew that he would now have to make a serious example of the plant growers. He needed to re-establish their control. It was necessary and would be done.

'And how dare they e-mail us and tell us that they were taking a further two weeks. The final, fucking insult was to give us twenty per cent to keep us happy. How the fuck dare they, the pair of cunts,' Rod screamed, his face turning purple.

'Calm down love, calm down, please calm down,' shouted Alan. God, if Rod got any more upset he would hurt himself.

Alan held Rod's hand and, slowly, his temper subsided and the colour in his face returned to normal.

'I'm not going to acknowledge the e-mail. Give it two days and treat yourself to a nice trip up North,' said Rod, his voice now quiet and controlled.

'Who shall I take with me?' Alan asked, certain that he knew the answer.

'Take Daisey and let him drive. Also, get a message to Wolf. Get him to confirm that it's Ferguson who controls the supply in Raymar and also get a home phone number,' Rod said.

Alan was pleased that Daisey would be making the trip with him. He was a handsome and wicked bastard who had the body of an angel.

Alan had decided that the trip would make a significant difference to their business and that serious lessons would need to be taught. He also decided that Rod didn't need to know about the details of the trip.

'Make sure that Wolf gets a good drink, you know how I arrange it,' Rod said.

Alan was a happy bunny. He was happy that the operation at Raymar had run its course and he was thrilled that he was going to be the one to pull the plug.

'What about that slimy cunt Ferguson?' Alan asked.

'Leave it up to you, just make sure that you come away satisfied that we are clean. Oh, just one more thing,' Rod said, smiling, 'There won't be any need to stay away overnight, will there?'

'Of course not, perish the thought,' Alan said, trying to keep a straight face.

'I can't understand why Rod hasn't replied,' moaned Tot, 'Still no news is good news, eh?'

CJ didn't reply, she felt uneasy about the whole affair. As usual, Tot had gone at the problem like a bull at a gate, without thinking it through. Ferguson was about as much use as a chocolate fire-guard, agreeing with everything Tot had said.

'Ferguson said that it will take about ten days to set it up. He said that he would tell the governor that the cons were moaning about the price of the plants and flowers, and that he had mentioned the problem to me. I suggested that I could still provide a service by selling the plants and flowers from a stall in the visitors centre. The visitors could then pay for the plants and flowers instead of the prisoners. I had also said that I would provide enough price lists for the prisoners to send out in their letters. He said that he was sure that the governor would go for it. She was a soft cow who would do anything for her beloved boys. Sounds like a plan to me,' Tot said, feeling completely happy with himself.

CJ thought hard about Tot's burst of mental activity. It did sound like a plan but she was deeply unhappy at not hearing back from Rod and Alan.

'OK, OK, it does sound like a plan but what about Rod and Alan?' CJ said, trying to keep her voice calm.

'They must be away or something. If they weren't happy they would have told us. Must be the thought of an extra twenty per cent that has kept them quiet. You know what Alan's like. He would be screaming like a big tart if he wasn't happy.'

'I suppose so,' CJ said.

'So it's a goer then?' Tot ventured.

'I suppose so,' CJ said and left to feed her expanding herd of cats.

'It's Terry,' Ferguson said.

'Really, I thought it was Big Bird,' CJ said, clearly unhappy to be speaking to him.

'Sarcasm doesn't suit you. Tell Tot that the governor has agreed. The price lists need to be ready to go out in the letters by the weekend. If that's done, he can start selling the following Wednesday. Tell him that I've started to put the word around already. It's going to be a winner.'

Before CJ could respond Ferguson had ended the call. She walked to the covered area where they kept the bags of Tot's Spot compost and relayed the call to him. Tot was as happy as a pig in muck.

About fifty five miles south on the M6, Alan and Daisey were tucking into a barely-edible lasagne and chips in a service area. It was a few minutes before 10 o'clock when Daisey parked the stolen Mondeo about half a mile from the garden centre. They had taken the car from outside a deserted supermarket. Their Mercedes was safely parked and would be retrieved after they had completed their work. They walked to the garden centre cursing at the mud which was caking their shoes.

When they reached the bungalow at the back of the centre they spent a few minutes making sure that there was nobody else hiding in the shadows. It was a three-quarter moon which made life a little easier for them. Daisey checked the window which was to the right of the front door. The room was in darkness. He made his way quietly past the front door and stopped at the left-side window. There was a light on but the curtains were almost, but not quite, closed.

Tot and CJ were watching TV, News At Ten was almost finished. They had their backs to the window and both had glasses in their hands.

Alan and Daisey had discussed the plan, repeatedly, on the drive up and were happy that they had covered all eventualities. Alan had brought Rod's trusty lump hammer and his own cutthroat razor. Daisey had a sawn-off shotgun. Both wore ski masks, black tracksuits and trainers, and thin leather gloves.

Tot and CJ were laughing at an advert featuring a fat man and a knitted monkey when they both heard soft but insistent knocks on the front door.

'Who the fuck can that be at this time of night?' slurred Tot.

'We won't fucking know unless you've got extra sensible deception, so answer the door,' CJ answered.

They both laughed. Tot got up and lurched to the door. He opened it and peered out. The lump hammer caught him on the bridge of his nose and he dropped across the door step. Blood gushed from his nose and he shuddered. He started to make strange, gasping sounds. He knew he was hurt but couldn't make sense of it. Had he walked into the door? Had he tripped over the door jamb? His face felt like it was going in different directions.

'Hello CJ, pleased to see me?' Alan said as he stepped over Tot and into the room. CJ was slow to react. By the time she managed to get to her feet, Alan had grabbed her by the throat and Daisey had the sawn-off pointed at her. CJ heard Tot moaning and managed to focus on him. She screamed and screamed.

'Shut the fuck up you stupid bitch,' Alan growled and punched her hard in the face. She fell backwards and banged her head on the edge of the coffee table. She was stunned but started to scream again. Alan kicked her on the side of her face and she felt herself going fuzzy. She started to feel sick as she drifted into unconsciousness.

Repeated slaps stopped the process and she felt warm liquid splashing on her face. As she started to focus she saw a man, whom she didn't recognise, urinating over her. Her jaw ached and her head was pounding. As she looked up Alan was staring at her with an amused look on his face. The man she didn't recognise was standing behind Alan.

'Oh my God,' she whispered as she saw Tot. He was sat, slumped on one of the dining table chairs he so hated. The man was holding Tot by the back of his sweatshirt. His face and sweatshirt were covered in blood. His left eye was closed and he sounded like he was muttering to himself. Daisey moved slightly to one side and back handed Tot on the side of his face. Tot sagged and went quiet. CJ roared like a wounded animal. Alan laughed, winked at Daisey and punched CJ twice in the face.

'Look at me bitch,' Alan said as he slapped her softly on her left cheek, 'And don't say a word.'

CJ was close to wetting herself and was trying to keep it in. She said nothing.

'Rod sends his love and wishes he could be here but he can't because he is a teeny weeny bit angry at being fucked over by you two,' Alan whispered.

CJ was about to answer when she caught another right hander from Alan. She tried to stay quiet but started sobbing as she looked at Tot.

'You must excuse my manners. Allow me to introduce my friend Daisey,' Alan said. Daisey smiled at CJ and bowed from the waist. CJ said nothing. She couldn't take her eyes off Tot.

'You've treated us with a complete lack of respect. You've insulted our intelligence by trying to buy us off with a trivial amount of money. Your fucking customers are treated better than we are. You really have shit in your nest, CJ,' Alan said and turned to Daisey.

'Wake that cunt up and make sure he can see out of his good eye,' Alan ordered. Daisey nodded and went to the sink. He filled a pint glass with water and threw the contents into Tot's face. Tot groaned and got a slap for his efforts.

'Can you see me Tot, can you?' Alan whispered. After a dig in the chest from Daisey, Tot nodded.

'Can you see CJ, can you?' Alan whispered. Tot nodded.

'Good, then remember this.'

Alan leaned forward and casually stroked his razor under CJ's chin. She frowned and touched her throat. It didn't hurt but didn't feel right. She looked at her hand. It was covered in blood. Frothy blood. She screamed and blood cascaded down the front of her blue Next top. The blood had also started to spray and Alan executed some neat footwork to avoid the red mess. Daisey laughed.

CJ was now grabbing at the wound with both hands but she couldn't stop the blood. As she lay on the carpet the blood was starting to pool around her head. It was warm and sticky. She looked up at Tot but the room was starting to go dark. Tot was staring at her with tears rolling down his face. She knew she must be dreaming and that she would wake up and laugh about it. Bloody Tot must have spiked her drink. But why was Alan here?

At just after eight o'clock the following morning Terry Ferguson received a phone call saying that Tot needed to see him urgently. He didn't recognise the voice of the caller so he phoned the garden centre. There was no answer. Ferguson grumbled about being got up so early on his rest day but he thought he might as well see what the problem was. He drove to the garden centre and found the gates locked. He thought it was strange because they were both early risers so, after climbing over the gates, he walked to the bungalow. The front door was ajar. He knocked, walked in and stopped. He stared. He saw CJ laying face down in what looked like a pool of blood. A big pool of blood. He saw Tot who was tied to a chair. His face was horribly swollen and the bottom half of his right leg was missing. There was blood everywhere. So much blood.

Ferguson stared and retched. He vomited down his shirt and trousers and on to his trainers. He couldn't stop. He thought he was going to faint. He sat down on the floor and then had to lay down. His head was swimming. He couldn't take his eyes off them.

As he lay there he heard a sound. As he turned his head he felt pressure on his neck. Then the pain came. He couldn't move his head.

'Hello Mr Ferguson, such a nice day for doing your garden. Anyway, as you can see our mutual friends have just gone out of business. A slump in the market you might say. No more pot plants, eh?' Alan announced in a sing song voice. This drew a peel of laughter from Daisey. Such a lovely boy. Ferguson wet himself and the smell of warm urine started to fill the room.

'Sometime in the future we may want you to work for us again. The emphasis being on the 'may'. Whatever we want you will do. Do you understand, completely understand?' Alan whispered.

'Yes, yes please don't hurt me,' Ferguson whined.

'Good, I'm pleased that we understand each other so I'll be off. Don't bother to get up or I will be forced to kill you. Understand?'

'Yes,' spluttered Ferguson through his tears.

The door closed and there was silence. Ferguson lay there for well over twenty minutes. He finally summoned the courage and slowly crawled to the front door. After struggling to open it he fell outside on to the path. He was covered in his own urine and the blood he had crawled through. He vomited again until he had nothing left. He got up and staggered to his car. He started the car, drove off and never looked back.

The news reached the prison later that day. The general reaction was one of shock. CJ and Tot were such gentle characters. Ferguson phoned in sick. The only person who wasn't remotely surprised was Wolf. From what the screws were saying it sounded like the place was a blood bath. Those London boys certainly knew how to hold a party. His main concern, though, was that the supply of drugs had dried up, like turning off a tap. He needed to give that some serious thought.

Alan phoned Rod to tell him that business had been successfully concluded. When Rod asked if Alan had been a good boy he lied and said that he had.

Chapter Thirteen

It was a nice day for a change. No rain. The sky was heavy and there was a nip in the air, but for the prisoners it was tee shirt weather.

The church service had gone relatively smoothly. Services at Raymar were not known for their lack of incident. One of the main reasons was the chaplain, The Reverend John Moss. He was five feet six inches tall and nearly as wide. He had been a chaplain in the Service for 16 years and had moved prisons when advised to do so. His sermons were of the fire and brimstone variety and were designed to pull no punches. It was said that he enjoyed giving offence, particularly to a captive audience which, of course, was the case at Raymar.

The chapel at Raymar had undergone a drastic refurbishment less than a week before the prison received its first prisoners. As in most prison establishments the chapel would be used by a number of different religious beliefs. The chaplain general of the Service had made a planned visit and was horrified to discover a major discrepancy in the building plans. If the chapel was to be used as built then, at confession, a prisoner would be seated where the priest should have been. The major embarrassment factor was allocated to the good Reverend Moss because he hadn't recognised the mistake. Some staff that had been at Raymar from the start would occasionally remind Moss of his faux pas and would be rewarded by a series of un-cleric-like outbursts.

The chapel had been designed to accommodate up to 100 prisoners, and staff, but numbers rarely rose above 30. A fifteen by eight feet stained glass window dominated the back wall behind the altar. The scene depicted pilgrims moving from darkness into light. One wag had likened it to a scene from the film Aliens. Moss was under no illusions about his reputation at Raymar but enjoyed his grace and favour cottage in a nearby village and the ministrations of selected young men when he felt the need. He considered prisoners to be heathens and understood that the free coffee and biscuits was a major reason for attendance at his services. Because of this he felt he was justified in using his sermons to castigate the heathens.

Twenty minutes into the service a loud, fruity fart caused some of the slumbering congregation to look around for the offending backside.

'Beef curry flavour,' offered one pilgrim.

'Na, definitely chicken supreme lightly flavoured with yesterday's beetroot and fried eggs,' ventured a fat skinhead sitting two rows from the front.

The exchange caused comment and titters from the congregation until Grove stood up and took a bow. Butterworth turned away but Masters, Lincoln and Perry led a spirited round of applause. Grove acknowledged the applause by releasing two more boxer-shredding offerings to the delight and amusement of the congregation. This, of course, did not include the Reverend John Moss.

Moss stopped in mid-sentence and glared at the congregation. He looked at the three officers who were at the service to maintain discipline. Two were studiously avoiding his gaze and the third was trying hard not to laugh.

'How dare you defile this House of God with your foul sounds and despicable words. I should pray for you all but I know that I would be wasting my time. This is a place for contemplation and soul searching not for your disgusting attempts at humour. Would Mr Grove, or whoever you are, care to enlighten us as to why you have felt it necessary to indulge in such childish behaviour?' Moss bellowed, feeling good at having silenced the moron who had dared to interrupt his sermon.

Grove stood, bowed, smiled, farted and went for it. 'As a vicar you're a fucking waste of space. This is a place for constipation not contemplation. We listen to you slagging us off. If you had tried it on with us away from this fucking place we would be giving you a number of well-deserved slaps. I will not be coming to this place again. I intend to sit in my cell and constipate, sorry, contemplate my sorry existence and how

I can become a better person. And then I might celebrate my new beginnings by having a hand shandy. Works for me,' Grove said. He bowed, farted one last time and sat down.

The applause was deafening. Moss started to speak but immediately gave up. He knew that he was wasting his time. A telephone call would be necessary to a mobile number in Carlisle and a suitable young friend would be needed to calm him down.

As Grove was escorted back to D wing he accepted the comments and back slaps from his friends with good grace.

It was still fine when the exercise period started. Prisoners from C and D wing made their ways down from their cells and out on to the shared exercise yard. The original architects of the prison had added the yard almost as an afterthought and had not given enough thought to the most important aspect of a prison: security. It was rectangular in shape and clearly would have benefited from greater CCTV coverage. The security staff understood the problems and did their best to supervise the exercise periods.

Grove joined Masters and Perry in a corner at the D wing end of the yard. Lincoln had decided to stay in his cell and watch the EastEnders omnibus. Sad bastard. Butterworth had decided to spend the period playing pool on the wing. He had never been a fresh air fanatic but was also aware that there was a possibility of something kicking off on the yard. Normally he would have enjoyed seeing some blood being splashed around and hearing bones breaking but not today. Playing pool against a Paki retard would be enough excitement for one day plus the fact that the winner would be the proud owner of a nice joint. He was certain that he would be that person.

'You really cracked me up this morning, you daft cunt,' Masters said as he passed a roll-up to Grove.

'Well, Moss should be crucified for the way he talks to us. He makes us sound like a bunch of retards and monsters. If anybody's abnormal it's that cunt,' Grove muttered.

Perry pointed to a prisoner who had just entered the yard from C wing. He was a white man in his mid-fifties serving a seven year stretch for unlawful sexual intercourse with a girl of 15. He was arrogant and disliked by most of the cons. He also owed Perry two joints and had made no attempt to repay the debt. Perry decided it was time to do a bit of debt collecting.

The prisoner in question was called Mick Siegal. He was born on the Isle of Man but had spent most of his life on the mainland. The other cons called him 'Mr One More' because whatever you had he always had one more. Siegal knew that the other prisoners thought he was a total waste of space but he didn't give a damn. He knew that he was a tough son-of-a-bitch and could handle himself. He was obsessed with sex. Nothing else mattered. If it had a pulse he would shag it. As a teenager he had served 20 months in Borstal after having been convicted of having unlawful sexual intercourse with an 18 month-old greyhound called Snoopy.

Siegal stood in the corner of the yard at the C wing end. As usual he was on his own. He always stood on the same spot because he knew that the CCTV camera had him in its sight. He wasn't surprised when he saw Perry walking towards him with a broad grin on his face. Perry was an OK con but because he was of the dark meat variety he couldn't be trusted. The joints that Perry had sold him were alright but no way could they ever take the place of a large Bushmills. He knew that Perry would want payment but he could fucking whistle for it. Times were hard so the cunt could wait.

'How's things then?' Perry asked as he leant against the wire and sparked up a roll up. He was playing the part of the relaxed soul man because he was in full view of his mates and the officers at the other end of the CCTV.

'Can't complain. Five star facilities, waiter service and fine wines. How the fuck do you think things are?' Siegal growled. He sensed that something was about to happen so the only thing to do was to go on the offensive. Perry stared at him and continued to smile. He noticed that, for all his front, Siegal had not mastered the ability to stop his hands shaking.

'Guess it's time that you paid me what you owe. You know the score, everything has its price and it's time you settled your account.'

'I'm skint so I can't pay. Maybe in a couple of weeks I might be able to do a bit but, for now, nothing. Nada. So be a good sooty and fuck off,' Siegal said and burst out laughing.

Perry said nothing. He turned, looked in the direction where Masters and Grove were stood and nodded his head. Grove nodded back, turned and pushed Masters in the chest. Masters winked and staggered backwards. Grove followed him and appeared to punch Masters in the face. Masters shook his head and lunged at Grove. They both fell to the ground, punching and kicking each other.

Perry stared at the CCTV camera. As it started to turn he turned, took one step forward and head-butted Siegal in the face. The blow caught Siegal on the centre of his nose snapping the bone instantly. He fell to his knees, blood gushing from his nose. Perry turned and ran towards Masters and Grove. By the time he reached them they had been separated by four members of staff who were supervising the exercise.

'What the fuck's going on?' the senior officer asked.

'It was him, Sir,' Grove said.

'No it wasn't, it was him, Sir,' Masters replied.

'It was him, bloody two timing bastard,' Grove spluttered.

'Why is he a two timing bastard?' the senior officer asked, clearly oblivious to the looks and smirks of the other prisoners who had run over to enjoy the entertainment.

'I told him, if I caught him wanking over Rusty again I'd smash his face in,' Grove said with a more than passable lisp.

'You bitch, you know I only have eyes for you,' Masters replied, his right hand on his hip.

'Who the fuck is Rusty, I don't know any prisoner called Rusty?' the senior officer said, clearly confused and running out of patience.

'He's not a con, he's that foxy Alsatian guard dog that we all fantasise over,' Grove lisped.

Masters now had both hands on his hips and was in the middle of blowing a kiss at Grove when they both collapsed in howls of laughter. The other prisoners started to laugh as did two of the officers. The senior officer was clearly not amused.

'So, you think you're a pair of fucking comedians do you, Morecambe and Wise?'

'No, more Arse and Hole me thinks,' Grove shouted to the obvious delight of all present except, of course, the senior officer.

'Well, fun over. You pair can cool your heels in the Seg overnight and wait for your adjudication in the morning.'

'Can we share a cell, Sir? Pretty please, Sir?' Grove lisped as they were led away.

The other prisoners, including Perry, dispersed and went on to enjoy what was left of the exercise period. Staff only discovered that something was wrong when one of the CCTV cameras swept back to its original position. Siegal was still on his knees with blood soaked into his shirt and most of his shorts. He didn't tell them it was Perry because, for the first time in his life, he was terrified.

Brian Lincoln would never admit it to a soul but he was finding his 18 year sentence hard going. He was happy enough being on D3 and he enjoyed the company of Grove, Masters and Perry. He thought that Buterworth wasn't the full shilling and secretly suspected that there was more to him than anyone knew.

Lately, when he opened his eyes as the screw kicked his door he no longer felt the urge to tell the bastard to fuck off. His dreams were peppered with flashbacks to his early days in Deptford and Peckham. One dream, which was becoming a bit of a disturbing regular, was about an incident which had happened when he was 12 years old.

He had caught a number 36 bus from Deptford and jumped off at the bottom of Rye Lane in Peckham. He liked Rye Lane because there was always something happening. He started to walk the Lane looking in the shop windows and saying hello to people he knew. The blacks ran most of the Lane and he always gave them due respect. Some of them were really naughty boys and pulled strokes that even Lincoln would think twice about.

Anyway, he had just passed Woolworths when a skinny white kid came round the corner and crashed into him, knocking him against a shop window. The kid had a black leather handbag in his hand which Lincoln thought strange until a small black woman came staggering round the corner screaming blue murder.

'You fucking piece of white shit, you fucking shit, taking me bag,' she screamed.

Lincoln was trying to regain his balance when the kid stood on his leg as he was trying to get away from the black woman. Lincoln grunted, straightened and punched the kid on the side of his head. By this time the black woman was trying to tear at the kid's face with her nails. For what seemed like an age the three of them were rolling about on the pavement. Lincoln managed to free his right arm and knocked the kid against the window with a short jab to the jaw. The black woman was struggling for breath and sat on the pavement swearing at the kid who had clearly run out of fight. Two Rastafarian boys who had witnessed the altercation, walked over and pinned the kid to the ground.

'Yo Momma, what will you be wanting us to do with this naughty boy?,' one of the Rasta's said, clearly enjoying the fun.

'I want you to rip his fucking head off, that's what I want,' she gasped, still fighting for breath.

'Would love to Momma but the filth wouldn't take too kindly to it, me thinks,' he answered.

'Leave it to me,' Lincoln said and got hold of the kid by his shirt collar. He dragged the kid round the corner and into a short alley at the back of Woolworths. As the kid started to speak Lincoln punched him in the stomach and followed it with two punches to the face. The second punch split the kid's bottom lip and loosened two teeth. The kid was on his knees when Lincoln kicked him in the face breaking his jaw. The kid rolled into a ball and was quiet. Lincoln turned and walked out of the alley. As he turned the corner the black woman was waiting for him.

'You are a good, good boy helping me as you did, 'she said and planted a kiss on his cheek.

The Rasta boys thought it was magic and were laughing their heads off.

Instead of taking offence and going ballistic with embarrassment, Lincoln thanked the woman, smiled at the Rasta boys and continued his walk up the Lane. What really disturbed him about the dream was the realisation that the act of helping the woman had been the last time he could remember that he had helped another person.

Lincoln was a regular at the gym and enjoyed the banter with the other prisoners particularly those who came from South London. One lad, who was built like a brick outhouse, was constantly moaning about the prison food and how he could murder double pie, mash and liquor. Manzies pie, mash and liquor. Nothing else would do. The thought of it actually brought a tear to Lincoln's eye and he had to make a hasty exit to the shower room before any of the other prisoners noticed.

His thoughts were increasingly dragged back to South London. Tony Masters, amongst others, was becoming irritated with him because he seemed to be in a world of his own. Grove, being Grove, decided to take the bull by the horns and have it out with him.

'Alright mate?' Grove said as they were walking back from the shop.

'Of course, why wouldn't I be?' Lincoln answered, wondering where the conversation was leading.

'It's just that some of the lads think that you're acting a bit fucking strange like,' Grove answered.

'Na, me guts have been playing up and I'm going to see the quack for some medicine. That should sort me out,' Lincoln answered, hoping that Grove would be satisfied and back off.

'So that's the strength of it. We thought you'd done a Butterworth and gone all religious on us,' Grove said, staring intently at Lincoln.

'Perish the fucking thought, I'll be as right as rain when I've seen the quack.' Lincoln laughed as he walked onto the Wing.

Later that day, during association, Grove reported back to Masters and Perry. Both seemed satisfied and didn't comment that Lincoln was, once again, sat in his cell watching television. Brian Lincoln was a man who normally had a good appetite, even for the muck that the prison dished out under the guise of food. But for some reason he was struggling to keep even a burger down. He had thought about really going to see the quack but he wouldn't put himself through the ordeal of having to be interrogated by Nurse Nelson before he actually got into the room. He also knew that any real problems that the cons had were freely discussed by the nursing staff in front of the other prisoners. No way was he going to stand for that. No, he would sort himself out as he had always done. If only the fucking dreams would stop and he could get a decent night's kip he would be as sound as a pound.

'I would like to introduce Tom Edwards who is joining the D wing team. Hilary Brand will be Tom's mentor for his first week, which should be more than long enough.'

Edwards had arrived at Raymar in a hurry. Mitchell Hagen had agreed to take Edwards as a favour to his opposite number in London. Edwards had been in the Service for a little over two years when he had stumbled upon information which had contributed to a target criminal receiving 35 years for a string of drug-related offences. Unfortunately for Edwards the criminal in question had sent a message indicating that he had the life expectancy of a cockroach. Although the reasons for his transfer should have remained confidential, trying to keep a secret in prison is about as likely as the Pope being caught drunk.

Edwards had been placed on D wing because the chances of Officer Jones returning to work was considered to be extremely unlikely. Although relatively junior in service the word from London was that he could handle himself if push came to shove. What hadn't been known in London was that

Tom Edwards liked to smoke cannabis after dinner and snort cocaine on his weekends off. Since his arrival in the North West he had been unable to secure any 'relaxation', and was very careful where he looked for the stuff. He knew that the obvious place was in the jail but he didn't want to draw unwarranted attention to himself, particularly with the hard-core prisoners on D wing. He wasn't addicted, he knew he wasn't, but he was becoming increasingly irritable with his wife. He wasn't normally a boozer but he had taken to fixing big vodka and tonics as soon as he got home from work. His wife never moaned because she was normally on her second or third. He knew that he had to sort it.

After that first week, Edwards felt that he was settling in at Raymar. The wing PO, Richard Watts, was alright for management and didn't constantly bitch if stuff wasn't done immediately. Hilary Brand had shown him the ropes and hadn't dropped him in it, even as a joke. Raymar was a major improvement on that shit hole of a jail in London. His only ongoing problem was the lack of 'recreation' to be had. Still, it wouldn't kill him to be clean for a few days even though it was costing him a small fortune in off licence bills.

It had been his habit, since joining the Service, to arrive at work a good half an hour before his shift started. It gave him the opportunity to have a cup of tea and, most importantly, to check if any of the staff lockers had been left unlocked. At least once a week there was always a little something to be found. Might be a letter, a photograph or a few quid. Stuff to be taken and hidden and possibly used in the future. Edwards had guaranteed his credibility by complaining to Watts, on his second week on the wing, that his locker had been opened and a few personal items stolen. Watts had apologised on behalf of the governor and asked if any money had been taken. Edwards said that a few quid had vanished but not to worry about it. Watts had thanked him and said that he would remember Edwards when the next batch of detached duty was up for grabs. Nice one.

It was Thursday morning in the second week of May when Edwards arrived on the wing at a couple of minutes after seven. He had visually checked the lockers in the staff room in the gate complex and there was nothing to be had. He made his second cup of tea of the day and went to check the cells so that the night auxiliary officer could get off early. He finally reached D3 and started to get responses as he kicked the doors. The responses ranged from a grunt to a full blown 'fuck off'. Edwards didn't mind the language because that was the norm for a long-term wing.

When he reached D.31 he kicked the door and waited for a response. He had no strong feelings about Brian Lincoln because he didn't know much about him. Apart from the fact that he was serving 18 years he was pretty much an unknown quantity to Edwards. The other prisoners on the spur would generally join in with a bit of banter and take the piss if given the opportunity. Edwards didn't mind because there was always something to be learned and, if it warranted it, entered on to a SIR.

Edwards looked in through the observation panel and kicked the door again. Nothing. He called down to the night officer to join him on the spur.

'I'm getting no response. He's in bed and appears to be asleep, but no response,' Edwards whispered, careful not to let his voice sound unduly concerned. He kicked the door twice more and waited for a response. Nothing.

'Romeo Mike November for Delta One, over.'

'Romeo Mike November receiving, over.'

'Romeo Mike November, I'm about to enter cell D.31 as I cannot obtain a response from prisoner Lincoln, over.'

'Delta One, is the night Officer with you, over?'

'Confirmed and will advise as necessary, over.'

'Received. All stations Romeo Mike November standing by.'

Edwards put his key in the lock and entered the cell. The smell of death was present, almost overpowering. Lincoln looked as though he was deeply asleep but was cold to the touch. Edwards pulled back the duvet and stared at Lincoln's naked body. The metallic smell of blood and the rancid aroma of faeces and urine rose up and assaulted his senses. Lincoln was laying on his left side. His hands were stuck together with what appeared to be dried blood. There were deep cut wounds on both wrists. The bedding was saturated with blood.

'Romeo Mike November from Delta One, over.'

'Romeo Mike November receiving, over.'

'Romeo Mike November, I require Hotel One and Oscar One to this location as soon as possible, over.'

'Received. All stations Romeo Mike November standing by.'

Brian Lincoln was pronounced dead by paramedics a little under an hour later and his body was moved to a hospital on the outskirts of Carlisle. Police arrived, took statements and removed a sheet of blood-stained paper which had been found under Lincoln's body.

After the Inquest was opened and adjourned, the coroner sent Governor Painter details of what was going to be considered as a suicide note. It read;

Dear All
I've thought a long time about this
I've had enough of living like this
This is no life
What a fucking mess
I just cant do it any more
Tell Stein that he's killed me the cunt
No more
Brian

Painter rang Mitchell Hagen. The suspected suicide, because that was the correct terminology until the verdict of the coroner's inquest was known, was another first for Raymar. Death, for whatever reason, always has a major impact on a prison. Prisoners, always ones to thrive on gossip, are careful in their comments in case it is thought that they are displaying a lack of respect. Staff, however, will discuss the incident endlessly, secretly relieved if they are not part of the subsequent investigation.

Hagen knew that he would have to give Raymar special attention for some time to come.

'Angela, it's Roger. Are you free for a couple of minutes if I wander over?'

'Sure. Problem?'

'Yes,' said Mason as he put his jacket on. He'd made one copy of the note which had been shoved under principal officer Watts' office door. It was always good to have insurance if things went wrong.

'Watts found the note when he went to his office on D wing just after eight this morning. He said that the note could only have been put there during yesterday evening's association period. Obviously, staff have access to his office. I have spoken to the staff who supervised the association period but none reported anything out of the ordinary. Apparently the main topics of conversation were Brian Lincoln, no surprise there and the Home Office plans to increase the tariffs for lifers,' Mason added.

'I was going to ask you about the tariff business. Do we need to take any special precautions with our lifer population? Area office wants a risk assessment completed by end of play today,' Painter said

'No problem, I'll have the assessment with you by mid-afternoon.'

'Thanks, now back to this note.'

Roger Mason handed it to her and she read it out loud.

To PO Watts and the Governor
You are going to start having problems soon Very soon
We like our relaxation but it's dried up
Nothing. Nada. Fuck all
Your backing us into corners you don't
want to back us into
Since Tot and his missus got despatched we've had nothing
You need to chill out and give us some room

> *Cut down the searches and Ill give you the name of the*
> *screw*
> *who made Tots scam work*
> *Ill know if your interested*
> *you ain't got long*
> *Later*

'I know I should know, but what the hell is relaxation?' Painter said, a confused look on her face.

'Drugs. Cannabis and cocaine are the drugs of choice in Raymar. Thank God that heroin isn't a factor here. We should be grateful for that.' Mason said, satisfied that his information was up to date.

'Our Mandatory Drug Testing figures are not giving cause for concern.' Painter said.

'No, but the Tot business is a major cause for concern. The note indicates that Tot was the supplier. Maybe that's the reason he and his wife were killed. Dreadful business but we could do with the name of the member of staff who was the middle man, if he or she actually exists,' Mason said, aware that he was being politically incorrect, but, what the hell. Painter didn't appear to notice, she was deep in thought.

'The note seems to indicate that the writer is trying to blackmail us or am I missing a trick?' Painter said, her head clearing.

'No, you're right and we can't ignore it. The place is dry, as dry as a desert. I've had most of the grasses checked and things are not good. We need to think strategically and not panic, if you don't mind me saying so.' Mason said, his face slightly flushed.

'You're right. Get the Senior Management Team together plus the security principal officer. We'll meet in the board room at 11 o'clock. No minutes will be taken. I want it to be an old fashion think tank, politically correct or not.'

'What about the area manager?'

'Fuck the area manager.'

It was probably one of the most extraordinary, extraordinary senior management team meetings ever held in a prison establishment. It would ultimately shape the careers of two of those present.

'No minutes will be taken. All opinions are welcome and will be given the same consideration and importance. Before I pass a document around the table I want to assure the meeting that if one word of our deliberations is leaked from this room I will find the person responsible and finish their career at this establishment. If anyone present wishes to leave, now is the moment to do so,' Painter said and looked round the room.

No one moved or spoke. Painter passed the note to the person on her left and waited patiently whilst it was read and passed around the room.

'What does Mitchell Hagen have to say about this?' asked the Head of Management Services. She was a non-operational grade who had achieved her present level of success by opening her legs for anybody who could advance her career. Male or female, any port in a storm. Her only vulnerable point was that she believed that everybody thought that she was a paragon of virtue.

'The Area Manager is not aware of the note and will remain unaware until I decide that the time is right to tell him. Does anybody have a problem with that?' Painter said, pointedly staring at her HOMS. She was becoming increasingly fed up with the stupid bimbo who had, somehow, achieved a recognisable qualification in management. Non-operational management, and it would stay that way. There were smirks around the boardroom table which Painter noticed but did not acknowledge.

The meeting lasted for a little over three hours. Painter spoke for thirty two minutes.

Nobody interrupted her because they were stunned into silence. When she finished the atmosphere was electric.

'Can we really voice our true opinions, governor?' the security principal officer said. He was a twenty seven year veteran who had been head-hunted by Mitchell Hagen. He had been transferred to Raymar six months before the first prisoners arrived and had been given free rein to set up the security department. His systems were simple and effective. His staff were loyal to him and he did not allow them to be rotated into different jobs. The original governor had wanted to include the security department in the staff rotation system but the Hagen had intervened and it didn't happen. When Angela Painter took command Hagen had said that security was paramount and there would be no changes to the present arrangements. Security principal officer Kevin Small had listened in silence but realised that if he didn't make sense of the situation then the prisoners would take control.

'Of course Kevin. As I said at the start of the meeting all opinions and suggestions would be given equal consideration. You know that I value your work so, please, share your thoughts with us.'

Small took a deep breath and stood. He always stood when he felt his temper rising to the surface.

'What you are suggesting is total lunacy. If we stop our search procedures it will not only be drugs that will come into Raymar. Many of our prisoners are serious players and regular users of firearms. Do we want guns in this place? I think not. Your suggestion of not searching visitors would lead to us losing complete control of what comes into the prison. If that Tot person was the conduit for drugs coming into Raymar then good riddance to bad rubbish. We have been aware, for some time, that a member of staff might be involved and I am confident that we will identify the individual without allowing ourselves to be blackmailed by a bloody prisoner. So what if the place is dry, that's the way it should be. It proves that we are doing our jobs. If we bow to pressure from the prisoners we will find ourselves in trouble, deep trouble. If anything, we should be increasing our vigilance not decreasing it. Towards the end of the nineteen eighties the inmates in many long term prisons were virtually out of control. It took the problems at Whitmoor and Parkhurst to shake the Service into action and restore the balance. In some places bloody battles were fought but we did regain control. Our record at Raymar has been good, up to now, because the prisoners know how far to go.

The attack on Officer Jones was unusual for Raymar and should be kept in context. If we adopted your suggestions the level of violence will increase because the prisoners will start to realise that we are giving in to them. These people are not like us. They are not normal. If they were they wouldn't be in prison. We should review our security files and transfer a few out. That would tell the players that we do mean business. We mustn't roll over.'

Small sat down and stared at the clock. He knew that he had probably said too much but he was past caring. That stupid woman was going to ruin Raymar and he would do what was necessary to stop it happening. He lowered his eyes and found himself staring at the deputy governor. Mason stared back and winked. Painter couldn't have seen it because she was sitting next to Mason. Small started to relax.

'These people are not animals. I'm sure that they would react in a favourable manner if we showed them that we were sympathetic to their problems,' Painter said. There was silence around the table for at least a minute. Finally Mason spoke.

'Why should we be sympathetic to their problems for Christ's sake? They're in prison because they can't live a normal life. They take, they don't give. I'm sorry, Angela, but I completely agree with Kevin Small. What you are suggesting is pure lunacy. I just hope that none of your suggestions find their way out of this room. If they do we really will be in trouble.'

Painter turned and looked at Mason. How dare he use her Christian name in a meeting. She was trying hard not to cry. She felt betrayed, let down. She was trying her best. Maybe promoting Mason to deputy governor hadn't been a good move after all. She thought that he would be progressive in his thinking, following her lead. Obviously not.

'I don't see that anything further will be gained by continuing with this meeting. Those of you who have voiced opinions are clearly against my suggestions. Those who have remained silent obviously don't care one way or another. I will consider what has been said and inform you of my decisions in due course. Remember what I said at the start of the meeting.

What has been discussed stays in this room. That is all.' Painter stood, turned and left the room. The silence was deafening.

Mason made the call as soon as he got home. Hagen listened with growing concern. He had thought that Painter had real potential but she was obviously losing her way. He was all for progressive thinking but she was taking things too far.

'Are you absolutely certain that you have told me everything Roger?'

'Absolutely, Sir. I don't want you to think that I am being disloyal to Angela but what she was suggesting is crazy. Kevin Small probably voiced what everyone was thinking.'

'Kevin is a good man and was right to say what he said. I don't think you have been disloyal. I would have been bloody angry if you hadn't made the call.'

'Thank you, Sir,' Mason said, the relief evident in his voice.

'Also, now is the right time for me to share with you a matter that is highly confidential and must remain that way.' Hagen spoke, without interruption, for 15 minutes and Mason could hardly believe what he'd been told. Sensibly, he remained silent but the significance of *why* he'd been told excited him.

'Finally, I will make an unplanned visit to Raymar just after lunch on Friday. Stay in your office until I call you. We never had this conversation.'

'Understood, Sir,' and the line went dead.

To PO Watts and the Governor
I know you've had your meeting
Wouldn't let her have her way would ya
All you had to do was cut some slack
Not good not good at all
Well get what we want
You know we will
Be a shame if people were to get hurt
Later

PS Screw Ferguson was the inside man greedy bastard.
Ask Noddy he knows fucking grass
Later

'How the fuck did he find out about the meeting?' Mason said.

'It's starting to circulate, news travels fast in prison as you well know.'

'How much do you know?'

'Most of it,' Watts answered. Mason didn't pursue it.

'Is Noddy a grass?' Mason asked.

'Yes, he's registered, on the list in your safe,' Watts said, trying hard not to laugh.

Mason felt foolish, he should have known. Another lesson learned.

'Have Noddy brought to reception at 8.30. Go down and ask him about Ferguson. Then tell him he's being transferred out for his own safety, because he's compromised,' Mason said, regaining his authority.

'What I'm about to tell you must remain between you and I. I know that Kevin Small is prone to running off at the mouth so you will not, under any circumstances, share what I am about to tell you with him or anyone else.'

'Yes, Sir,' Watts replied, wondering what was coming next.

'In the early 90s, headquarters was backed into a corner and forced to come up with radical ideas to stem the flow of drugs coming into our prisons and to address the increasing levels of violence being used against both staff and prisoners. Most of the ideas never saw the light of day but one did. A small number of life-sentence prisoners were, shall we say, "recruited".'

'Recruited,' Watts spluttered.

'Yes, recruited. Now let me finish without further interruption.'

'Yes, Sir, sorry Sir,' Watts replied, embarrassed at being spoken to like he was a naughty school boy.

'I used the word 'recruited' because nothing else really describes the situation. The lifers, in question, were all subject to a long tariff, in most cases 30 years and upwards. The deal was as follows. In return for providing high-grade information and agreeing to be moved to prisons experiencing problems, the lifers would have their individual tariff reduced. These prisoners were selected because of their personalities, abilities to merge in with the population and an almost overpowering wish not to die in prison. They are called 'projects'. A silly name but one which was selected by the director general personally. Only the governing governor, and one other senior member of staff, in each establishment, are privy to this information. Some governors use them, some don't. Ours doesn't. I believe that this is a resource that is vital in our fight against illegal drugs..

Watts was stunned into silence. He had heard rumours, as others had, but had dismissed the concept as unworkable. The significance of how Mason knew about the 'projects' and why he had shared the information, was completely lost on Watts. Mason could see the confusion in the other man's eyes and knew that, under no circumstances, would he divulge the whole truth.

'Do we have a 'project' in Raymar?' Watts whispered.

'Yes, the prison barber, Johnny Scapes, and we will start to use him in the coming days. I'll see you at the morning meeting.'

'Will do,' Watts said and went back to his office.

'Well, is it true?' Mason asked.

'Yes, I'm afraid so,' Watts replied, 'Noddy said that it was common knowledge amongst the users. Apparently Ferguson has made a tidy packet over the past twelve months. He also said that he thought Nurse high and mighty Nelson may have been having a tickle but that was just a vague rumour. He said the prisoners hated her and were probably trying to stitch her up. Apparently the stuff was distributed from the healthcare centre.'

'What have you done with Noddy?'

'Segregation Unit. Said he wants a move down South so I'll arrange for him to go to Wormwood Scrubs and then onwards to Parkhurst. Said he'd get cut if he went back on the wings.'

'Fair enough.'

'When is Ferguson on duty?'

'Late shift today.'

'Wait for him at the Gate, with PO Small, and bring him to my office.'

'Will do. Will we tell the Governor?'

'Not yet, leave that to me.'

After Watts had left his office, Mason telephoned Mitchell Hagen.

'Thanks for the call Roger, have you told Angela?'

'No, she's on a day's leave.'

'Fine, leave it like that. See you tomorrow,' Hagen said.

Ferguson was escorted to Mason's office, informed of the allegations and suspended on full pay whilst the investigation ran its course. He never said a word. He was escorted back to the gate. He went through and walked to his car without a backward glance.

Chapter Fourteen

Friday arrived under black clouds heavy with rain. Angela Painter greeted the gate staff at twenty minutes to nine and found Roger Mason waiting for her in her office. He told her about the note and about Ferguson's suspension. She nodded her agreement with his actions and said that she had a mountain of paperwork to get through and asked him to chair the morning meeting at nine o'clock. Mason left her office perplexed. He had expected to be told off for not phoning her about the note and the suspension. She had barely spoken to him. He wondered what would happen when the area manager arrived.

Mitchell Hagen pulled into the staff car park just after 1.30.

'Good afternoon, Sir. We weren't expecting you today,' the gate senior officer said.

Hagen smiled, collected a set of keys and said nothing.

'Governor, it's the gate. The area manager is on his way to your office.'

'Are you sure?' Painter said as she grabbed for her organiser.

'Absolutely Governor.'

'Thanks,' Painter said and put the phone down. There was nothing in her organiser and she couldn't ask her secretary because she was on leave. Silly girl had obviously forgotten to put the visit in the diary. Painter would take her to task the following Monday.

'Mitchell, what a pleasant surprise. My secretary has obviously forgotten to inform me of your visit otherwise I would have been prepared for you,' Painter said, trying to hide her embarrassment with a smile. She walked forward to shake his hand which he ignored.

'Don't blame your secretary, I wasn't planning to visit until I was told about your extraordinary meeting which took place earlier this week. Would you care to explain, Mrs Painter, or shall I take you through the un-minuted meeting? How shall we do it?' Hagen said as he sat down behind her desk.

Painter was stunned. She felt her cheeks burning. She remembered Hagen's words when he had installed her as governor of Raymar. He'd said that mistakes could generally be rectified but that he never wanted to find out about something important via a third party. He said he would find that unforgivable. Painter felt herself starting to panic. What could she say?

As she struggled to compose herself, Hagen spoke. He took her through the meeting in so much detail that she sat in silence. When she asked who had told him about the meeting he ignored her as if she hadn't spoken. She struggled to concentrate on what he was saying and felt the bile trying to rise in her throat. Her head was spinning.

'Are you listening to me, Mrs Painter? Concentrate.' Hagen said, his voice heavy with sarcasm.

'Yes, yes I am,' Painter whispered.

'So, I find myself in the position of not being able to trust one of my senior governors. You were advised to tell me of the meeting and chose to ignore the advice. You were seriously considering going against Service policy on searching and preventing the spread of illegal drugs. Your actions would have put both staff and prisoners at risk. Fortunately, a concerned member of your staff ignored your threats to end a career and had the good sense to contact me. Your actions would not have been progressive; they would have been the actions of a highly paid governor who had lost the plot. Tell me I'm wrong,' Hagen said, his voice literally dripping with sarcasm.

As Painter was about to speak, Hagen picked up her internal telephone and dialled a four figure number.

'Roger Mason.'

'Roger, Mitchell Hagen. Come over to Mrs Painter's office.'

'Yes, Sir, on my way,' Mason said.

Suddenly it all became clear. What on earth had she been thinking? Trying to get pregnant had dominated her every waking hour and Hagen was right, she had lost the plot. She had tried to exert her will on her senior management team and had failed. Failed miserably. And Roger shit cunt Mason had told tales. The bastard. The fucking bastard. She couldn't believe that she was swearing in her head. She never used such dirty words.

'So, I am placing you on gardening leave until I decide what to do with you. What you were planning was a dereliction of duty which, if proven, could end your career in the Service. Your actions will be investigated by another area manager. You will be contacted and interviewed about your apparent misconduct. Collect your personal items and leave the prison. Now.'

As she stood up there was a knock on the door.

'Come in Roger,' Hagen said.

The door opened and Mason entered. He looked sheepish and wouldn't make eye contact with Painter. As she walked past him she called him a traitor. The tears were running down her cheeks as she heard Hagen welcome Mason as the acting governor-in-charge of Raymar. She walked to the gate and pushed her keys down the shute. Although she was aware that the staff were staring at her nothing seemed to register. She walked to her car and sat for a few minutes until the sobbing had stopped. She drove home and was almost bursting to use the toilet when she parked the car on the drive. As was her almost obsessive habit she used the pregnancy testing kit. It was positive. She tested again. Again, positive. She tested a third time. Again, positive. She cried and cried. Fuck the Prison Service, she was pregnant. Yesssssssssss!

Seven days into Roger Mason's reign as acting governor-in-charge, the security information reports were arriving in the security department at an increasing and alarming rate. Papers were arriving from the wings, healthcare and even one from the chaplain. He was concerned that his orderly was spending increasing amounts of time in the company of the gang elements in the jail. Attendance at his bible classes was on the increase but he felt as though the prisoners were just using the chapel as a meeting place. The prisoners were talking quietly amongst themselves but fading into silence if he approached them. Even Butterworth wasn't his usual grovelling self.

PO Small was taken off all other duties and told to concentrate on the flood of reports. He was looking for patterns and trends and was coming up with absolutely nothing. His informers were producing little of value but one thing was becoming abundantly clear. Fear was descending on Raymar like a fine mist. The informers confirmed it but either couldn't, or wouldn't produce names. Still, Small beavered away and reported to Roger Mason twice a day. Mason was still thinking about a way to approach Scapes without raising suspicions amongst both staff and prisoners.

Wolf was angry, and frightened, in equal measures although it wasn't apparent to all but the closest to him. Only one prisoner had been allowed to get close to Wolf and he was called Curtis. Just Curtis.

Curtis was serving a 14 year sentence for savage assaults on two drunken holiday makers in a bar on the Costa Blanca in Spain. The two hapless victims had spent an entire evening subjecting Curtis to a torrent of abuse about his singing. Apparently, he snapped when the older of the two, Douglas Myles, became abusive to a waitress named June. It became apparent, during the subsequent trial, that Curtis and June were romantically linked. With no previous criminal record, he had successfully appealed and had been allowed to serve his sentence in the UK prison system.

Curtis was a respected face in Raymar. He was rarely troubled by the other prisoners but would sort aggravation with a savage simplicity. During the first year of his repatriation he was at a long-term institution in Leicestershire. Another prisoner called Terry had taken the piss out of him as he was learning to lift weights in the gymnasium. Curtis had initially ignored the comments but, by the third day the other prisoners using the gymnasium were laughing at his expense. The following day Curtis went to the gym at his usual time and waited patiently by the bench press area. Terry arrived and walked over to Curtis. He pushed Curtis hard in the chest and told him that he would fuck his arse if he didn't vanish.

Curtis smiled, leaned forward and caressed Terry's face with his right hand. The blade was sharp. Terry shook his head and only realised that his right eye wasn't in its usual place when his left index finger found its way into a soggy mess. Curtis was still smiling when he punched Terry in the stomach and dropped him to the ground with a right hook. Terry was trying to make sense of the situation when Curtis sat astride him and pushed something into his mouth. Terry tried to shout but he started to choke. He thought that he had bitten his tongue but he hadn't. He'd bitten his right eye in half and swallowed it. It took a couple of seconds for him to realise what had happened and he started to vomit. Curtis climbed off of him, smacked him hard around the face, smiled and walked away. He looked back to see Terry on his knees trying to sort through the mess on the floor. To Terry's credit he never fingered Curtis but the incident was discussed and pored over for months. If the governor had used the 'project' system, Curtis would have received an extra 10 years for his efforts that day.

The legend followed Curtis down the years and came to Wolf's attention in Raymar. Wolf liked Curtis and both men knew the other's reputation and gave the due respect. Wolf arranged to meet Curtis in the healthcare centre waiting room. He had two major problems. The suppliers from the Smoke had not made contact about restarting the supply of drugs. But, more worryingly, Mother hadn't written for over a week. He had tried ringing her mobile but it went straight on to answer phone. What the hell was going on? He'd lost his temper the previous evening after lock up and had ripped his biker magazine into a hundred pieces.

The following morning Wolf was escorted to the healthcare centre and locked in the waiting room. Curtis was the only other prisoner in the room.

'How's tricks Wolf?' Curtis ventured. Wolf looked troubled.

'Could be better, lad, could be better,' Wolf answered trying to keep his voice even.

Curtis waited for Wolf to continue. He was acutely aware that time was against them and that Florence fucking Nightingale Nelson would be coming for one of them to take him to see the quack.

'Big problems, lad, big problems,' Wolf whispered.

'How can I help?'

'Those London boys are ignoring my request for gear and I've got a lot of angry customers.'

'So fucking what? I've got some irons in the fire which I was going to tell you about. Fuck 'em, let 'em wait. Now, what's the real problem? It ain't like you to worry about pressure.'

Wolf stared at Curtis and knew that he needed help from a friend.

'I can't reach Mother. No letters and I can't get her on the dog,' Wolf answered.

Curtis now knew how serious the situation was. He knew that, normally, Wolf wouldn't give a flying fuck about a bit of pressure from the junky cons. He would smack a few heads and bring them back into line. But his worry about Mother was messing with his head. He wasn't thinking straight which was dangerous at the best of times.

'I've got a few favours owed me on the out. I can pull a few in and check that Mother is OK. Would that help?' Curtis asked.

Wolf thought about it. He didn't normally ask for help because it was a sign of weakness but he was fucking desperate.

'Yes lad, do it and I owe you one.'

'No you don't, it's a freebie for a friend,' Curtis replied, knowing that Wolf was a sound investment for the future.

As the men were shaking hands Nurse Nelson walked in.

'Mr Curtis, you're first to see the doctor,' Nelson said, the tone of her voice clearly indicating her dislike for the pair.

'I've changed me mind. I had a spot on the end of me knob but my dear friend here sucked it off for me. So, no harm done, eh?'

'You disgust me, Curtis,' Nelson sneered, 'Wolf, you're next for the doctor.'

'I've changed my mind. I had a knob on the end of my spot but my dear friend here sucked it off for me. So, no harm done, eh?'

'You are a disgusting pair of animals and I won't forget how you've wasted my time,' Nelson shouted as she stormed out of the waiting room.

'That went well didn't it? I'll be in touch,' Curtis said and smiled one of his special smiles.

After the Monday morning meeting Mason convened a special Senior Management Team meeting to listen to Small's report.

'Ladies and Gentlemen, this has not been an easy task but my findings will be of interest to you,' Small said, playing to the crowd.

Mason was about to speak but decided to hold his tongue. Fresh blood was required in the security department but there were the present problems to be dealt with first. He would add it to the list for discussion with the area manager.

'I think that we can all agree that drugs, or the lack of, are causing the tension on the wings. Many of the SIR's confirm that. The place is not completely dry but it's only blow that's doing the rounds at inflated prices. Gang activity is causing the increase in tension with the related fear factor. A number of SIR's report that a new drug source is being worked on but, as of this morning, no names have come to the fore. Our regular informants confirm the substance of the SIR's but cannot, or will not, go any further. So, I suggest the following: One. Over the next seven days we will target the major players on each of the wings with the aim of transferring at least a dozen early next week. We need to be sure that our information is sound to avoid a major backlash. Two. We should reduce movement off the wings to the minimum. Activities such as evening classes, bible study and evening gym sessions should be curtailed whilst we are identifying the major players. Three. Notices should be displayed on the wings to the effect that activities are being limited due to staff shortages. It will be interesting to see which prisoners are most vocal about the cutbacks. That's my report, sir,' Small concluded and sat down.

'Thank you Mr Small, excellent work. I agree with your recommendations. See that the notices are in place by lunchtime. Also, see that your report is emailed to area office. Meeting concluded,' Mason said.

On the Thursday morning Wolf was given a message telling him to meet Curtis in the gym that afternoon. Wolf had booked a weights session for the afternoon so that wouldn't be a problem. He still hadn't heard from Mother but he knew that he had to keep his head down. He'd heard the whispers doing the rounds about the increased security activity and he didn't for one moment believe that the evening activity cutbacks were due to staff shortages. Fucking screw bastards.

At 2.15 he joined five other prisoners on the ground floor of the wing and was escorted to the gym. Physical education instructor Smith was supervising the weights session and Wolf nodded to him. Wolf suspected that Smith was a turd burglar and had been trying to think of a way to use the knowledge to his advantage. Shortly after 2.30, Curtis arrived. Wolf smiled a greeting but Curtis just nodded. His expression was grim. Wolf knew that he had to be patient but the suspense was doing his head in. He knew that he had to speak to Curtis before his head exploded.

'Mr Smith, got a minute?' Wolf shouted.

Smith walked over.

'Yes Wolf, problem?'

'No. Me and Curtis have been having a wager as to who can bench press the most weight. Being as Curtis is a pansy bastard it's obvious that I will win but he don't trust me. Can Curtis spot for me for ten reps and I'll do the same for him? It will prove that I ain't cheating and will stop Curtis moaning,' Wolf said with a big smile.

'No problem, I'll send Curtis over,' Smith said and winked at Wolf.

Curtis ambled over. Smith watched as they greeted each other. He went into the office and thought no more of it.

'What's the news then?' Wolf asked.

'Not good, brother,' Curtis replied, looking down at his feet.

'Tell me then, for fucks sake,' Wolf grumbled.

'Mate of mine, Hank the Wank, went round to your place early Monday evening. So, he's sat in his transit when, just after eight your missus turned up.'

'What do you mean, turned up?'

'I'm just getting to that,' Curtis replied testily.

Wolf said nothing.

'She rolled up on the back of a bike. Flash, Japanese thing with shiny bits. She gets off as does the geezer on the front. They take their helmets off and Hank recognises your missus by the tattoo round her neck.'

Wolf could feel his face starting to redden.

'Go on,' Wolf whispered.

'The geezer takes hold of your missus and sticks his tongue down her throat. Hank said she looked like she was loving it. Anyway, after a minute or so he pats her on the arse and says that he will see her tomorrow. She asks him in but he says that he can't because he has a bit of business to deal with. She kisses him and says 'I love you Monty'.'

'Monty, who the fuck's Monty?'

'Don't know.'

'Are you sure that's what happened?' Wolf spluttered. He was finding it hard to breathe.

'Yes mate. I made Hank repeat it to me. He can be a bit of a tosser but he's reliable. He wouldn't dare tell me porkies. He went round there last night and the same geezer was in the house. Hank said that they were at it on the carpet in the front room with the fucking curtains open as well. I phoned him this morning from the screws' office. I told the PO that my brother was ill. Stupid cunt believed me. I'm sorry mate, I know how much she means to you,' Curtis said.

Wolf was staring at Curtis but he wasn't seeing him. The banging in his head was now a steady throb. He nodded and turned his back on Curtis. He bent down and, very slowly, removed the discs from the weights bar. Curtis watched Wolf and decided that he needed to put some distance between them. As he walked away Smith came out of the office and walked towards Wolf.

'Who won the wager then?' Smith said, patting Wolf on the shoulder.

Wolf ignored him and stared at the bar in his hands.

'I said, who won the wager then?' Smith persisted.

Wolf turned and pushed Smith in the chest. Smith fell backwards over the weights bench. Wolf raised the bar over his shoulder and walked towards Smith. The gym orderly later recounted that the sound Wolf made as he beat Smith with the bar was similar to the noise a dog makes when it's bollocks are clamped in a vice. Scary stuff.

After the fourth blow was struck the orderly pressed the alarm bell. After the eighth blow was struck three prisoners wrestled Wolf to the ground as the staff burst in through the gym doors.

Smith was unconscious. His arms were broken in several places which probably saved his life as he tried to protect his face. His skull was fractured in several places as was his nose, jaw and collar bone. He lost most of his teeth.

Wolf was moved, under restraint to the segregation unit. Despite repeated questioning, Wolf remained silent. He cried but was silent. Always silent. Curtis was questioned by the governor leading the investigation. He said that Wolf had started acting funny as they were lifting weights. Curtis decided to call it a day. As he walked away he saw Wolf attack Smith. Sick bastard.

The following Monday, Small gave the senior management team an updated report.

'Good morning ladies and gentlemen. First, the attack on Mr Smith seems to have taken a lot of the tension out of the jail. Although Smith was popular with some of the prisoners, others were starting to question his motives, if you know what I mean.'

There were nods and smirks which Mason chose to ignore.

'It would appear that prisoner Wolf was trying to set up a new drug supply into Raymar and was putting intense pressure on our junky community. My most reliable informant has confirmed that blow is still doing the rounds but in manageable quantities. My staff will be doing selective cell searches this afternoon. We will be transferring a number of prisoners but I am conscious of the need to maintain the status quo on the wings. I recommend that we return to normal on the activities front,' Small concluded.

'Thank you Mr Small, excellent work,' Mason said. 'Let's get Raymar back to normal. I want to be able to tell the area manager that we are back on track to meet our performance targets,' Mason concluded.

It never occurred to anyone sat around the table to enquire about the health of physical education instructor Harland Smith.

Later that day Small met with his most reliable informer. The meeting took place in the healthcare centre waiting room during the tea time lock up period. The prisoner had pressed his cell bell and told the officer that he felt unwell and needed to see a doctor. Shortly after, Small arrived in healthcare. He told the nurse that the prisoner in the waiting room was a scum bag and was overdue a warning about his behaviour, which was about to be rectified. The nurse agreed. The prisoner was a nasty piece of work and needed to be put in his place. Small let himself into the waiting room.

'You did well this week, very well,' Small said as he handed the prisoner three packs of Drum rolling tobacco.

'At your service Mr Small, as always,' the prisoner chuckled.

'Is there anything else going on that I need to be concerned about?' Small asked.

'Keep an eye on the cons on D3. Masters, Perry and Grove are tasty bastards and Butterworth is a seriously messed up cunt. A word to the wise, eh?'

'Thanks, I will.'

'Any idea when we might receive our first shipment up from the Smoke?'

'I've put feelers out but it's taking longer than planned. Things should be back to normal in a week or so. We won't need the healthcare orderly this time; Nurse Nelson says she's more than capable of sorting things.'

'Cheers Mr Small, always a pleasure doing business with you.'

With that Small left Curtis waiting to see the doctor.

Just after 07.00, four days later, Watts let himself into his office on D wing and found a small envelope on the floor. He opened it, read the note inside, and rang extension 200.

'Governor.'

'Sir, I need to see you right away.'

'Mr Watts, one of the most irritating things about being governor-in-charge is that everybody wants a piece of my time. I've started coming to work early to deal with the mountain of paperwork which is trying to suffocate me. Can't this wait until after the morning meeting?' Mason said, the frustration clearly evident in his voice.

'No, Sir.'

'What's it about?'

'Project, Sir.'

'Come to my office immediately and accept my apology for sounding like a bore.'

'No problem, Sir.' Watts was knocking on Mason's door a little over five minutes later. 'Come,' Mason shouted. Watts walked over to Mason's desk and handed him the note.

To The Governor.
PROJECT

I am taking a huge risk in writing to you. You will know, by now, that I have a real interest in being of assistance to you in any way that I safely can. As you will be aware, my tariff is now 25 years and I am hoping to make a further improvement during my stay at your prison. So far, this has not been possible because I have not been approached. I found it necessary to approach your predecessor, Ms Painter, but she wasn't remotely interested. I thought about writing to Mr Hagen, but I considered that to be a step too far, for now.

I am going to give you the following information in the hope that I will be rewarded with a further reduction in my tariff.

Four days ago your head of security met with prisoner Curtis. The meeting took place in the healthcare centre during the tea-time lock up period. Curtis was given a substantial amount of rolling tobacco, by Mr Small, for information provided on a number of matters. This, in itself, will not interest you greatly but what I am now about to tell you will. As the meeting was drawing to a close, Curtis asked Mr Small when the first consignment (drugs) would be arriving from the Smoke.

Mr Small assured Curtis that it would be soon and that things would return to normal. Mr Small also said that the healthcare orderly would no longer be used because Nurse Nelson had everything in hand. Curtis also advised Mr Small of the following, 'Keep an eye on the cons on D3. Masters, Perry and Grove are tasty bastards and Butterworth is a seriously messed-up cunt. A word to the wise eh.' Those are the exact words because Curtis taped the whole conversation on a Sony Dictaphone which came into my possession a short time ago.

I will be happy to share the whole of the recorded conversation with you subject to the following concessions,

1, That you acknowledge my 'project' status and allow me to attempt to reduce my tariff further.

2, That prisoner Curtis will not be subject to any form of recognition or punishment. All he asks is that he be allowed to marry his fiancée, June, on a day of his choice in the prison chapel. Being of the Roman Catholic faith he will not require the ministrations of Reverend Moss.

Curtis will continue to assist me in my quest for a better life and he will, of course, continue to receive a steady supply of Drum rolling tobacco.

As is now apparent, Mr Ferguson is not the only bad apple in your barrel. Also, Mr Edwards should be considered to be 'on the turn'.

If you agree with this proposition please arrange for me to be taken to Curtis's wing, at 9.30 am, to cut his hair. If this doesn't happen then I will know that my time at Raymar is coming to an end and, of course, the Dictaphone recording might vanish forever. JS.

Mason and Watts looked at each other in stunned silence. When Mason broke the silence they discussed every aspect of the letter, both re-reading it again. As they left Mason's office, at five minutes to nine, Mason instructed Watts to arrange, by whatever method he saw fit to use, to arrange for Scapes to be taken at 09.30 to cut Curtis' hair. Because he had a dental appointment in Carlisle he also instructed Watts to ring area office, inform Hagen's staff officer of the note and request his presence at a meeting he intended to hold at midday at Raymar. Watts missed the morning meeting but met the target time of 09.30 by the skin of his teeth.

Chapter Fifteen

Later that morning, Masters was let back on to D wing by Officer Brand after having made his way back from the education department. As she walked in front of him he couldn't resist staring at her figure. Why the female officers felt the need to wear trousers was beyond him. He'd been studying her for a few days, wondering if it was worth the risk of trying to chat her up. Grove had offered the opinion that she might be up for it but there would be an awful lot to lose if he had got his sums wrong.

'Is it Miss, Mrs or Ms then?' Masters asked, trying to keep an edge of sarcasm from his voice.

'Are you speaking to me, Masters?' Brand answered wondering where the conversation was going.

'No, I'm fucking talking to myself, I do that a lot you know. I always start the day by asking myself if I'm going to be a Mrs, Miss or Ms for that particular twenty four hours. Of course I was talking to you,' Masters said, knowing that he was probably going to face an adjudication the following morning.

Brand surprised him. 'Listen Masters, as far as I'm concerned I could be Mother Teresa if it pleases you. I could also be Deputy Dawg or Lily Savage if that would float your boat. Probably a mixture of all three if your file is correct. But right now, I'm just over four hours from two weeks annual leave so shut the fuck up and go to your cell or I'll have you moved to the segregation unit.'

Masters could feel his cheeks warming up and, for the first time for a long time, was lost for words. Fucking slag.

Brand shouted up the stairs to unlock D3, turned, went into the wing office and slammed the door.

Masters found his voice. 'Enjoy your holiday cause I'll still be here when you return, then we'll have a real conversation.'

'Who are you talking to?' Watts said as he unlocked the gate to enter the wing.

'Nobody PO, just the fucking wall, just the wall,' Masters muttered and walked towards the stairs to go up to his cell.

Watts laughed and went to his office. Just another boring Friday afternoon. Weekend off starting in about 75 minutes. Great.

Masters walked on to the spur and towards his cell. The door was open, a policy which he didn't agree with but the screws said it saved time that could be better used elsewhere. Selfish bastards. There was no way that it would happen in a remand jail. Fucking hell, your belongings would have vanished inside ten minutes. As he pushed the door open he knew that there was somebody in there. It was Raymond Butterworth and he had his hand in a drawer.

'What the fuck are you doing?' Masters said, not quite realising what was going on.

Butterworth said nothing and moved towards Masters.

'I said what the fuck are you doing?' Masters said, things starting to become horribly clear.

Butterworth was now starting to push past Masters, grunting with the effort.

'You thieving cunt,' Masters yelled and pushed Butterworth in the chest sending him sprawling backwards. Butterworth hit the wall but seemed to bounce back up. Masters stared into his eyes and saw that he was spaced. Out of his tree. Butterworth staggered forward and lost his balance. He fell and rolled on to his left side, facing away from Masters.

Masters moved forward and Butterworth turned. Butterworth had a blade in his right hand.

'Coming for you boy, coming for you,' Butterworth slurred and moved forward.

Masters was tuned now. Everything was sharp. Everything was real. Butterworth had shown him the ultimate disrespect by trying to rob his cell. The ultimate crime, the ultimate sin in prison.

'Come on then you cunt, bring it on you fucking low life scum bag,' Masters said, now back in control of his feelings. That slag Brand had upset him, got inside his head. She had upset him and would pay. A shagging would not be enough. Her screams would not satisfy. He would eat her fucking soul.

But for now, Butterworth would do. The fucking useless wanker. How dare he try to rob him and then pull a blade. What was the world coming to? Where had the standards gone? Masters moved forward. Butterworth raised his right hand and looked like a cartoon killer. Masters snapped. He grabbed Butterworth's right wrist and dragged his arm down. Butterworth was grunting again. Masters smashed him in the face, getting a good connection just below his nose.

Butterworth staggered backwards and tried to regain his balance. He dropped the blade as he cradled his face in his hands, blood leaking through his fingers.

Masters hit him again and he fell forward still holding his hands to his face. Masters kicked him on the shoulder and leaned over him. He picked the blade up. It was a plastic eating knife but, by fuck, it was sharp. Masters rolled Butterworth over and sat astride him. He punched him twice around the sides of his head which just made Butterworth grunt and grunt. Masters ripped open Butterworth's shirt. He had no tee shirt on. He was sweating like a pig and stank like one.

Masters stabbed downwards and the knife entered just below Butterworth's breast bone. There was a gurgling and hissing sound and the slight aroma of shit. Butterworth started to open his mouth but Masters clamped his left hand over it. Blood started to shoot upwards and hit Masters in the face. He took his hand from Butterworth's face to wipe the blood from his own face. Butterworth forced himself upwards and pushed Masters backwards. The pain in his chest and stomach was intense. He felt as though he was on fire. He started to feel dizzy and thought he was going to throw up. Masters was trying to regain his balance as Butterworth started to shout.

Grove and Perry arrived at D wing gates. They rang the bell and after a minute or so Officer Edwards came out of the wing office and let them in.

'How was the gym today lads?' Edwards said, trying to gain some ground with two of the more difficult long-termers on the wing.

'Well, actually, it stank of screw piss and sweat. The female changing room was particularly ripe. Staff sports day was it? Still, we cleaned it up so that it was nice for the people it was built for. Us,' Perry said, aware that he was upsetting the new screw and loving every second of it.

Grove burst out laughing and sprayed spit over Edwards' tie which set Perry off into a fit of the giggles.

Edwards felt his face starting to get hot and was lost for words. He knew that he should say something, warn Perry about his language but the moment was lost so he turned away and went back into the office. Perry and Grove made their way up to D3 laughing at the way they had jazzed the screw.

As they walked on to the spur they heard what sounded like a strangled scream. The noise was coming from the direction of Masters' cell. When they entered it looked like the aftermath of a road accident. Butterworth was laying on his back with his feet wedged under the bed. His chest area was covered in blood and he was desperately trying to stem the flow. Masters was trying to get up but he was slipping in the blood. He looked like a spastic ballerina. His face was covered in blood. He turned as he heard them enter his cell.

'What the fuck is going on here?' Grove said, looking back over his shoulder to see if there was anybody else on the spur. There wasn't.

'I found this cunt in my cell on the rob. He's spaced out on something. He tried to do me with a blade but I took it from him and stuck him,' Masters said, trying to regain his composure.

'What has he done to your face?' Perry asked.

'Nothing, it's his claret not mine.'

'Are you sure he was on the rob?' Grove asked.

'Yea, I caught him with his hand in the drawer.'

Grove stared at Butterworth, who was groaning. Grove smiled, took a step forward and kicked Butterworth in the face. Perry kicked him on the top of his head.

'Thanks lads, but enough. I've got to move him out of here before the screws turn up or I'm in deep shit,' Masters said, wiping the blood from his face with a towel.

'We'll help,' Perry and Grove said, sounding like Peters and Lee.

Edwards, Brand and Watts were finishing cups of coffee and preparing to serve the evening meal.

'If you feel that they have stepped over the line of acceptable behaviour then you must bring them to task. I suggest that you go up on D3 and speak to them individually. If you pull them whilst they are waiting to be served they'll try and score points with the other prisoners,' Watts said.

'Sounds like a plan to me,' Edwards said.

'I suppose so,' Brand said

'You don't sound too sure,' Watts said trying to get a flavour of what was bothering Brand.

'I should have pulled Masters at the time instead of trading childish sarcastic remarks with him.'

'Hindsight is a wonderful thing but not common in this job. You need to regain the upper hand or he'll try and lean on you when you come back from leave.'

'I suppose you're right,' Brand said feeling ever so slightly stupid. She wished that the conversation hadn't taken place in front of Edwards.

'OK, go up and get it sorted. I'll get the orderlies ready to serve up. Don't take too long.'

Watts said. Edwards and Brand made their way up to D3.

'The cunt weighs a ton and it's double hard trying to stand up in all this claret.' Grove said trying not to sound as worried as he felt.

'Where can we put him?' Perry said

'In his own cell. We need to get cleaned up double quick,' Perry said, trying to get Masters moving.

'You're right, let's do it,' Masters said, things clearing in his head.

Edwards and Brand walked on to the spur. They heard excited voices coming from the direction of Masters' cell. They looked at each other and walked forward.

As they entered the cell they saw Masters, Grove and Perry trying to pick something up from the floor. Masters heard their footsteps as they entered the cell. Everybody froze, then Masters spoke.

'No drama, we found him in my cell. Somebody has chinned him, used a blade by the looks of it. Poor cunt.'

'It's Butterworth,' Edwards said, trying to make sense of what he was seeing. Butterworth was looking pale and wasn't moving, not moving at all.

Brand was trying to move but her feet felt like lead. She knew that she desperately needed to use the toilet. She was terrified.

'We were about to shout for help when you turned up,' Perry said, the realisation of how serious things were beginning to appear.

Brand stared at the three of them. She couldn't miss the blood on Masters' face and she didn't miss the blood on the floor and on Grove's and Perry's trainers. Oh fuck.

'They've killed him. My God, they've killed him,' Brand screamed.

Edwards seemed to wake out of a dream and turned towards the door.

'No need to be so hasty Mr Edwards, it wasn't us who did the cunt,' Masters said, instantly realising that he had shot his mouth off. Fuck.

Edwards heard what Masters said. Brand heard what Masters said. They all heard what Masters said.

Edwards turned and stared at Masters and he knew. He knew that he had to get away, get out of the cell. He glanced at Brand who seemed to be trying to speak. Edwards turned again, his decision made. He had reached the door when he felt the blow on the back of his neck which knocked him to the floor. He rolled over and looked up. Perry was standing over him, with Grove close by.

'You stupid cunt, it wasn't us for fuck's sake,' Perry shouted.

Edwards knew that he had to try to get away again. He lurched forward and literally fell out of the cell. Perry and Grove both tried to get through the door way at the same moment and fell into each other. Edwards landed on his knees and the pain was bad. He tried to stand and only made it up on one knee. He pushed himself up and forward as Perry was trying to grab his right ankle. Edwards looked up and saw the alarm bell push.

Brand looked at Masters who was staring at her. His face still had blood on it and it was matted in his hair. Butterworth still hadn't moved. She turned and started to walk as if she was in a dream. Edwards staggered forward and reached for the bell.

Masters moved forward and grabbed Brand by her hair. He pulled her towards him and then threw her on the bed. He kicked the door and it moved. He kicked it again and it slammed shut. Brand screamed and wet herself. Masters stared down at her and spat.

'You can scream all you like bitch but you ain't going anywhere,' Masters said.

Perry and Grove saw what Edwards was doing and looked at each other. Survival was kicking in. They looked at each other again, nodded and ran to their own cells. The doors slammed shut within a second of each other. Edwards pressed the bell.

'Attention all stations, general alarm, D wing third level.'

'Attention all stations, general alarm, D wing third level.'

'Acknowledge Oscar One, over.'

'Oscar One received.'

'Acknowledge Victor One, over.'

'Victor One received.'

'All stations, Romeo Mike November standing by.'

Richard Watts was standing by the hotplate, with Officer George Marcus who was on loan from B wing, when he heard the general alarm. D3. Fuck.

He shouted at the hotplate orderlies who ran to their cells and slammed the doors. He ran, with Officer Marcus, to the stairs and started to climb, concerned about what he was going to find.

When he reached D3 other staff were arriving on D wing. What he found, initially, confused him. The place was quiet, unusually quiet. There was no shouting, no radios blaring out. Tom Edwards was sat with his back to the wall under the alarm bell. No sign of Hilary Brand. Edwards was crying, his head in his hands.

'What's happened Tom?' Watts asked as he knelt down.

Edwards didn't answer.

'Speak to me Tom, speak to me,' Watts urged, feelings of dread starting to fill his head.

Edwards looked up, tears streaming down his cheeks.

'Masters has got Hilary in his cell. He's also got Butterworth and I think he's badly hurt,' Edwards whispered, 'Cutler and Perry are in their cells. They were involved. They hit me, the fucking bastards.'

As Edwards finished speaking a senior officer from A wing arrived on the spur. As he started to speak, Watts put his right index fingers to his lips and gestured the man to come to him.

'We might have a hostage situation in Masters' cell D.33. Hilary Brand might be in the cell. Prisoner Raymond Butterworth might also be in the cell and be badly hurt. Also prisoners Perry and Grove might have been involved. They should be in their cells. A lot of 'mights' at the moment I'm afraid. Stay here and secure the area. Nobody else comes on. George, go to Masters' cell door and ask if everything is alright. Sound concerned but not aggressive. Ask to speak to Hilary but don't insist. If Masters tells you to fuck off, don't reply but remain near the door. I'm taking Tom Edwards downstairs to make some sense of what he's told me,' Watts whispered. He gently helped Edwards to his feet and walked him downstairs.

He took Edwards into his office and sat him down. Watts picked up the phone and rang the emergency control room (ECR).

'This is PO Watts on D wing. We have a potential hostage situation on D3 so, until further notice there will be radio silence concerning anything to do with D wing. Ring each wing manager and inform them of the situation. Ring the nurse-in-charge and ask her to come to my office immediately. Find the duty governor, Andy Leitch, give him my regards and ask him to come to my office as soon as possible.'

The controller acknowledged the call and set about his tasks.

Watts sat down with Edwards and listened in silence as he recounted what had happened on D3. As he was finishing, Nurse Dalton, duty governor Leitch and PO Small, who was Oscar One, arrived in his office. They, in turn, listened in silence as Watts recounted what Edwards had told him and the initial actions he had taken. Watts could barely contain his anger at Small but satisfied himself that the bastard had it coming and now would not be the time to show his hand.

'OK, first things first. We need to be certain what we are facing. Get the list of trained hostage negotiators from the ECR and find out who is on duty. Get the best one here as soon as possible. We will need to set up a first aid station here as soon as possible. When the negotiator arrives he or she will go up to Masters' cell and ascertain the depth of the problem. Mr Small will detail security staff to check Grove and Perry's cells to ascertain what we may be facing in that direction. Can you think of anything else we should be doing at this juncture?' Leitch asked. Nobody raised any other issues so they got to work.

Andy 'Jock' Leitch had worked in the Scottish Prison Service before making the journey south with his wife and three young children. The staff knew him as Jock and he actively encouraged the familiarity. Although he could come across as dour he had the respect of both prisoners and staff. He was good company at staff functions because he had an almost endless supply of stories. A real Dr Who.

Ten minutes later, Officer Max Williams was sat in Watts' office. Williams was in his early forties and had been involved in a number of hostage situations down the years. He listened in silence until asked if he had any questions.

'OK, just a couple of things, Sir. I will need a pad and pencil to pass messages. I will use George Marcus to hand messages to. A control and restraint team will need to be on the spur but out of sight. We will need a list of negotiators and a rota established. But, first of all I'll go to the cell and see what the problem is. OK, Sir?'

Leitch and Watts nodded and Williams made his way up to D3 accompanied by Small.

Leitch phoned Roger Mason who, in turn, phoned Mitchell Hagen. It was agreed that Mason would make his way back to the prison and ring Hagen as soon as Max Williams had ascertained the extent of the problem. A little over forty minutes had elapsed since Edwards had pressed the alarm bell.

Perry was sat in his cell thinking about his options. They would come for him. Did he fight or not? Probably not. Nothing to worry about. The screws would unlock his door. He would do exactly as he was told. He might get a slap or two but he would allow for that. Plenty of time to complain later. He would say that he had pushed Edwards out of the cell. Grove would have to look after himself. Masters was a mad cunt for doing what he had done. He would be locked up forever and Perry made his decision to see that Masters took all the shit himself. Yes, decision made.

Grove was debating his options and finally decided that he would be the perfect prisoner unless they started to give him a kicking. It was simple. Masters had the female screw locked in his cell with what remained of Butterworth. Even a thick cunt could see who the guilty party was. Masters was the right man for the job. He had won the audition for the part of fall guy at

Raymar. Almost funny but not the time for laughter yet. Soon though.

Masters was staring into space. He had tied Brand up, using her tights, and had punched her twice in the face to stop her shouting. A smelly sock in her mouth had completed the process. Daft cow. He'd decided to have a bit of fun, finger-pie fashion, but the bitch smelled of piss. Not guaranteed to make the old man stand to attention was it?

Butterworth had stopped bleeding but looked decidedly ill. So what, the cunt shouldn't have been a cell robber. Lowest of the low. Cutler and Perry had proved their worth, slimy pair of wankers. Run out on him. Still, he would make them pay. All in good time. Masters knew that they would come for him. He was fucked as far as Butterworth was concerned because a stabbing attracted a few extra years but Brand might be useful to him. He moved her so that she couldn't be seen when a screw looked through the spy hole. He thought better of it and blocked the spy hole. He sat and waited.

He'd done a lot of waiting over the past few months, or it felt as though he had. It was as if he knew something was going to happen. To complicate matters he hadn't been sleeping very well. He felt as though his head was having a conversation with itself. If he tried to join in then the conversation would stop so he contented himself with listening. Some of it made sense but most of it was twaddle. He'd thought about going to see the quack but that would show weakness. Anyway, there couldn't be anything wrong. When doing a lot of times things often went wrong in the nut department, all the old cons had said that. He was Tony Masters for fuck sake! There wasn't a man alive who would dare to fuck with him and live to tell the tale. He was The Man. The screws knew it as did the other cons.

'Tony Masters, my name is Max Williams. I normally work on C wing and I don't often get to work over here. I've been told that problems have occurred in the last hour or so and I want to help. I've been told that Officer Hilary Brand is in the cell with you. Is this true?'

Masters thought about how to answer.

'I told the other shaky cunt that I wanted to speak to Watts. Where is he?'

'Mr Watts is busy at the moment and he's asked me to speak with you. I want us to have this conversation because we both don't want this situation to get out of hand, do we?' Williams persisted, his voice calm and non-threatening.

Masters had been expecting threats and shouting but the Williams screw had unsettled him.

'Tony, can I call you Tony, let's start again. Call me Max. Is Officer Brand in the cell with you?'

'Yes, she's here. She was after a shag but I had to let her down. Not really in the mood for romance with a fucking dyke.'

Williams had heard a rumour about Hilary Brand but he didn't let it show in his voice.

'So, can we agree that Hilary is OK?'

'Sure, why wouldn't she be?' Masters growled.

'No reason. Can I speak to her?'

'Not at the moment, but she's fine.'

'Thanks Tony,' Williams said, scribbling on the pad held against the wall next to the door.

He passed the note to Marcus who passed it to another officer at the top of the stairs.

'I was also told that Raymond Butterworth was in your cell when the problems started. Is he OK?'

'Yea, no problems,' Masters answered, aware that things were tense.

'Great, can I speak to him?'

'No, he's got a big sulk on and won't talk.'

'Thanks Tony. Are you OK?'

'Never better. Anything else?'

No, thanks Tony. I need to take a leak. Be back in a few minutes. OK with you?' Williams asked.

'Whatever.'

Williams moved over to the door leading to the stairs and wrote slowly:

I am satisfied that Brand and Butterworth are in the cell.
I was not allowed to speak to either of them.
Masters sounded calm. I need to know more about Masters.
We need information from Perry and Grove if they were in the cell.
I have told Masters that I need a piss. Brief me in the next 10 minutes.

Williams passed the note to Marcus and waited at the top of the stairs.

When Roger Mason arrived back from the dentist his first task was to ring D wing. He spoke to Leitch and to Watts and was satisfied that it was a real hostage situation. He instructed two senior officers to convert the boardroom into a command suite. He phoned Mitchell Hagen who, in turn, phoned headquarters. He spoke to the Midlands area manager, Phil Crouch, who was five days into his week as duty gold commander in the event of a serious incident. A hostage incident, particularly one involving a member of staff, was about as serious as it got.

The headquarters incident command suite was opened and the chain of command was established. The gold commander would have ultimate responsibility for the management of the incident. Roger Mason would assume the role of silver commander and would be based in the command suite at Raymar. Also in the command suite would be staff to record the progress of the incident and the actions taken. Mason would also be advised on the readiness of C&R staff, should there be the need for a planned intervention. There were contingency plans for the management of just about every type of incident and Mason would constantly refer to them. The gold commander also had a complete set of the Raymar contingency plans. The duty governor would adopt the title of bronze commander, incident scene.

PO Small remained at the top of the stairs leading on to D3 spur. There would be no verbal communications within earshot of the cells on the spur. Small had staff with him to relay messages down to Watts' office where Leitch was based. Nurse Dalton had set up a comprehensive emergency first aid station in the staff rest room next to Watts' office. Medical Officer Dr Alan Hall was on his way to the prison with a police escort. A police advisor, of Inspector rank, was also on his way. He would join the others in the command suite.

Mitchell Hagen hated feeling powerless. He had despatched his staff officer to the prison for the midday meeting but, for now, he would be his eyes and ears at the incident scene. He would not go himself because that would undermine the authority of the Roger Mason. Although Mason had only held the reins for a matter of days, Hagen had confidence in him and his team. More importantly Hagen knew that he could trust Phil Crouch at headquarters. Crouch was a seasoned campaigner and a steady hand in a crisis.

As a detailed set of instructions were handed to Williams a team of advanced control & restraint-trained staff (C&R) moved silently passed him and into cell D31, formally occupied by the late Brian Lincoln. Two other C&R teams were stood at the top of the stairs leading on to the spur. Max Williams walked forward and stood outside Master's cell.

'Tony, it's Max. I'm back and about half a stone lighter,' Williams said, allowing an amused edge into his voice, 'How are things?'

'How the fuck do you think things are, eh?' Masters growled. The full force of the situation was starting to get to him.

'Sorry, just asking. You will hear some noise in a couple of minutes. We are going to move the other prisoners so that they can have dinner,' Williams said, sounding sincere.

'If I get the slightest inkling that you are trying to come in I'll cut miss dinky tits a new smile and fuck her while I'm doing it. Understand?' Masters shouted.

'Absolutely, Tony, you have my one hundred per cent assurance that we have no intention of coming into your cell,' Williams replied and waved to PO Small who was stood in the doorway. Small turned on a music box which was plugged in just inside the door. A CD of Dire Straits was playing just loud enough to block out speech but not loud enough to cause alarm.

Small stood outside D32 and looked in through the spy hole. Grove was sat on his bed facing the door.

'Terence Grove, this is PO Small. If you are prepared to leave your cell right now raise your right hand.'

Grove raised his right hand and stood up. One of the C&R teams waiting at the top of the stairs moved forward and stood off to one side of the cell door. Small unlocked the door and opened it.

'When you leave your cell staff will walk you into empty cell D36. You will be searched, handcuffed and taken to the ground floor. You have my word that force will not be used against you if you follow my instructions. Do you understand?'

Grove nodded.

'Answer me so that I am satisfied that you understand.'

'Yea, I understand,' Grove muttered.

'Walk forward.'

Grove walked forward. Small backed out of the cell and moved to one side. Grove left the cell and was surrounded by four officers in black suits and helmets. He looked at Masters' cell and decided that it was not a good moment for sarcasm. Max Williams was stood, out of sight, in Butterworth's cell. Grove said nothing. He was taken into cell D36. He was stripped searched and given a new set of clothes. His hands were placed behind his back and he was handcuffed. Not a word was spoken which Grove found slightly frightening. He was taken down the stairs and on to the ground floor. IMB Chairman Crossland was there and asked him if he had any complaints. He shook his head. Nurse Dalton asked him the same question. Again he shook his head. He was taken to an empty cell and locked in. He sat on the bed wondering what was to come next.

Small stood outside cell D34. Perry was stood facing the door, his back to the window. Small went through his prepared speech and received the same responses. Things went the same as with Grove until Perry looked over at Masters' cell.

'You've fucked up big time Masters, you fucking muppet. Sticking Butterworth was not a smart move. Shagged the screwess yet?' was as much as Perry was able to shout before he was wrestled to the ground. He was dragged through the door and down the stairs under restraint. He was taken past Crossland and Dalton and out of D wing. Seven minutes later he was being strip-searched in the segregation unit.

'Who was that, Max, what was he shouting? I ain't done nothing to Butterworth, the cunt's sulking. Answer me!' Masters shouted. He was starting to feel funny, his head felt hot. Williams was back outside the door, composing himself before he spoke.

'It's OK Tony, Perry didn't like being told what to do so we wrapped him up, you know the score,' Williams answered.

'What was he saying? What was he saying?' Masters shouted, a tinge of hysteria in his voice.

'Some rubbish about you shagging Officer Brand. We told him that he was talking rubbish, you wouldn't do anything like that,' was Williams measured reply. He knew that Masters would want more.

'What was he saying about Butterworth?' Masters shouted.

'We couldn't understand him, he was babbling like a baby. Nothing for you to worry about Tony. My word. Sound,' Williams answered.

'If you're lying to me somebody is going to get hurt, I ain't joking!' Masters shouted, shaking his head. His head felt funny. He was hungry.

'You have my word, Tony. I'm being straight with you. You can trust me.'

As Williams was speaking, Raymond Butterworth started to cough. As he coughed, bright, frothy blood started to spray from his mouth. Blood ran from his nose. Hilary Brand was staring at him and she knew. At that moment Raymond Butterworth, aged 57 and serving life sentences for the murder of his wife and her lover, died.

Brand tried to scream but was eating the sock. Masters turned as Brand's face was turning a dark red. She was choking. Masters grabbed her by the hair and pulled the sock from her mouth. Brand started to scream as Masters punched her on the jaw. She drifted into unconsciousness.

'What was that Tony, does Officer Brand want to talk to me?'

'No, she's just had a coughing fit. She's OK now.'

'Thanks Tony, I know you won't hurt Officer Brand or Raymond Butterworth. I trust you as I hope you trust me,' Max Williams said, and didn't believe a single word that Masters and himself had said. He scribbled notes on to his pad, with the word URGENT, URGENT at the top of the page. He passed it to Marcus who, getting a nod from Small, took the stairs two at a time down to the ground floor.

Watts had interviewed Grove and was horrified at what he was hearing. Grove told him everything, being careful to ensure that Masters was completely implicated and that it was Perry who had hit Edwards.

Leitch read Williams's note with alarm.

Masters is becoming hysterical
He heard what Perry was shouting
He won't let me speak to Hilary or Butterworth
He is engaging with me but only just.

I'm very concerned about the health of Hilary and Butterworth.

My considered opinion is that we should be prepared to intervene soon.

Leitch phoned the command suite and gave Mason a detailed report on the information received from Williams and Grove. Mason digested the information and phoned Phil Crouch.

Brand had come round and was starting to whimper which was getting on his nerves. His head was starting to feel really strange. Must be because he was hungry.

'Stop moaning cow or I'll slap you again,' Masters whispered in her ear.

Brand stopped whimpering and was trying to speak. Masters put his head closer to her face as he strained to understand what she was saying.

'Roger, Phil Crouch.'

'Yes, Sir,' Mason answered.

'Are you satisfied that the information received from your negotiator and prisoner Grove accurately reflects the seriousness of the situation?'

'Yes, Sir, I am,' Mason replied without hesitation. He had thought long and hard about how he would answer the question when it came.

'In that case prepare to enter the cell if it becomes apparent that there is any further deterioration in the situation. You have my authority to proceed. Do you understand?' Crouch asked.

'Yes, Sir,' Mason answered.

'Speak to me the moment you initiate any action.'

'Understood,' answered Mason and ended the call. He phoned Leitch who made a careful note of the instructions. Leitch made his way up to D3 and gestured to Small. As Small read the instructions he gestured to Williams to join them. Williams read the instructions. Not a word was spoken.

Small made his way silently to D31 and showed the instructions to the senior officer in charge of the intervention team. The rest of the team read the instructions and nodded their understanding. They made their way carefully out of the cell and waited in front of Masters' cell. Leitch stood to the left of the cell door with his cell key in his right hand. Williams stood to the right of the door, his pad in his hand. The team,

Leitch and Williams would be replaced after 60 minutes to maintain readiness.

Brand had regained consciousness and was staring over Masters' right shoulder at Butterworth, her eyes welling up with tears. She was trying to speak.

'What the fuck are you saying, bitch?' Masters shouted. 'How can I hear you with my head pounding? Fucking speak up.'

They heard him. Leitch tensed. He carefully placed the key in the lock. The officer with the shield was a step behind him. The other three were in position.

Brand focused on Masters' face and saw a white froth coming from the sides of his mouth. His breath stank. She took a deep breath.

'BUTTERWORTH'S DEAD, YOU'VE KILLED HIM, YOU FUCKING BASTARD!' Brand screamed and tried to move her head away.

Masters reared back, looked at Butterworth and knew instantly that she was right. It felt as though his head was starting to explode and it was down to the bitch who was screaming at him. He lunged at her.

CLICK. Leitch was turning the key in the lock.

Masters heard the sound but couldn't focus. He knew that he should know the sound. Recognise the fucking sound. The blood was pounding in his head. The smell of piss and shit was overpowering.

There was a grating noise as the door started to open.

Masters caught Brand by the throat and was frantically grabbing at the blade which was on the floor and just out of reach. Brand had started to struggle and scream. She was kicking and trying to bite and scratch.

Masters was touching the handle of the blade as the shield hit him. Hands grabbed at Brand and threw her off to the left. The shield was in his face, on his chest and against his legs. The shield pushed him and crashed him against the back wall and he fell. He roared in pain as they held him by the wrists, his face pressed against the floor. He roared because they had lied to him. He roared because he hadn't killed the bitch.

As they lifted him up he found himself looking into Raymond Butterworth's cold, dead eyes.

Chapter Sixteen

'Scapes, you're wanted in the Governor's office. Short back and sides is it?" Officer Richard Head shouted.

Scapes smiled and laughed because he knew Head expected it.

They reached the Governor's office and Head knocked on the wood panelled door.

"Come."

Head opened the door and ushered Scapes in.

"That will be all, Mr Head, this will only take a couple of minutes," Roger Mason said.

Head turned and closed the door behind him.

Mason beckoned Scapes forward and handed him a mobile phone. He pointed at a single Gitanes cigarette on the desk, smiled and left the room. Scapes pocketed the cigarette and spoke into the phone, "Hello."

"Scapes, you will recognise my voice but do not acknowledge my name," the cultured voice instructed.

"Yes," Scapes whispered.

"I have good news for you."

"Yes?"

"The minimum length of time you will now be required to serve before you become eligible to be considered for release on license has been reduced to 22 years. Keep up the good work."

"Thank you, Sir, I will.

To be continued......